THREE DRAGONS DOOMED

A Donald Youngblood Mystery

THREE DRAGONS DOOMED

KEITH DONNELLY

HUMMINGBIRD BOOKS
Gatlinburg, Tennessee

Hummingbird Books
A division of Harrison Mountain Press
P.O. Box 1386
Gatlinburg, TN 37738

Designed by Todd Lape / Lape Designs

Library of Congress Cataloging-in-Publication Data

Donnelly, Keith.
Three dragons doomed : a Donald Youngblood mystery / by Keith Donnelly.
pages cm
ISBN 978-0-89587-627-0 (alk. paper)
1. Youngblood, Donald (Fictitious character)—Fiction. 2. Private
investigators—Tennessee—Fiction. 3. Serial murderers—Fiction.
4. Mystery fiction. I. Title. II. Title: 3 dragons doomed.
PS3604.O56325T55 2014
813'.6—dc23   2014012555

Printed in the United States of America
by the Maple-Vail Book Manufacturing Group
York, Pennsylvania

To Tessa,
Charge not slowly into old age,
but together, at full speed

Prologue

Saddle Boot, West Virginia, was growing. An online retailer had purchased some cheap land and built a giant warehouse. The town boasted a new Dollar General store and two new service stations. McDonald's had arrived, followed by Bojangles'. There were job opportunities. The population had increased by five thousand in the last four-plus years. Local businesses were upgrading, renovating, and expanding. Handymen and carpenters had as much work as they could handle. Homes were being built. Outside town, a new subdivision was in the early stages of development, roads were being cut, and lots were being surveyed. That's where Sheriff Dave Phillips had been summoned this hot July day.

Sheriff Dave stood with the county medical examiner looking down on the cocoon of semi-clear plastic as the crime-scene techs scurried around doing what crime-scene techs do. The cocoon looked like a combination of old shower curtains and heavy-duty industrial plastic wrap bound with duct tape. A bulldozer had brought it to the surface early that morning, and the job foreman had called the sheriff's office. The shape beneath the wrapping gave a strong suggestion that the package contained a human body. The size suggested the corpse was male. The smell that escaped when the foreman started to unwind the duct tape removed all doubt it was a body. The odor was gut-wrenchingly strong for those who got too close.

"We're done with the scene, sheriff," one of the techs said.

"Okay," Dave Phillips said. "Load it up and take it to the county morgue."

The tech nodded, disgusted at the prospect of touching the thing.

"You two help him," Sheriff Dave said, glaring at two young deputies. *Rank does have its privileges,* he thought.

"And handle it with care," the M.E. said. "Looks like it's been in the ground a long time."

"How long before you know something?" Sheriff Dave asked.

"I can tell you a few things later today," the M.E. said. "Probably won't know all of it for a week or so. I'll have to send it to the state boys for a DNA profile. See if we get a hit on any of the databases."

Dave Phillips nodded. The summer had been quiet so far, and he wanted it to stay that way. Not likely: this probably was a murder, and murder was not his strong suit. In fact, Saddle Boot had not had a murder since he'd been sheriff.

"Who could have done this?" the M.E. asked, more to himself than Sheriff Phillips.

"Anybody," Sheriff Phillips said. "Lots of old logging roads run through this area, and lots of hunters know these woods; lots of ways in and out. He could have been killed in the next county or the next state, for all we know. Anybody could have buried the body here. The killer is probably long gone, maybe even dead."

The two men were silent, each lost in his own thoughts.

"Well," the M.E. said, "guess I'll get on back." He lumbered toward his wagon, his shirt drenched from the humidity.

"I'll drop by this afternoon," Dave Phillips called after him.

The M.E. waved and kept walking down through the woods to where he had parked his SUV. Dave Phillips watched him go, then turned away and walked over to the foreman, a big guy with a ruddy complexion, a barrel chest, and forearms like Popeye's.

"Work around this taped-off area for a while," Dave Phillips said. "We may want to have another look at the scene."

"No problem," the foreman said. "We have plenty to do."

"I'll let you know when it's okay to finish here. Give me your cell-phone number."

The foreman rattled off his number, and the sheriff input it into his own cell phone and pressed *Send*. He heard the ring in the foreman's pocket and disconnected.

"Okay, I'll call you," Sheriff Dave said. "And keep your guys away from the crime scene."

"Will do," the foreman said. *The last thing I need is trouble with the law*, he thought.

◆　　◆　　◆　　◆

"What have you got?" Sheriff Dave asked the M.E. The sheriff had just come from the Saddle Boot Diner, where he had enjoyed a big burger with fries, an indulgence he allowed himself about once a week. Tramping around the woods at the crime scene had made him hungry.

"As we guessed, the body was a young male," the M.E. said. "Probably late twenties to early thirties. The way the body was wrapped really slowed decomp, so it's hard to tell how long he was in the ground. At least five years, maybe as many as twenty. Thank God it wasn't airtight, or all we'd have would be a pile of bones and mush."

"Cause of death?"

"I'm guessing the heart was punctured with a sharp instrument from behind. Enough skin was left on the back of the corpse to see tiny puncture wounds spaced evenly at an angle across his back. Looks like he might have been stabbed with a pitchfork."

"Pitchfork?"

"Yep." The M.E. nodded. "If you find it, I might be able to match it up."

"Fat chance of that," Sheriff Dave said.

"One other thing," the M.E. said. "He was naked."

"Naked?"

"Yep. Not a stitch of clothing on him. Who kills a man and then takes his clothes off?"

"Maybe he was naked when he was killed."

"Doing what?"

"Doing who might be a better question," Sheriff Dave said.

◆　　◆　　◆　　◆

Late that afternoon in the privacy of his office, Sheriff Dave Phillips sat and thought about the apparent murder. By his own admission, Sheriff Phillips was not a crack investigator, but he could add two plus two. He didn't have to be a genius to figure out that murder by pitchfork was probably not premeditated. Pitchfork probably meant farm, which probably meant barn, and the three or four closest barns to the crime scene were miles away. The old Malone farm might be the closest. He would start there. Will Malone had died, and his wife had left town. Sheriff Phillips had no idea if the Malone barn was still standing, but tomorrow he'd go have a look.

Then he remembered the Tennessee Bureau of Investigation agent who had asked about the Malones four or five years ago and wondered if there was a connection. He rummaged through his file where he kept business cards and finally found it. T. Elbert Brown was the guy's name, a retired TBI agent. He had come to Sheriff Dave's office with some younger guy. What was his name? He couldn't remember. *It won't hurt to give Mr. Brown a call*, Sheriff Dave thought.

1

We were at the lake house. The clock on the nightstand on my side of the bed read 3:00 A.M. when the phone woke me that Monday. A phone call in the middle of the night is never a good sign. Best-case scenario: it's a wrong number. Worst-case scenario: it's bad news. The phone was on Mary's side of the bed, and she answered it before it rang a second time. It wasn't a wrong number.

"Yes," she said sleepily.

Ten seconds of silence.

"Okay," Mary said. "I'll be rolling in fifteen minutes."

She hung up. Mary is my wife and a detective on the Mountain Center, Tennessee, police force.

"What?" I asked. Donald Youngblood, private investigator, man of few words.

"Dead body," Mary said, throwing off the covers on her side. "Downtown in the alley behind King's Department Store."

"Want some backup?" I asked, turning on my bedside lamp. Mary's lamp went on at the exact same time.

"As long as it's you," she said. "Let's move."

"I'll use the hall bath."

◆   ◆   ◆   ◆

Ten minutes later, after leaving a note on the kitchen counter for our teenage daughter, Lacy, we were rolling. It was a warm, clear July night. The humidity was tolerable; later, it wouldn't be. Mary placed her portable flasher in the center of the dash as we pulled out of our driveway and headed toward trouble. I smiled to myself. The drive normally took fifty minutes to an hour, depending on traffic. With no traffic and Mary at the wheel, it would take forty or less.

When we arrived, two patrol cars were at the scene, lights pulsing red and blue. An SUV driven by the chief of police, my longtime friend Big Bob Wilson, pulled in ahead of us. Mary maneuvered in behind the SUV and turned off her flasher as Big Bob got out of his ride.

"Turn off those damn strobes," Big Bob said. "They'll give me a headache. Leave your headlights on."

The red and blue pulsing lights disappeared, leaving only the car headlights and a nearby street lamp to illuminate the body. The blond female was lying on her side in the middle of the alley not fifty feet from the back door of the department store. Her eyes were closed. She could have been sleeping. Mary and I walked over to the body as Big Bob talked with his younger brother, Sean, and another officer, John Davis, who I deduced had found the body.

"Did you check for a pulse?" I overheard Big Bob ask.

"Yes, sir," John Davis said. "No pulse. She was cold."

"You didn't move her or touch anything else?"

"No, sir."

"Okay," Big Bob said. "Go back on patrol. We'll handle it from here. Sean, you stay."

I heard the patrol car back down the alley as we knelt to get a closer look at the body. The woman was clothed in jeans and a T-shirt. She wore sneakers. A watch was on her wrist and a ring on one of her fingers, but it was not a wedding band. I guessed she was in her mid-thirties. Her purse lay a few feet away.

"I don't see any wounds," Mary said.

"Wasn't robbery," I said. "Her purse wasn't taken."

"You're right. It doesn't look like robbery," Mary said.

"Looks like she was dumped. I bet she was killed somewhere else."

"Maybe she was walking down the alley and died of a heart attack," Mary said. "Just dropped in her tracks. It kind of fits."

"You believe that?" I asked.

"Not really," Mary said.

I heard the click of the big man's leather heels on the concrete, coming toward us.

"I'm going home," Big Bob said. "Mary, this is your case. Call Wanda Jones and get her down here, and get the crime-scene guys. Don't let Wanda touch the body until the crime-scene guys are finished. You know the drill."

"Okay," Mary said, walking away from us as she pulled out her cell phone.

"Sean, tape off the entire alley and stay here until everyone's finished."

Sean nodded and walked toward his patrol car.

Big Bob turned to me. "I hope to hell this isn't a murder. That's all I need."

"Mary said the woman might have just dropped," I said.

"It fits," Big Bob said. "But I'm not that lucky."

We stared at the body.

"Murder, sure as shit," Big Bob said, disgust dripping from his voice.

"Most likely."

"Feel free to stick your nose in," Big Bob said. "We'll need all the help we can get."

"Only if your lead investigator asks me," I said.

Big Bob chuckled. "I heard that," he said, and walked to his SUV.

◆   ◆   ◆   ◆

Wanda Jones, medical examiner and good friend to both Mary and me, arrived thirty minutes later, looking sexy as hell. I had always thought Wanda was the best-looking woman in Mountain Center. Then Mary moved to town.

"Hey, handsome," Wanda said.

"Hey, yourself."

Mary was within earshot, watching the crime-scene techs. "I heard that. Quit flirting with my husband."

"No way," Wanda said. "It's too much fun."

A dead body lying in the alley, and they're cracking wise, I thought. Maybe that was just a defense mechanism. Wanda had seen plenty of bodies. I could never think of anything funny to say around a dead body.

"All done here," one of the techs said.

Wanda and Mary approached the body. I leaned against the front of Mary's truck and watched. This was Mary's show, and I wasn't about to interfere unless asked. They rolled the body over. Wanda looked at the head and neck, opened one eye and then the other.

"What do you see?" she asked.

"No bruising on the neck, but her eyes are bloodshot," Mary said. "She might have died from asphyxiation."

"You're probably right," Wanda said. "I'll know more when I get her on my table."

"There appears to be bruising on her wrist," Mary said.

Wanda took a closer look. "I think so."

Mary got up, put on a pair of latex gloves, and went to the woman's purse. She picked it up by the strap, walked over to me, and put it on the hood of the Pathfinder. She carefully slid the top zipper open, did a little rummaging, and zipped it closed. She then did the same with two side zippers.

"Everything you'd expect except her billfold," Mary said. "No ID, no credit cards, no money. Whoever did this did not want us to ID her right away."

She walked the purse to one of the techs and came back to the Pathfinder.

"Nothing more I can do here," she said. "I'll talk with Wanda later today and get to work on identifying the body."

She turned away and took one last look at the dead woman. When she turned back to me, her face was hard, and I knew she was pissed.

"Take me home," she said.

2

By the time we got back to the lake house, it was five o'clock—too late to return to bed, although Lacy and our two standard poodles, Jake and Junior, were still asleep. I showered, shaved, dressed, drove back to Mountain Center, and went to my office. The town was waking up, but the traffic was still light. I parked in my space in the lot behind the Hamilton Building, punched in my security code, and went up the back stairs. My office was on the second floor. One floor below was Harrison National Bank. I came out into the main corridor near the elevators and pushed the down button. I glanced down the hall at my office door and was a little saddened by the sight:

CHEROKEE INVESTIGATIONS
Donald A. Youngblood
Private Investigator

My partner and friend since college, Billy Two-Feathers, had asked me to remove his name, finally deciding it was time to move on. Billy was now a full-time deputy sheriff in Swain County, North Carolina. Much had happened since we opened the office. Our lives, constantly evolving, had led us in different directions, though we were still good friends and always would be.

I took the elevator down to the first floor. When the door opened, the security guard was standing there with his gun at his side.

"Don't shoot, Sam. It's me."

Sam, a retired cop from Atlanta, had been on the job for about a year. Ted Booth, president of Harrison National Bank, had come to me looking for recommendations. A call to Jim Murphy, retired Atlanta police detective and husband to one of my ex-girlfriends, had netted Sam Watson. Sam was recently retired and looking to supplement his pension. He took the interview and got the job. He and his wife were thrilled to move to a small town.

"Sorry, Mr. Youngblood," Sam said, holstering his Glock. "I didn't know anyone was in the building."

"I came up the back way and thought I'd go over to Dunkin' Donuts. Want some coffee? It's on me."

"Sure," Sam said. "Black, please."

Sam unlocked the door to let me out, and I crossed the street, went inside, and ordered a coffee with cream and sugar and a toasted poppy seed bagel with cream cheese for me and a black coffee and a couple of donuts for Sam.

He was waiting by the door when I returned. I handed him his bag as I entered.

"Enjoy, Sam," I said. "And there's an extra treat inside."

"Thanks, Mr. Youngblood."

I heard the rustle of the bag being opened as I got on the elevator.

◆　　◆　　◆　　◆

Early mornings in the office were quiet. I relished quiet. Quiet was good. I had my fill of hustling, bustling offices when I worked on Wall Street. I enjoyed my time there. I made lots of money, learned the ways of the big city, and benefited from the experience. At heart, though, I was a small-town guy. So I returned to my hometown. I became a private investigator and continued to handle investment accounts for an exclusive list of clients because most of the time a private investigator's work is boring.

The last two years, my private investigation business had been highly successful. I didn't need the money, but I did need the work. I wanted a sense of purpose and some excitement with maybe a modicum of danger tossed in for good measure. In the last five years, I had certainly found more excitement and danger than I bargained for.

As I ate the bagel and drank the coffee, I went online and checked the prices of some stocks I was tracking. The market was vacillating around thirteen thousand, and I was hoping for a temporary dip so I could pick up a few bargains. I checked my email—mostly junk that never seemed to find its way to my spam folder. I opened an email from T. Elbert Brown, mentor, friend, and ex-TBI agent. T. Elbert was now confined to a wheelchair, thanks to a drug dealer's bullet many years ago.

Donald,
Come by and see me when you can. I got an interesting
phone call late yesterday. We need to discuss.
T.

T. Elbert rarely invited me over; rather, he just waited until I showed up. I usually arrived about once a week bearing gifts of coffee and bagels or donuts, which we consumed on his front porch while discussing whatever subject came up.

I checked my calendar and wrote back,

See you at 3:00.

◆　　◆　　◆　　◆

Midafternoon was hot and muggy—a typical July day in East Tennessee. I drove out of the parking lot, took a left on Back Street, then another left on North Street. North Street was a former U.S. route, the main north-south thoroughfare through Mountain Center when I was growing up. Then a bypass was built around the city, and outlying shopping centers sprang up like dandelions north and south of town. North Street became just another lightly traveled city street with sparse local traffic.

A mile up North Street, I turned right on Olivia Drive and drove the two miles to T. Elbert's house. I executed a perfect U-turn and parked in front. T. Elbert was in his rocker on the front porch. I made my way up the concrete walk and the few stairs to the porch. A pitcher of dark liquid, a small bowl of sliced lemon, and an extra glass were on a small table next to an empty rocker. I sat.

"Have some sweet iced tea," T. Elbert said.

Normally, I would have declined, but since he had gone to the trouble, I poured myself a glass, added a lemon wedge, and took a drink.

"Good," I said.

T. Elbert smiled. "I make good iced tea."

"You do."

We rocked in silence. I had to play his game. He had something, and I had to ask for it.

"So tell me," I said, acting appropriately annoyed.

"Remember Sheriff Dave Phillips?" T. Elbert asked.

I knew immediately that could not be good news. "Saddle Boot, West Virginia," I said.

"That's him. He called."

We rocked. He was going to make me pull it out of him.

"So what did he want?"

"He remembered our visit a few years back," T. Elbert said. "And he remembered we were asking about Tracy Malone. Seems a body turned up not too far from where Betty and Tracy Malone lived. He wanted to know if our investigation back then could be connected to the body."

"Interesting," I said, acting casual as I took another drink of iced tea. "What else did he tell you?"

"That the body was wrapped in plastic, which made it hard to tell how long it was in the ground," T. Elbert said. "A construction crew unearthed it while grading a road for a subdivision."

I wrapped him up good so the smell wouldn't get out and carried him deep into the woods and found a nice little open area where the soil was soft. I dug a grave and buried him deep.

T. Elbert watched me as I silently recalled the words of Will Malone. That conservation I would never forget.

"Remember what you said to me after we left the Malones'?" T. Elbert asked.

"I said, 'T. Elbert, this is one time I need you not to be curious,' or something close to that," I recounted.

"Verbatim," T. Elbert said, dragging the word out. "And I never asked."

We were quiet a minute or two. T. Elbert was letting me sort it out.

"Did Sheriff Phillips question Will Malone?" I asked.

"The sheriff told me Will Malone died last year from cancer," T. Elbert said.

The news shocked and saddened me. I had thought that, at some point, I might tell Lacy about her great-uncle, might take her to meet him. That idea died with Will Malone.

"What about Thelma Malone?" I said, knowing T. Elbert would have asked.

"Moved to Florida, the sheriff thinks. He has no idea where."

We sat silent for a while.

"Anything you need to do about this?" T. Elbert asked.

"I'll have to give it some thought," I said.

◆   ◆   ◆   ◆

That night, I sat at the kitchen bar at our downtown Mountain Center condo drinking an Amber Bock. Mary sat across from me with a glass of Smoking Loon Chardonnay. We had finished dinner, and Lacy was in her room. Mary and I had adopted Lacy soon after we were married, fast approaching two years. Mary was saying something to me, and I wasn't hearing it. I was lost in thought, recalling the words of Will Malone the last time I had talked with him about Betty Malone, Lacy's grandmother, and Tracy Malone, Lacy's mother. I remembered most of it, some of it word for word.

Betty Malone had come knocking on Will's door late one night. "*We go to bed early,*" I remembered Will saying, so he knew it couldn't be good news for Betty to get him out of bed. Thelma was a sound sleeper and didn't hear the knock, Will said. So Will got out of bed and went down and opened the front door, and there stood Betty "*lookin' like she had seen a ghost or somethin'."* Those were Will's exact words. She had begged Will to come with her. She said there had been an accident. So Will got in her truck, and they drove to Betty's barn. The trip took only a few minutes on an old road, long since grown over, that connected their farms.

They went inside the barn, and there lay Johnny Cross "*dead as a doornail*" and Tracy Malone huddled in a corner "*white as a sheet, starin' off into space like she was in another world. Johnny was this drifter Betty took up with. God knows why good women take up with bad men."*

Betty had said that she came home from a PTA meeting and found Johnny raping Tracy. So she had stabbed "*the son of a bitch with a pitchfork."* According to Will, those were her exact words.

Will wanted to call the sheriff, but Betty begged him to just get rid of the body, and nobody would know the difference. Will figured Betty was ashamed of the whole thing and wanted to save Tracy the embarrassment of having to talk about getting raped, so he said okay.

Will told Betty to take care of Tracy, and he would take care of the body. He used an old shower curtain and some duct tape and wrapped Johnny up so the smell would be contained, then carried him deep into the woods. He found a nice little open area where the soil was soft. Will dug the grave and "*buried him deep."* He then returned to Betty's farm and told her it was done. Betty told Will they would never speak of that night again.

About two months later, Betty told Will she was leaving town. She said she would stay in touch, but Will knew she wouldn't, and indeed she hadn't.

I had asked Will Malone if he thought it was really rape.

"*I don't know,"* I remembered him saying. "*Betty had a bad temper, and Tracy was a little wild."*

Will said Betty had panicked when he mentioned calling the sheriff. He said he believed her story at the time, but over the years he began to have doubts. "*Maybe Betty caught 'em in the act. Maybe I helped cover up a murder."* I definitely remembered that verbatim.

"Don," Mary said loudly enough to break my train of thought. "Are you listening to me?"

"No," I said. "Sorry. We need to talk."

In a marriage, "we need to talk" is never a good way to open a conversation. Mary went a little pale.

"Not about us," I said quickly. "We're fine."

"Well, that's good to know," Mary said, slightly annoyed. "You scared me. Talk about what?"

"A phone call T. Elbert got today."

I recounted my conversation with T. Elbert. Mary drank her wine and listened. She knew about the death of Johnny Cross. We had agreed it would be our secret; that we would not tell Lacy she was either the product of a rape or that her grandmother, whom she dearly loved, was a murderer. We both thought the latter, but there was no way to be sure.

"What do you think I should do?" I asked Mary.

"Keep your mouth shut," Mary said. "You were the only one who Will Malone told about that night, and Will Malone is dead."

"Thelma knows."

"I doubt she would tell that her dead husband covered up a killing. But it might not be a bad idea to find her and give her a heads-up," Mary said.

"I'll do that."

Some skeletons in the family closet need to stay there, I thought.

3

At midmorning the following day, I called Scott Glass. Scott was the special agent in charge of the Salt Lake City FBI office. I had met Scott at the University of Connecticut the day before I met Billy. Scott, Billy, and I were on the basketball team. They were on scholarship, and I was a walk-on. I was asked to walk off, and they went on to be stars.

Except for being six-five, Scott looked nothing like a basketball player. He had a geeky, lanky, awkward, studious look that belied the fact that he was one of the best three-point shooters ever to wear the UConn blue and white. Scott's dark, curly hair and glasses had earned him the nickname "Professor." He was always grinning as if he knew something no one else did, and he loved to play little mind games. Over the years, a few of my cases had crossed paths with his. His star was shining bright at the FBI, and I had helped to add a little luster to it. That allowed me to cash in favors now and then.

"How's it going, Professor?" I asked when he answered his private line.

"Hey, Blood, what's happening?"

"Typical FBI agent. Answer a question with a question."

"We are well trained," Scott said. "I bet this isn't a social call."

"I need a small favor," I said.

"Anything within reason."

"See if you can find a Thelma Malone who used to reside in Saddle Boot, West Virginia, but is probably now living in Florida. She's probably in her sixties or seventies, so if you find more than one, try to verify their ages."

I realized Mary could probably do this, but I didn't want to take her focus away from her murder investigation.

"She's related to Lacy?"

"Only by marriage," I said. "As far as I know, Lacy isn't aware she exists."

"Interesting," Scott said.

I knew he wanted more information. "It's complicated," I said.

"I bet."

"When it's resolved, I'll tell you all about it."

"You better," he said. "I'll email you the info."

"Thanks, Professor," I said. "How's Deena?" Deena was a Salt Lake City police officer Scott had been dating for a while now.

"We're great," he said. "She's moving in as soon as her lease is up."

"Sounds serious."

"Looks like it. I'm long overdue to settle down. Funny, isn't it? You end up with a cop, and I end up with a cop. Explain that one, Blood."

"What can I say? Girls with guns are pretty damn sexy."

"And then some," Scott said.

♦   ♦   ♦   ♦

Fifteen minutes later, sexy walked into my office, poured herself a cup of coffee, and sat in front of my desk. From time to time, she surprised me with an impromptu visit.

"Kind of quiet with Gretchen on vacation," Mary said.

Gretchen was my Jill-of-all-trades super assistant. Mary had found her, and I had resisted hiring her. Now, Gretchen was indispensable.

"Want to get naked and do it on the couch?" I asked. *Might as well take advantage of an empty office.*

"I prefer king-sized beds," Mary said.

"I don't think one will fit in here."

Mary laughed. "Then you'll have to wait."

"A guy's got to try."

"I would expect nothing less. Now, try to refocus."

"Okay," I said. "You want to tell me about your case."

"I do," Mary said. "I checked all reported missing persons in the states of Tennessee, Kentucky, Virginia, North Carolina, South Carolina, and Georgia. No hits."

"Maybe she hasn't been missing long enough."

"Maybe. So we ran her prints."

"And got nothing," I guessed.

"Right."

"So you'll do the DNA thing."

"We will," Mary said. "But it will take awhile. So, for now, all I can do is show her picture around to hotels, restaurants, gas stations and anywhere else I can think of and hope I turn up something."

"You might give Peggy Ann Romeo a heads-up," I said. "She could do a story for the six o'clock news. She could say something like, 'If anyone has seen this woman, please call the Mountain Center Police Department.'"

"Not a bad idea."

Mary drank her coffee, and I stared out my office window thinking about the dead body in West Virginia and finding Thelma Malone.

"I've got Scott working on locating Thelma Malone," I said.

"I figured as much," Mary said. "Easier for him than me."

"Might have to go to Singer Island."

"I figured that, too. Unfortunately, I can't come with you."

"A pity."

"It is," Mary said, standing. "I'll see you at the condo."

I escorted her to the outer office door and watched her walk down the hall to the elevator. I greatly enjoyed the view.

◆   ◆   ◆   ◆

That night, Mary fixed chicken pepperoni—chicken breasts pounded flat, rolled up with fontina cheese and pepperoni, coated with Italian bread-crumbs, skillet-fried, and served with marinara sauce. Wild rice and my infamous Caesar salad accompanied the entrée.

We had just finished when the local news came on. Mary unmuted the TV. "Murder in Mountain Center?" was the headline. An artist's rendition of the dead woman appeared on the screen. She looked very much alive.

Peggy Ann Romeo's voice-over: "An unidentified body of a female thought to be in her mid-thirties was discovered early this morning in an alley behind King's Department Store. Police have reason to believe the unidentified woman was murdered."

All of a sudden, a video replaced the picture. Peggy Ann Romeo stood beside none other than Mary.

"I'm here with Mountain Center police detective Mary Youngblood. What can you tell us about the murder?"

"It appears the victim was strangled at an unknown location and then dumped in an alley downtown," Mary said. "She had been dead less than twenty-four hours when we found her. There is no way to confirm if she was murdered in Mountain Center, but we also cannot rule out that possibility."

The dead woman's picture reappeared on the screen with the phone number of the Mountain Center Police Department.

Peggy Ann's voice-over again: "Please call this number if you can identify this woman or have any information pertaining to her murder."

"That's what we need," I said. "Another Youngblood on television."

"You had your fifteen minutes of fame," Mary said. "Now it's my turn."

"You're welcome to it. If I'm never on television again, it will be too soon."

4

The email from Scott came the next morning. The FBI computers had located three Thelma Malones in Florida who were about the right age. One was in Gainesville at a regular street address, one in Orlando in an apartment complex, and one in a retirement community near Melbourne. I looked at a map of Florida. If I drove, I could make stops in Gainesville, Orlando, and Melbourne. But if I flew to Singer, I could do Melbourne first. And the retirement community made the most sense. So I called Roy Husky.

Roy was part of my inner circle. We had met during the Fleet case and over the years had become close friends—not as close as Big Bob or Billy, but close nonetheless.

"Hey, Gumshoe," Roy said. "What's happening?"

"I'm working something," I said. "I need to go to Singer. Let me know when the jet is available."

"Hang on," Roy said. He put me on hold, and I heard soft jazz. About the time I started to enjoy the music, he was back. "Jim says eight o'clock tomorrow morning." Jim Doak was Fleet Industries' number-one pilot.

"I'll be there," I said.

"Need any backup?"

"I would think not. But thanks for asking."

◆　　◆　　◆　　◆

That night, we sat on the balcony of our Mountain Center condo. My watch read 8:05. The sun was setting, and our east- facing balcony offered a wooded view with an unusual twilight glow. I hated daylight saving time. I would rather wake up in daylight and observe darkness an hour earlier. I understood the economic concept, but it didn't change my thinking. I was a winter person. I loved snow, cold weather, extreme elements, and time spent on any ski slope. I didn't mind short days. Mary was a summer person. She loved long days, sun, warm breezes, and days spent on any beach. We got along anyway.

"I talked to Wanda today," Mary said.

"Anything new?"

"She found traces of chloral hydrate in the woman's blood work."

"No alcohol?"

"No," Mary said.

"Somebody slipped her a nonalcoholic Mickey?"

"Apparently so."

"Any hits from the news broadcast?" I asked.

"A few proposals of marriage. But nothing to help the case."

"Next time you're on TV, be sure to display your wedding band for the camera."

Mary laughed. She had a five-carat diamond I had given her on our wedding day that she kept locked in a safe at the lake house. She never wore it on the job. She took it out of the safe on Friday nights, wore it all weekend, and locked it up on Monday mornings before she started her workweek.

"I'm done with TV," she said.

There was a tap on the sliding glass door to the balcony. The door opened, and Lacy and Biker McBride came out. Biker had been dating Lacy for a while. I had not been thrilled with the idea at first, but Biker was growing on me. Billy accused me of being prejudiced because Biker drove a Harley. That was probably true. Fortunately, Biker had turned out to be a pleasant surprise—a solid kid from a good family who cared very much for Lacy.

"We're going out for ice cream," Lacy said.

I looked at Biker. "Take her car."

"Will do," he said. "We won't be gone long."

"Be careful," Mary said.

"Jeez," Lacy said. "Relax, you guys."

The sliding glass door closed, and they vanished into the shadows.

"How long is that going to last?" I asked. When it came to Lacy, Mary knew all.

"Long time, I think," she said.

"Really?"

"Really."

"Huh," I muttered.

5

Out of gratitude from Joseph Fleet, Jim Doak had been flying me around the country on Fleet Industries' jet number one for over five years. Fleet Industries had two jets, and neither one seemed busy. Never hurts to have backup, especially if you can afford it, and Joseph Fleet could definitely afford it.

Jet number one was a Learjet 60 that had been completely refurbished a few years back. It felt like home; I was totally spoiled. I made an annual contribution toward fuel and maintenance, much to the chagrin of Mr. Fleet, who had more money than I did and wanted none of mine. Roy told me once that Fleet donated the money I paid to charity. That was fine with me; I wanted to pay my way.

Two hours after departing Tri-Cities Airport, we landed at Palm Beach International. The Florida humidity greeted me indignantly as I exited onto the hot tarmac. I made a hurried retreat to air conditioning as Jim taxied away for his departure to Miami to pick up a client. He promised to retrieve me the next day for my return to Mountain Center.

I rented a Lincoln Navigator from Hertz, found I-95 North, and headed to Melbourne. Two hours later, I was at the front door of Unit 21 in a retirement community not far from Exit 180, hoping to find the Thelma Malone I was looking for. I knocked and waited, knocked and waited some more, and was about to leave when I heard the lock turn. The door opened slightly, the chain still attached. A single eye peered at me through the opening.

"May I help you?" the voice that went with the eye asked.

"Thelma Malone?"

"Yes."

"From Saddle Boot, West Virginia?"

"Mr. Youngblood? Is that you?"

◆   ◆   ◆   ◆

We sat at the kitchen table. Thelma had prepared sweet tea, and we had exchanged pleasantries that included my condolences for the death of her husband, Will. Thelma seemed glad to have a visitor.

"I gather you were not just in the neighborhood," she said.

"No," I said. "I came to see you."

"That's nice. How did you find me?"

"Florida Motor Vehicle Department. You have a current driver's license."

"Yes," she said, pleased. "I still drive."

She waited. I took a drink of the cold sweet tea.

"A body was found a few miles from your farm," I said. "More than likely, it's Johnny Cross."

"Oh, dear," she said. "Should I be worried?"

"No. You didn't do anything wrong, and I don't see how anyone could connect it to Will."

She paused. A distant look came over her, as if she were trying to recall a memory.

"They could," she said. "If they're real smart."

"Explain," I said. I drained my glass.

"The motorcycle and Johnny's leather jacket are hidden in a secret cellar in our barn," she said. "Beneath many bales of hay."

"That could be a problem."

We were quiet for a moment. I could hear the clock on the kitchen wall ticking.

"What about the pitchfork?" I asked.

"Long gone," Thelma said. "Will went fishin' a few days later and took the pitchfork with him. He said nobody would ever find it. I didn't want to know the details."

"Do you still own the property?"

"Yes," she said.

I finished my tea and thought about the situation. Thelma poured more tea and was quiet.

"Would you like to sell the farm?" I said.

"And all the possessions therein or thereon," she said.

"Yes."

"To someone of your choosing."

"Yes."

"So you can legally remove what you might want to remove."

"You catch on fast," I said.

"I've had some time to think about it." She took a drink of tea. "I've had the farm appraised, and I'll want a fair price," she said with a smile. "But you don't really need to buy it. I could give you permission to take whatever you want."

I really wanted to buy the farm. I had it in the back of my mind that I someday might give it to Lacy and tell her the history, minus the death of Johnny Cross, of course.

"I think it is best if we buy it," I said. "It would look less suspicious if the new owner shows up to move some things. Sheriff Phillips is a little nosy."

"He is that," she said.

"We'll pay whatever you're asking."

"Why? Why go to the trouble? This isn't your problem."

The moment of truth was at hand. I hesitated. I was about to utter the words, but Thelma Malone beat me to them.

"Tracy had a child, didn't she? And Johnny Cross was the father."

"Probably the father," I said.

"Son or daughter?"

"Daughter."

"Where is she now?"

"She's been adopted."

"Adopted," she repeated. The word seemed to fade away like a puff of smoke. She was thinking. It didn't take her long to connect the dots.

"You," she said.

A sharp cookie, my mother would have called Thelma Malone.

"And my wife," I said. "Mary."

"My God," Thelma whispered. "What's her name?"

"Lacy."

"Does she know about Will and me and all the rest?"

"No."

Thelma Malone paused as if trying to come to a decision.

"Probably best that she doesn't," she said.

"Probably," I said. "I'm still working that out in my head."

◆　　◆　　◆　　◆

The rest of the day and into the night, I was on my cell. After some thought, I decided to ask Roy to be the front man on the purchase. I was vague on the whys and wherefores.

"Be glad to," Roy said. "Should I ask why we're doing this?"

"Not now."

"Doesn't matter," Roy said. "I'll do it. Owning a farm sounds nice. I've never owned a piece of property. How much am I paying for it?"

I told him.

"I can cover that myself," he said. "Any reason I can't keep it?"

"None, as long as Lacy's name is on the deed as co-owner."

"Fine with me," Roy said.

"You'll be getting some paperwork in a few days."

We discussed the details. Roy agreed he would use Joseph Fleet's Amelia Island property as his home address. I didn't want a Mountain Center address raising a red flag.

After we hung up, I called Rollie Ogle.

"I need a real-estate lawyer near Melbourne, Florida, to handle a sale on a piece of property in West Virginia," I said. "The seller is in Florida. The buyer is Roy Husky, and the deal is as confidential as we can keep it."

I explained the details. Roy wanted a farm, and I had found him one, but he wanted to keep the purchase a secret.

"A secret," Rollie said, knowing something was afoot.

"Don't be too curious about this one, Rollie."

"Right. We'll probably need to get more than one lawyer involved, since we're dealing with two states."

"Whatever you need to do," I said. "I want to make it as easy as possible for the seller. Bill me for your time."

"Gladly," Rollie said. "What's the seller's name?"

I ignored his question and pushed on. "You set up the Florida lawyer, and I'll handle it from there."

"I see," Rollie said. "The less I know, the better."

"Who said lawyers aren't smart?" I said.

◆   ◆   ◆   ◆

Rollie Ogle quickly lined up a Florida real-estate attorney to act on Thelma Malone's behalf. I called Thelma, gave her the lawyer's name, and told her to be in touch. She said she would call immediately.

The price was set. The property would never officially be on the market. Our story: Mr. Husky, a friend of the family, had made a fair offer, and Thelma had accepted. The transaction would be completed as soon as possible. If we fast-tracked it, we should be able to get it done in a couple of weeks. I hoped the title search didn't turn up a problem.

The sale would undoubtedly be in the local paper in Saddle Boot, but that shouldn't raise suspicion, since Thelma had already moved to Florida and the locals probably expected her to sell.

As soon as the sale was final, someone would retrieve the bike and the jacket. Wanda Jones should be able to get something off the jacket to do a DNA screen. I hoped I had all the bases covered.

◆   ◆   ◆   ◆

"I wish I were there," Mary said.

"You're not alone in that wish."

"Tell me about your day."

I told her. I was sitting on the balcony drinking a beer and looking east into the darkness. Lights from various ships dotted the ocean.

"Thelma Malone is a pretty smart cookie," Mary said.

"Exactly what my mother would have said. It makes the whole thing a lot easier." I took another drink of beer. "Any luck on identifying the dead body?"

"None," Mary said.

6

We landed at Tri-Cities Airport around noon the next day. My Pathfinder was parked near the Fleet Industries hangar, allowing me to make a quick exit from the airport and get to the office in the early afternoon. Gretchen was still on vacation. She'd been a little vague on where she was going and who she'd be with. I hadn't pressed. Gretchen held her personal life close. I knew little about it.

I checked my messages and email. An email from Roy let me know the purchase of the Malone farm was well under way. I checked the Street.

The Dow was still bouncing over and under thirteen thousand. I stayed in a holding pattern.

Late in the day, my phone rang.

"We need you in my office," Big Bob said—no preamble, no explanation. I knew it was important.

"On my way."

◆   ◆   ◆   ◆

Mary was in Big Bob's office when I walked in.

"Look at this," Big Bob said, handing me a sheet of paper.

The note was printed in an unusual typeface. I read it to myself and then aloud:

Having trouble identifying the body? I'll give you some help. The main thing is that the answer is right in front of you. Good luck trying to figure it out.

"This is more than bizarre," I said. "How did you get it?"

"In the mail," Mary said.

She handed me the envelope. It was addressed to the Mountain Center Police Department and marked to the attention of the chief of police. The postmark was Washington, D.C.

"Washington," I said.

"We noticed," Big Bob snarled. "We need you to solve the puzzle. You're good at that. What does it mean, the answer is right in front of us?"

I read the note again. "You think the killer wrote this or someone is just jerking you around?"

"Hard to tell at this point," Big Bob said.

"Who else knows about this note?" I asked.

"The three of us," Big Bob said.

"I think we should keep it that way," Mary said.

"I agree," Big Bob said, looking at me.

"No problem," I said.

I took one more look at the note. Mary and Big Bob were quiet.

"Maybe she's from Maine," I said. "The note says, 'The main thing is that the answer is right in front of you.' Maybe that's the clue."

"Maine," Big Bob said, looking at Mary.

"It's a start," Mary said.

"Okay," Big Bob said. "Get our computer guy on it. Have him search out missing person reports in Maine and see if any fit our vic."

"Will do," Mary said. "I'll get Jackson right on it."

"Jackson," Big Bob said. "Right, get Jackson on it."

I watched her go down the hall and up the stairs to the second floor.

"Christ have mercy," Big Bob said, watching me watching Mary. "Stop ogling. You're married to the woman."

Lucky me, I thought.

7

Monday morning, Roy, T. Elbert, and I sat on T. Elbert's front porch eating sausage and egg biscuits from the Mountain Center Diner and washing them down with Dunkin' Donuts coffee. I rationalized the biscuits by reminding myself that I was meeting Mary and Lacy after work for a four-mile run on the Mountain Center Country Club nature trail. Roy brought us up to date on his acquisition of the Malone farm, acting rather pleased with himself that he was finally going to own something. T. Elbert sat quietly with a puzzled look on his face, trying to figure the whole thing out.

"I should have bought something a long time ago," Roy continued. "I shouldn't need you to tell me to buy something."

"You're doing me a favor," I said.

"I'm doing myself a favor. I've spent my whole adult life working for Mr. Fleet. I've never owned anything. I like the idea of owning land."

"Squire Husky," T. Elbert said.

Roy smiled and took a big bite out of his second biscuit.

"So what are you-all not telling me?" T. Elbert asked.

"I don't know any more than you," Roy said. "Don wanted me to buy the place, so I bought it."

They turned their gazes on me and waited. Some secrets are best held close, but there comes a time when you have to trust your friends. I knew my time for being secretive had ended, as far as Roy and T. Elbert were concerned.

"You know I would trust both of you with my life," I said. "But there are some things you're better off not knowing, especially things you can do nothing about. However, since you're both peripherally involved in this, I feel I owe you the whole story."

I took a bite of biscuit, drank some coffee, and organized my thoughts. I turned my chair slightly toward them and leaned forward.

"Lacy's grandmother killed Lacy's father," I began. "At least she killed the man I think was Lacy's father. Hopefully, we'll be able to prove or disprove that in the near future. Of course, Lacy doesn't know any of this."

An eerie silence filled T. Elbert's porch. For a few seconds, it was as if we were in a vacuum.

"Go on," T. Elbert said quietly.

I told it the way Will Malone had told it to me. Maybe not word for word, but close. They listened with concerned looks but made no comments. When I was done, there was more silence.

"Why do you want the farm?" Roy asked.

"Johnny Cross's motorcycle and leather jacket are hidden beneath the flooring in a section of the barn where they stacked hay," I said. "With any luck, the bike and jacket are still there. Once this deal is done, I need you and Oscar to go up there and bring them back."

"We can do that," Roy said.

T. Elbert was quiet, processing. I thought maybe I was about to get a lecture on messing with a crime scene. I didn't.

"Well," T. Elbert said, "whether or not the killing was justified, the killer is dead. The victim is long dead. Whatever justice could be served by opening that can of worms has long since been served. I cannot see any good coming from anyone else knowing about this. Do what you have to do to protect Lacy. That's my advice."

"Mine, too," Roy said.

I nodded and drank the rest of my lukewarm coffee.

"Does Mary know about this?" T. Elbert asked.

"Yes," I said.

"Billy?" Roy asked.

"Yes."

"Anyone else?" T. Elbert asked.

"Except for Thelma Malone," I said, "no one I know of."

"And we all have Lacy's best interest at heart," T. Elbert said, almost choking on his words as he said them.

That was the moment I knew how deeply T. Elbert cared for Lacy. Not only Mary and I had adopted her. Those in our inner circle had, too.

"We do," I said.

8

That same morning, I was in my office doing what I do best—playing Spider Solitaire on the hardest level. Gretchen was still on vacation, and I was taking the opportunity to be lazy. I had won two straight games when I heard my outer office door open and close.

Mary walked in. She wore black slacks and a white form-fitting sleeveless top. Her detective's badge was on her belt. She came around my desk, pulled the armrests up on my chair, spread her legs, and sat in my lap. She leaned down and kissed me. I kissed her back and reached underneath her top to unhook her bra. She slapped my hand away.

"Every kiss doesn't lead to sex," she said, kissing me again.

"Sorry," I said. "I forgot."

She gave me a final quick kiss and removed herself to one of the chairs in front of my desk as I tried to catch my breath.

"You're here twice in a week," I said. "What's up?"

"Just keeping an eye on you while Gretchen is on vacation."

"Uh-huh."

"And I wanted to tell you what our computer guy found out from Maine."

"Which was?"

"Nothing," she said. "No missing female fitting our description."

"Maybe she hasn't been reported missing yet. Maybe she was single and had a job where she didn't have to go to an office every day."

"Maybe," Mary said. "Or maybe she wasn't from Maine."

"Maybe that, too."

"So what's the big clue that's right in front of us?"

"Maybe there is no clue," I said. "Maybe whoever wrote the note is messing with you."

"Maybe, but I don't think so."

"Neither do I. I'll give it some more thought."

"Please do," Mary said. "If you come up with something useful, there'll be a reward."

"Like what?"

"Use your imagination."

"I can imagine a lot," I said.

"I bet," Mary said.

◆   ◆   ◆   ◆

That afternoon, I did come up with something useful. I was working on a general report for my financial clients. I wanted to spruce it up with different typefaces, using some bold, some italics, and a bit of color. I didn't bother to count them, but Word 2013 probably had over a hundred typefaces to choose from. Combine that with sixteen different sizes, boldface, italics, and color, and the possibilities were endless. Quite by accident, I stumbled on to the typeface used in the note sent to the Mountain Center Police Department. Then I was pretty certain where the dead woman was from.

I locked the office, went down the back stairs to the Pathfinder, and drove to the police station. I could have called, but it was a slow day, and I wanted to break the news face to face.

Mary was at her desk. I made eye contact and gave a nod toward Big Bob's office. Big Bob was on his computer. He looked up from his desk as we walked in.

"Did your computer guy come up with anything?" I asked.

Big Bob looked at Mary.

"Jackson," Mary said. "No, nothing yet."

"I don't think he will," I said. "I don't believe the dead woman is from Maine."

"Then where is she from?" Mary asked.

"Manhattan."

"Manhattan," Big Bob repeated flatly. "How did you come up with that?"

"The clue wasn't in the wording. It was in the typeface. The typeface he used was Broadway."

Big Bob looked at Mary. "Go tell the computer guy to check Manhattan."

"Jackson," I said.

"Whatever," Big Bob grumbled.

◆　　◆　　◆　　◆

That night, Mary and I cooked at the lake house. What started as dinner for four turned into dinner for six. Hannah, Lacy's best friend, was spending the night. Lacy wanted to invite Biker. So Hannah wouldn't feel left out, she also invited Alfred Lucas, known around school as "the Brain." Alfred was *kind of* Hannah's boyfriend, whatever that meant. He had gained status in school because he hung out with Biker.

I enjoyed the pleasant evening on our upper deck as I grilled two pounds of boneless chicken breasts slathered with a miso sauce. Mary prepared corn on the cob and made deviled eggs and Gorgonzola potato salad. We ate on the lower deck watching the sun sink slowly in the west between scattered clouds. The females carried the conversation. Every now and then, the males were asked to contribute.

When we finished, Biker, Alfred, and Hannah went down to the dock to fish. Lacy lagged behind. I knew something was up.

"Susan wants Lacy and me to come out to visit her before Lacy's senior year starts," Mary said to me.

Susan, Mary's daughter from a previous marriage, had graduated from Wake Forest and moved to San Francisco.

"California," Lacy said. "Isn't that awesome?"

"It is," I said. "Guess I'm not invited." I tried to look forlorn.

"You could come, too," Lacy said.

"He's kidding," Mary said. "He'd be bored out of his skull."

"Gotcha," I said to Lacy.

She gave me a punch on the shoulder. "I knew you were kidding. I was just playing along."

"Uh-huh. Sure you were."

She smiled at me as she got up from the table. "See you guys later," she said. She went down the steps to the boat dock and joined the others.

"That girl is crazy about you," Mary said.

"And you," I said.

"I know."

We drank sweet tea and observed the young people below, listening to their laughter as night descended on the lake.

"So when's this trip to California?"

"In a couple of weeks, I hope," Mary said.

"How long will you be gone?"

"Probably two weeks."

"What about your dead body?"

"Not much more I can do about that," Mary said. "We're almost certain she wasn't killed in Mountain Center. I've interviewed employees from every hotel, motel, restaurant and gas station in the area. No luck."

"Did you check bed and breakfast places?"

Mary stared hard at me.

"Of course you did," I said.

She smiled.

"Think of something I haven't thought of," Mary said.

"Probably can't," I said.

We heard yelling from the dock. Lacy had hooked a fish and was reeling it in while the rest of the group rooted her on. Mary and I, caught up in their excitement, for a time forgot all about the unidentified body.

9

I sat at my table in the Mountain Center Diner. I had parked in my usual spot behind my office building and walked down the alley and through the back entrance, marked **Employees Only**. Doris had spotted me within twenty seconds of my sitting down. Twenty seconds later, I had a pot of coffee and a one-owner newspaper.

"Are you going to wait to see if Roy or Big Bob shows up?" Doris asked as she poured coffee into a heavy white mug with Mountain Center Diner printed on the side in navy blue.

"Might as well," I responded. "I'm not in any hurry."

I was finished with the first mug and my head was buried in the paper when the noise level dropped by about half and I knew Big Bob Wilson had arrived. He sat in his usual spot, and the noise returned to normal. I wondered how many people in the diner had, for a brief moment, thought the Mountain Center chief of police had come for them. Doris brought another mug and poured him a cup of coffee. She took our orders and hustled away.

"Breakfast is on me," Big Bob said, an occurrence that happened less often than a harvest moon.

"What's the occasion?"

"Your reward for being so damn smart. Our computer guy got a hit on a missing Manhattan female who fits our dead body. We're sending pictures and dental records for confirmation, but it feels right."

"So how did she get from Manhattan to Mountain Center?"

"Good question," Big Bob said. "The precinct captain I'm dealing with said he'd try to establish her last known location, and we'd go from there. If it wasn't Mountain Center, then it's somebody else's problem. I have enough of my own."

"Does Mary know?"

"Sure. I called her first thing. She's out of the office working a break-in. She told me you'd probably be here."

Our food arrived, and we dug in. The conversation turned to sports and then to local politics. The mayor, who Big Bob had always considered a major pain in the ass, was giving him grief about his budget.

When we finished, Doris took the plates away and poured Big Bob a second mug of coffee, which was unusual for him since he was always in a hurry.

"What else?" I asked.

Big Bob lowered his voice to a soft growl. "Peggy Ann Romeo has been snooping around trying to find out if we've identified the body yet. Think I should tell her anything?"

"You should tell the newspaper and TV people right away that you have a credible lead toward identifying the body and you'll let them know as soon as it's confirmed," I said. "If you identify the body quickly, maybe you won't get any more notes."

Big Bob thought about that for a moment. "I'll have Sean leak it to the paper and Mary leak it to Peggy Ann," he said. "That way, they'll both owe us."

"You're a sneaky devil," I said.

"I am," he grinned.

·   ◆   ◆   ◆   ◆

When I finally got to the office, Roy was at the conference table drinking coffee and reading the *Wall Street Journal*.

"Got any tips for me?" I asked.

"Facebook is going public," Roy said. "Can you get me in for a thousand shares?"

"Probably," I said. "But they'll be overpriced. If I were you, I'd wait. I'll bet they eventually go under the initial offering."

I took a mug from the cabinet and opened the Keurig coffeemaker to reveal that Roy was drinking Green Mountain Breakfast Blend. I removed the used K-Cup and inserted a Green Mountain Wild Mountain Blueberry. I closed the top and pressed the far right button to brew the maximum. A minute later, I added cream and raw sugar and joined Roy at the table.

"What's the latest on the sale?"

"They're doing the title search," Roy said. "As long as that goes okay, we should get the deal done next week. As soon as that happens, I'll take Oscar and go up and get the bike and the jacket. I'll take a big enough truck that I can clear some of the furniture out. I'll bring it back and donate it to a local church. We'll put the bike up front and pack around it in case anyone wants a look inside."

"Sounds like a plan. Too bad I can't be there."

"Best that you're not," Roy said.

I knew he was right, but I really wanted to be there when they uncovered the bike.

"Tell the O-man to take some pictures," I said. "I want to see the hay-stack, the hiding place, and lots of angles from inside the barn."

"Could be risky if someone gets his hands on the camera," Roy said.

"Not if Oscar removes the chip when he's finished and hides it in the truck."

"No wonder you earn the big bucks," Roy said, nodding. "You're always thinking, Gumshoe."

10

Two days later, the confirmation on the dead body came from New York. I sat in Big Bob's office that morning and listened to the details.

"Ashley Hill was her name," Big Bob said. "She was a nurse at Sloan-Kettering Hospital in the city. She was divorced, lived alone. The last time anyone saw her alive, she was participating in her third day of a nurses' convention in Baltimore. She checked into the Baltimore Marriott at BWI Airport but never checked out. Her clothes, cosmetics, and luggage were still in her room. New York has Baltimore involved, since she was last seen alive there. It's a mess."

"Looks like you're off the hook," I said.

"Thank God."

"So somebody killed her somewhere between Baltimore and Mountain Center and dumped her body here," I said. "Why?"

"Must be a reason," Big Bob said. "Hell if I know what it is."

"Maybe someone will write us a note and tell us."

"That would be nice," Big Bob said.

◆   ◆   ◆   ◆

That evening, Mary and I sat on the lower deck enjoying the sunset and having our final drink of the evening—a white wine spritzer for her and a Sam Adams Light for me. Lacy and Hannah were on the lake fishing and due back before dark. I guessed they had about a half-hour.

We were discussing the Ashley Hill case. The story confirming the identification had run on the six o'clock local news. Since it was simulcast over the Internet, anyone could watch it from anywhere. I wondered if Ashley Hill's killer had done so. The story would also be in the *Mountain Center Press* the next morning.

"So somebody kills her and brings her body to Mountain Center for us to find," Mary said, thinking out loud. "Someone has an agenda. Dumping her in Mountain Center wasn't just a random act."

"Probably not," I said.

"How long does it take to drive from Baltimore to Mountain Center?"

"About eight hours," I said.

"You checked it out?"

"I did."

"So somehow our killer drugs her, gets her in his car, strangles her, and brings her here. And on the way drives through Washington, D.C., and mails the note."

"Looks like it," I said. "The timing is right."

"Doesn't make any sense," Mary said.

"Murder never does."

11

I was in the office early the following Monday when the phone rang. Caller ID was no help, telling me only that the call was "out of area."

"Cherokee Investigations," I answered in my very best radio voice. *Professionalism is all.*

"Whoever you are," Gretchen said, "put my boss on the phone."

"The golden voice thou hearest is I, Donald Youngblood," I said in my best Shakespearian.

Gretchen laughed. "Glad to hear you're in a good mood," she said. "I have a favor to ask."

"You want to extend your vacation."

"How'd you know?"

"Only reason you'd call. Where are you?"

"South," she said, sounding rather pleased with herself. "Way south."

"So how much longer?"

"Another week."

"Must be a guy."

"Could be I'm just having a good time," Gretchen said.

"What about your kid?"

"The kid is being well taken care of," Gretchen said. "Thanks for asking."

"I still think it's a guy," I said.

"Could be."

I took that as a yes.

"Enjoy," I said.

◆　　◆　　◆　　◆

An hour later, the phone rang again. This time, I knew who it was.

"What's up?" I answered.

"Very professional, Gumshoe," Roy said.

"Caller ID allows me a certain amount of freedom when answering the phone."

"Which wouldn't happen if Gretchen weren't on vacation."

"True," I said.

"When is she coming back?"

"Who knows? She just asked for a week's extension."

"Must be a guy," Roy said.

"We're hard to resist."

Roy laughed. "Yeah, lucky us."

"You didn't call just to kibitz."

"The deal is done," he said. "Lacy and I now own real estate."

"Congratulations. When do you plan on seeing what you purchased?"

"This weekend," Roy said. "Oscar and I are going up early Saturday morning. We'll spend one night and be back Sunday. I'll be in touch."

"The Lacy thing will be our little secret," I said.

"Except that it's public record," Roy said.

"But not around here," I said.

"Good point." Roy said.

◆   ◆   ◆   ◆

Another hour, another phone call. This time, it was Big Bob.

"Get your ass over here," he growled.

"What's wrong?"

"Another damn note."

"On my way," I said.

◆   ◆   ◆   ◆

Note in hand, I read,

> **The boys in JC will need some help identifying the body. Here's your clue. Traveling through deep snow is easier if you have help.**

"I called the Johnson City chief of police, and sure enough, they had a body dumped in a downtown alley two nights ago," Big Bob said.

"A couple of nights after the news reported you had identified the Mountain Center body," I said.

"Exactly. It's like the killer was waiting for us to solve the first note, then he gives us another one. Why us?"

"Don't know," I said. "But you can bet there's a reason."

"I told the JC chief about the note. He wasn't too happy about it being sent to us. He said they'd work on it."

"Good. Let them have it."

Big Bob ignored that comment. I knew him well enough to understand he wanted us to solve the note.

"Our computer guy says the typeface is Georgia," Big Bob said. "So we're going to start there."

I resisted saying the computer guy's name was Jackson.

"I doubt it's that simple," I said. "Our killer is playing games. He won't use the same clue twice. Where was the postmark from?"

"Same as the last one. Washington, D.C."

"Did he mail it before or after he dumped the body?"

"Before," Big Bob said. "So what do you think?"

"I'll need some time," I said. "Did you share all this with Johnson City?"

Big Bob smiled. "Not all of it."

No big surprise there, I thought.

◆　　◆　　◆　　◆

That afternoon in the office, I put the phone on auto-answer and started poring over the note. I was sure the last line was the clue. The first line was the killer's reason for sending it to Mountain Center. Johnson City's needing help had nothing to do with it. There was another reason that would be revealed to us later—I was sure of that, too.

I made a general list of things that would help in traveling through snow. Then I got more specific. I listed all the four-wheel-drive SUVs, all the makes of snowmobiles, all the manufacturers of snowshoes and cross-country skis that I could find online. To my surprise, I found at least six SUVs whose manufacturers had named the models after cities. They were all west of the Mississippi and well out of reasonable driving distance. If our second victim was from one of those cities, she had probably been abducted from somewhere else, like maybe a convention in a city within driving distance of Mountain Center. *Another nurse?* I wondered.

Late in the day, I came up with another idea. What made it easier to get through snow? A sled! I took more time researching sleds. Then it hit me: dog sleds. Huskies!

I had a sinking feeling; I hate coincidences. The University of Connecticut's mascot was a Husky. I did a search and found out that Washington, Northern Illinois, Northeastern, Southern Maine, and a branch of the University of Wisconsin also used Huskies as their mascot. All except Washington were within a twelve-hour drive. That seemed a place to start. I made a list. Connecticut was at the top.

I called Big Bob.

"I have a list," I said. "I'll fax it over. It's not definitive."

I filled him in on the details.

"We got zip from Georgia, so we'll start on Connecticut," Big Bob said.

I hope to hell it's not Connecticut, I thought.

12

The weekend rolled around. Nothing much had happened. No hits on the second dead body. Connecticut drew a blank, as did the rest of my list. I was missing something.

Lacy was filling in at the Mountain Center Diner and had left early Saturday morning to help Doris open. Mary and I sat at the table on the lower deck drinking coffee and listening to the lake wake up—our favorite time of day.

"A little cool this morning," Mary said.

"I love it," I said. "Fall is coming."

"I bought some Black Angus filet mignon for you to grill tonight."

"Sounds good. We haven't had steak in a while."

We listened to the irritating call of a blue jay close by and the hammering of a woodpecker farther away. A clean-smelling breeze was coming off the lake. The sky was crystal blue and dotted with puffy white clouds. Altogether, a perfect morning.

"Lacy is staying at Hannah's tonight," Mary said, gently stroking my forearm.

"I know. Might I be in for a treat later?"

"For certain," Mary said.

I smiled and drank coffee and wondered if anticipation really was 90 percent of satisfaction.

I finally decided participation was all.

❖   ❖   ❖   ❖

I spent the day working on the upper deck. I could have hired the job done, but I was never satisfied with someone else's work when I knew I could do it better myself. I power-washed the deck boards, then turned my attention to the rails. I sanded the tops with an electric sander, then stained them with a top-of-the-line redwood stain. It was late after-noon when I finished the rail tops. I still had the bottoms and the pick-ets to do. Staining the pickets was tedious and would take hours and hours. After that, I would tap down any nail pops, then sand and stain the deck boards. The work would take time, but the end result would be worth it.

Dirty, hot, and sweaty, I went through the back door into the kitchen and sat at the bar, exhausted. Without asking, Mary fixed me a glass of sweet iced tea with lemon. I drank it down with gusto.

"Want another?" she asked.

"Please!"

As I took more time with the second glass, I noticed six steak fillets sitting on the counter.

"Who's coming for dinner?"

"It's a surprise," Mary said.

"What time are they coming? Or is that a surprise, too?"

"By the time you take a shower, get dressed, get everything ready for grilling, and have a beer, they'll probably be here."

I finished my iced tea, slipped off the barstool, and headed upstairs. I was sure Maggie and Billy were two of the four, but I had no clue as to the other guests.

◆　　◆　　◆　　◆

A half-hour later, I reappeared downstairs a new man. I went on the deck, uncovered the grill, lit it, set the temp on high, then went back inside. I opened a Sam Light and sat on a barstool and watched Mary wrapping bacon around the fillets. She noticed me watching.

"Like what you see?"

"You bet. The steaks look great."

"You weren't looking at the steaks," Mary said, taking a sip from her glass of wine.

"You're right. I was looking at your very fine derriere."

"You can have a closer look later," she said, and went back to her bacon wrapping.

A minute later, there was a knock on our front door.

"We're here," Maggie said, coming down the hall into the kitchen.

Billy followed silently. Maggie and Mary hugged. Mary and Billy hugged. Maggie came around the bar and gave me a hug. Billy and I nodded at each other.

"How are you, Don?" Maggie asked.

"Fine, Maggie. How are you?"

"I'm great."

"Where's Little D?" Mary asked.

"With his nanny," Maggie said.

"You have a nanny?" I asked, failing to hide the surprise in my voice.

"That's what we call her," Maggie said. "She's an older Cherokee woman I've known a long time, and she insists on baby-sitting whenever we go out so we can have some alone time."

"Nice," I said.

"Very nice," Billy said.

◆　　◆　　◆　　◆

Billy and I sat at the table on the lower deck with the umbrella tilted at just the right angle to keep the sun off us. We played catch-up on recent events in our lives. The conversation turned serious when I filled him in on matters in West Virginia, including the bike and the jacket.

"Nothing good is going to come from that," Billy said.

"I'm just trying to see nothing bad comes from it," I said.

"Any thoughts about hindering a murder investigation?"

"There's nothing to hinder," I said. "We know who did it. Why she did it is another story, but since she died years ago, there's no justice to be served."

"Manpower is being wasted on the investigation," Billy said.

I didn't want to argue the point any further, so I ignored the comment. "I might want you to take a look at the bike."

Billy shook his head. "Not me. Murdered man's bike is bad medicine."

I didn't know whether he was putting me on or not.

Billy smiled. "But keep me in the loop."

I heard the sound of tires on gravel and decided to pursue that conversation another time.

"You know who the other couple is?" I asked as I heard car doors slam at the front of the house.

"No," he said. "Don't you?"

"Mary said it was a surprise. She didn't even tell me you and Maggie were coming, but I pretty much had that one figured out."

"Maggie told me to keep quiet," Billy said. "I do as Maggie says."

"Good strategy."

After we heard the storm door open on to the upper deck, our surprise guests came down the stairs, beers in hand, grinning widely. I was shocked: Wanda Jones, followed by Bruiser Bracken.

I had met Bruiser, a former NFL lineman, my senior year at UConn, then lost track of him until I ran into him in Vegas while working the Malone case. We had stayed in touch since then. Bruiser was in a long-distance relationship with Wanda, one I was sure would fail. Mary said they would make it. I had a strange feeling I was about to be proven wrong again.

"Long way to come for a cookout," I said.

"Actually, I came for a job interview," Bruiser said.

I looked at Billy. He shrugged. I looked at Bruiser. He smiled.

"Two plus two equals . . . ?" he said.

I paused. There was only one possibility. "Fleet Industries," I said.

Bruiser pointed his index finger at me.

"What can you tell us?" I asked.

"Roy said I could tell you all of it," Bruiser said. "But it's confidential, so it stays in our little group."

I nodded.

"Fleet Industries has landed a government weapon-parts contract that's top secret. It's worth a fortune. Every employee's background will be thoroughly researched, and they'll have to sign no-tell contracts. Those who do will receive lucrative bonuses. I'll be in charge of security. I'll set up cameras to monitor all manufacturing areas and have an operations room much like in Vegas. I'll have a team working with me. I may bring in a couple of guys from Vegas who I've worked with who are really good about spotting odd behavior. We'll be the eye in the sky. It's part of the contract. I'm interviewing with Mr. Fleet tomorrow, but I think the job is mine. I'll use you and Billy as references, if that's okay."

"Sure," I said.

"No problem," Billy said.

Joseph Fleet already knew Bruiser, so I guessed he was just following procedure, as far as the hiring process was concerned.

We heard giggling from inside the house. Bruiser looked toward the kitchen and smiled.

"One other thing," he said. "Wanda and I are getting married."

When you're wrong, Youngblood, you're really wrong, I thought.

◆   ◆   ◆   ◆

Night fell on the lake as we ate, drank, laughed, traded stories, and thoroughly enjoyed each other's company. At some point, Wanda told me she had communicated with the Johnson City M.E. and that his report on his dead female matched hers perfectly. Two murders with the same MO. Two notes. Did we have a serial killer in our midst?

◆   ◆   ◆   ◆

Later that night, after everyone had gone, the blond goddess attacked me. I was beat, and Mary was wired. Guess who won that battle?

"I'm too tired," I said, knowing she would not take no for an answer.

"We'll see," Mary said, pulling her oversized nightshirt over her head. Her hand slid down below my waist. "Feels like there's life in the old boy yet."

Within seconds, she was on top of me and I was inside her, lost in a world of pleasure. Mary never ceased to amaze me. How long we made love that night I couldn't say, but I remember, just before falling asleep, congratulating myself on having the good sense to marry an amazing woman.

13

When I arrived at the office Monday morning, the door was unlocked and Roy Husky sat in his usual spot at my conference table reading the *Mountain Center Press*. A mug of coffee and a bagel were keeping him company and slowly disappearing. A Dunkin' Donuts bag was sitting by my Keurig coffeemaker.

I inserted a Dunkin' Donuts K-Cup in the Keurig, placed a mug underneath, and pushed the button to brew a ten-ounce serving. I peeked in the bag: a toasted sesame seed bagel with cream cheese. A minute later, I was adding half-and-half and raw sugar to my coffee. I sat at the table.

"Thanks for the bagel," I said, taking my first bite.

"My pleasure," Roy said.

"How was the trip?" I asked.

I drank some coffee.

"No problems," Roy said, handing me an envelope full of pictures.

I took my time looking at them. I was most interested in the ones taken inside the barn. The bales of hays were stacked high. I watched them diminish as I went through the pictures until the bales were gone and a wooden floor was revealed. In the next shot, the floor was gone, revealing the motorcycle. I wondered how Will Malone had managed to get it into its hiding place. I didn't wonder long. The next picture showed the bike being lifted out by a sling and rope from overhead pulleys attached to a joist.

"How hard was it to get the bike out?"

"Not as hard as it looks in the picture," Roy said. "The pulley system Will Malone installed worked really well. No doubt, he used it to move bales of hay around."

"Did you find the jacket?"

"Not at first," Roy said. "It was tucked away in a corner of that hidey-hole, folded up in a sheet and covered with loose straw. We almost missed it."

"Where is it?"

"Hanging in your office closet."

"What else did you bring back?"

"Most of the furniture," Roy said. "Oscar is taking it to the Methodist church today. There's a Spanish family in need of furniture. We're going back up this weekend or next to get the rest of it."

"What did you think of the place?"

"Loved it. I'm psyched about doing something with it. I think I'm going to knock down the house and put up one of those log cabin homes—something decent, maybe a three-bedroom."

I took another drink of coffee and finished my bagel. "Where's the bike?"

"Still on the truck," Roy said.

"Can you hide it someplace safe?"

"Sure. What are you going to do with it?"

"I haven't figured that out yet," I said. "Billy thinks it's bad medicine."

"He could be right," Roy said.

◆   ◆   ◆   ◆

Near lunchtime, I got a call from Joseph Fleet. I had expected I might hear from him.

"Mr. Fleet is calling for you, Mr. Youngblood," his female assistant said. "He'll be right with you."

"Donald," Joseph Fleet said, "how have you been?"

"I'm fine, Mr. Fleet. How about yourself?"

"Fine, fine," he said hurriedly. "Sorry for the short notice, but I was wondering if you're available for lunch."

"I am."

"Can you meet me at the club at one o'clock?"

"I'll be there," I said.

◆   ◆   ◆   ◆

The Mountain Center Country Club had all the comforts of home, and then some. Tennis, golf, racquetball, swimming, and a running trail for sports enthusiasts, plus a very fine restaurant for those who enjoyed fine dining. It offered much more, of course, but I rarely took advantage of any of it except for the restaurant and the racquetball court. Lacy took golf lessons from the club pro, Tony Price. Mary occasionally brought Wanda Jones for lunch or dinner but usually came to the club with me only to eat or play racquetball.

The restaurant was on the third floor overlooking the eighteenth hole of the club's championship golf course. Joseph Fleet sat at a corner table by the window, his back to me.

"I know you like to have full view of the room, so I saved you the premier seat," he said after we shook hands.

"Thanks," I said. "I must have been a gunslinger in a former life."

We ordered club sandwiches, iced tea, and a side of fries to share. I knew what Fleet wanted, but he was going to take his time getting there.

"I haven't seen you in a while," he said. "Have you been staying out of trouble?"

I smiled. "Of course not."

"I didn't think so. I heard you made a trip to the Pentagon. The reason why was a little vague."

"You have good sources," I said.

"Anything you can share?"

"Sure," I said. "I can tell you all about the Pentagon trip."

He waited. The iced tea arrived. I didn't know how to answer. I trusted Joseph Fleet, but he didn't need to know the details of the Crane case. He saw me hesitate.

"Forget it, I shouldn't have asked," he said. "I expect you'll treat it with the same discretion as you did my case."

The first big case I had worked on was what our Cherokee Investigations files called the Fairchild case: the investigation of the disappearance of Sarah Ann Fleet Fairchild. Some of our big cases made headlines, and some were shrouded in secrecy. The Crane case was in the latter group.

"I can tell you that it was for a high-profile client, that justice was served, and that the outcome was bittersweet," I said.

That pretty much described the outcome of his daughter's case, too. He nodded, a distant look on his face, then turned away and looked out the window. Below, three men and a woman were lining up putts on the eighteenth green.

"Do you play golf?" Joseph Fleet asked.

"No," I said as our food arrived. "But Lacy plays, and she's pretty good, from what Tony Price tells me."

Fleet took a bite of his club sandwich, and I did the same from mine. Then we tried the fries, which were great as always.

"Roy told me about his purchase," Fleet said.

"He was doing me a favor."

"That may be true, but I think he's pretty happy about being a landowner."

"He does seem to be getting into it."

I took another bite of my club and ate some fries.

"I guess you know why I invited you to lunch," Joseph Fleet said.

"I do."

"Tell me what you can about Bruiser Bracken. All I know is what I've heard and observed at our Thanksgiving soirees."

I talked. He listened. We both ate. I painted a vivid picture of my first encounter with Bruiser and how we had become friends at UConn. Then I described how I had lost touch until our chance meeting in Vegas and the role he played in the Malone case. By the time I finished, the food was gone and our plates had been removed.

"Bruiser is one of a few close friends I would trust to cover my back," I said in closing. "I'd hire him in a heartbeat and pay him whatever he wants."

"Good enough for me," Joseph Fleet said, drinking the last of his iced tea. "I'm going to make him an offer at four o'clock today."

◆　　◆　　◆　　◆

Back in the office, I sat and thought about events of the past few weeks and about what my next move should be. I had Johnny Cross's jacket and was having second thoughts about taking it to Wanda Jones for a DNA profile. Was that what I really wanted to do?

Then I thought about Mary's murder investigation. It seemed to be out of her jurisdiction, so she was off the hook. Mary and Lacy would be leaving soon to visit Susan in San Francisco. The recent note to the Mountain Center Police Department was odd, but since the dead body was found in Johnson City, it was also out of MCPD's jurisdiction. It seemed there was nothing much for me to do about the two dead females, but I kept coming back to the notes and the strange feeling I had that someone was personally involving me.

Then I came up with an idea.

I went to my Palm Pilot and looked up a phone number. Michael Addison was a professor of economics at UConn who was not much older than I was. Maybe that's why I had tried to take every course he taught when I was there. He had a reputation as a ball breaker; many business majors called him "the Grim Reaper" because of what he did to their GPAs. As an econ major, I couldn't avoid Professor Addison and was pleasantly surprised at how good a teacher he was and how much he challenged me. Since graduation, we had stayed in touch. We talked about once a year and never kept score on whose turn it was to call.

I dialed his direct line.

A young female voice answered. "Professor Addison's office."

"Is Michael in?"

"Who's calling, please?"

"Donald Youngblood, world-famous private investigator."

She giggled. "Yes, I think I've heard of you. One moment, please."

A few seconds later, he picked up. "Don! How the hell are you?"

"I'm good."

"How's married life?"

"It's great. You should try it sometime."

"Not a chance," Michael said. "Although if I could find a babe like your wife, I might take the plunge."

"Liar. You're having too much fun with the coeds."

"There is that," he laughed. "I sense this is more than a social call. You usually call at night."

"I need a favor, Michael," I said. "I'm assisting in an investigation involving an unidentified murdered female, and one of the clues leads me to believe she might have attended UConn."

"Ah, a murder investigation. What can I do?"

"If you can, send me a list of all graduating females from 1995 through 1999."

"No problem," he said. "I'll assign it to a graduate assistant. Should have it in a couple of days."

"Don't go into any great detail about why you want the list," I said. "We might be dealing with a real nut case."

"Spooky," Michael said. "I like it."

◆ ◆ ◆ ◆

Late that afternoon, I took a look at Johnny Cross's leather jacket. It was black, soft, and beautifully crafted, but the thing that caught my eye was the embroidered gold dragon covering most of the back. The label inside read,

FORZINI & SONS
ROME, ITALY
1989

The jacket showed some wear, but not a lot. Johnny Cross had taken good care of it.

I put it back into the black clothes bag Roy had brought it in, locked up the office, and headed down the back stairs. Destination: the office of the county medical examiner.

◆   ◆   ◆   ◆

"Hey, good lookin'," Wanda Jones said when I walked in.

"I notice you're flirting with me again."

Wanda used to flirt with me unmercifully until Mary and I married, then she stopped.

"Well, Mary told me to keep an eye on you while she's out of town, so I thought I'd give you a little incentive to hang around."

"Shame on you," I said. "You're about to be a married woman. Where is the big fellow, anyway?"

"Dennis is going back to Vegas to get his affairs in order. It may take awhile. He called me a few minutes ago. He accepted the Fleet Industries job."

Dennis was Bruiser Bracken's given name. People he knew in Vegas called him Dennis, but old habits from college died hard. Bruiser said that Dennis, coming from me, just didn't sound right.

"That's great," I said. "I should probably keep an eye on you while he's gone."

"No need," Wanda said. "I've got what I want."

"Have you set a date?"

"Not yet. We're in no hurry."

"I'm real happy for you two, Wanda. I really am."

"Thanks."

For a second, I thought her eyes got misty, but she recovered quickly.

"Enough bullshit," she said. "Why are you here? Did you bring me something?"

I was still holding the black clothes bag. I hung it on a nearby coatrack.

"There's a leather jacket inside," I said. "Get anything off it you can that might yield a DNA profile. Don't talk about this to anyone. If I decide I want you to run a profile, I'll let you know."

We stared at each other. I knew she wanted to know more, but I wasn't ready to share.

"You're working a case?"

"Kind of," I said.

"Okay, but at some point, I want to know what's going on."

"At some point," I said.

14

Michael Addison called two days later.

"I've got the list," he said.

"That's great, Michael. Thanks."

"It's pretty extensive. I'll attach it to an email."

"I'll be looking out for it."

"Let me know if the girl is on the list."

"Woman," I said.

"Right. Woman. Please let me know if the *woman* is on the list."

"I will, Michael," I said. "Thanks again."

I hung up and called the Mountain Center Police Department. Big Bob's sister, Susie, answered.

"Hey, Don. How's it going?"

"Fine, Susie, how about yourself?"

"No complaints. Want to speak to big brother?"

"Actually, I want to speak to your computer guy, Jackson."

"Jackson," she said, as if trying to place him. "Hang on a minute."

After maybe ten seconds of silence, a voice said, "Jackson."

"Jackson," I said, "my name is Don Youngblood."

"Yes," he said. "It's a pleasure to speak with you, Mr. Youngblood. No luck on the search so far. I guess that's why you're calling."

He seemed flustered. Well, after all, he was talking to a famous private investigator.

"Not exactly," I said. "I have a new list for you. You'll have to expand your search."

"Specific names?"

"Yes."

"How many?"

I told him.

"That will take some time," he said, less flustered than annoyed.

So much for fame, I thought.

◆   ◆   ◆   ◆

Even from my office, I heard the click of the big man's leather boot heels on the marble floor in the hall. The outer door opened and closed, and in a few seconds Big Bob Wilson was seated comfortably in one of the two oversized chairs in front of my desk.

"I heard you talked to our computer guy," Big Bob said.

"I did. I hope that was okay."

"Sure. How did you come up with the new list?"

I told him.

He handed me a folded business-sized envelope. "This came in the mail."

I opened it and read,

**You're taking too much time. Hurry up or I'll
give you another one to work with. Maybe
that hotshot Mountain Center PI can help you out.**

I had a really bad feeling when I read the last line. It was getting personal.

"You think this is about you?" Big Bob asked.

"I don't know," I said. "But if we identify the body from the list I gave Jackson this morning, then I think it is. I just can't figure out why."

15

Early the next morning, I was going seventy-five miles an hour on Interstate 81 South toward Knoxville with Johnny Cross's leather jacket hanging in the backseat on the passenger-side hook. I had picked up the jacket that morning from Wanda.

"I pulled two different hair samples off the collar and did some scrapings from the collar and cuffs," Wanda had told me. "The scrapings might be a waste of time."

"Let me guess. One of the hair samples was dark and the other blond."

"Good guess."

"Anything else?"

"Did you know there's a monogram inside the cuff on the left sleeve?"

"No, I didn't."

Wanda had shown me the monogram: *JCD*.

Interesting, I thought. It was not a traditional monogram—first initial, larger last initial, and middle initial. The initials were all the same size. I was guessing it was a modern monogram—first initial, middle initial, and last initial. That raised a question. Was Cross really Johnny's last name?

I passed the exit for Morristown. A few minutes later, Interstate 81 ended, connecting to Interstate 40. Traffic started to build as I approached Knoxville. Once I was in the city and off the interstate, I easily found the house I was looking for: a baby-blue split-level on a dead-end street in an upscale neighborhood. The house was recently painted. The once-white shutters were now a darker shade of blue. The owner knew I was coming. I went up the steps to the front landing and knocked on the door. It opened a few seconds later.

"This must be important for you to drive all the way down here," Amos Smith said, looking at the clothes bag slung over my shoulder.

Amos, known as "Teaberry" when he was in prison for forgery, was a black man in his early fifties, neat, well groomed, and a Harvard graduate. He was smart and resourceful and had a good sense of humor. I had known Amos for a while now and considered him a friend, just outside my inner circle.

"For me?" he asked, looking at the bag.

"Not exactly."

"Well, come on in and tell me what 'not exactly' means," Amos said, his cultured speech slow and measured.

I followed him down to the lower level and into his office. It hadn't changed since the last time I visited. I removed the leather jacket from the bag and hung it on a beautiful wooden coatrack while Amos made coffee. The gold dragon on the back of the jacket was facing us. Amos moved slowly from the coffeemaker to his desk, set my coffee in front of me, and sat, never taking his eyes off the jacket.

"Beautiful," he said. "Top quality, no doubt handmade."

We drank coffee and exchanged small talk.

"How's the neighborhood?" I asked.

"Still nice. Very ethnic: Caucasian, Hispanic, Asian, and me. I am the token African-American."

"How does that work out?"

"Fine," Amos said. "We all have two things in common. We have money, and we are well educated. Once they found out I am a Harvard grad, my skin color got considerably lighter."

"Funny how that works."

"It is," Amos said. "But they're not bad people, once you get to know them. A few are good friends."

"Restores my faith in humanity."

Amos laughed. "Money can do that." He took a drink of coffee. "I know etiquette requires a certain amount of chit-chat, but I am dying to know about that jacket."

"If you're interested, I need you to make a trip," I said. "All expenses paid. I need to find out who the jacket was made for."

"Where am I going?"

"Rome, Italy."

"Oh, yeah," Amos said. "I am definitely interested."

"Excellent."

"And you think a face-to-face is required," he said. "And that I might have to spread a little cash around to get all there is to get."

"You're a quick study," I said. "Must be that Harvard education."

"I doubt it. I learned more in jail that I did at Harvard."

"Now, that's a scary thought."

"Isn't it?" Amos said.

◆   ◆   ◆   ◆

Amos and I went to breakfast at a place of his choosing and worked out the details of his trip. The place turned out to be a swanky Internet café. I ordered a sausage and egg croissant, roasted red potatoes with rosemary, and the mildest coffee available. Amos ordered a dark-roast coffee and a chocolate croissant. I was envious. Amos appeared not to have one ounce of excess fat on his body.

He booted up his laptop and searched the web for flights to Rome.

"Go first-class," I said as Amos worked his mouse.

"I don't think so."

"Why not?"

"The first-class tickets are all over ten grand."

"You're kidding."

"I wish," Amos said. "I would love to go first-class, but I'd feel guilty about it. Business class will do just fine. It's a little less than five grand."

Obviously, I was out of touch with the price of airline tickets. Flying in a private jet can do that to a person. Then again, I had not flown overseas in the last twenty years.

Amos booked an afternoon flight two days hence on US Airways with a stopover in Charlotte, North Carolina. He would arrive in Rome early the following morning.

"I appreciate your frugalness, but I insist you book a really good hotel," I told him.

"No argument from me," he said as breakfast arrived. "I'll work on that later."

"And take plenty of pictures."

"My pleasure," Amos said.

16

Breakfast out on consecutive days was usually not in my plans, but the next morning I was in the Mountain Center Diner early. The morning crowd was straggling in, generally looking ragged and complaining about the heat, which was supposed to reach a record.

I was engrossed in *USA Today* when I heard Doris say, "Good morning, Chief Wilson."

The big man walked to my table, threw his Cowboy hat in an empty chair, and sat. He didn't look happy. Doris brought a pot of coffee and an empty mug, poured the mug full, and took our orders in silence, apparently sensing Big Bob was in a serious mood. I stared at the scowl on his face.

"What?" I asked after Doris left.

"Our computer guy got a hit off that list you gave him," he said. "She graduated UConn in '97 and was reported missing a few days ago. Johnson City PD has been advised and is working on a confirmation."

"Ah, hell," I said. "Don't tell me that."

"Hate to," Big Bob said. "But there it is. It would be one damn big coincidence if it wasn't her."

"I was hoping to be wrong about that one." A wave of trepidation washed over me like the ocean tide rolling in. What had I done to set these events in motion?

"What does it mean?"

"It means the note was for me," I said. "It's personal, and I have no idea why."

"Where do we go from here?" Big Bob asked.

"I don't know. But we need to draw him out."

I assumed our killer was male. There are very few female serial killers, and none I had heard of who killed only women. But I knew from experience that nothing was for certain. I had been surprised on more than one occasion.

"How?" Big Bob asked.

"The most obvious way would be through the press," I said. "I'll have to think about it. Since you let the Johnson City PD know you identified the body, I'm sure it will make their paper."

We were silent, drinking our coffee.

"You know," Big Bob said, "you draw trouble like shit draws flies."

"Not a gift I'm proud of."

"And another thing," he said, obviously annoyed. "What's Mary doing taking a two-week vacation? That's going to stretch us pretty thin."

"You had plenty of notice."

He made a mumbling sound.

"She could resign," I said. "That would solve your problem. Or you could demote her back to patrol."

He looked like he wanted to hit me. Then the look softened. "You know I'm not letting Mary leave MCPD. So what's your point?"

"My point is that you have a lot more to worry about than who is or isn't on vacation. You're always going to have to deal with that."

"Yeah, I know," the big man said. "I'm just in a foul mood."

Doris delivered our food. I barely tasted it, preoccupied with thoughts of another killer on the loose who had somehow drawn me into the eye of his storm.

When we finished, Big Bob stood and tossed enough bills on the table to cover his breakfast. I usually paid, but I knew he was in no mood to accept charity.

He picked up his hat and placed it squarely on his head. "Don't make this worse than it already is," he said. He walked out before I could respond.

I had no idea how I could make it worse. I also had no idea how I could make it better.

◆　　◆　　◆　　◆

Caller ID read, "Private caller." No number.

"Cherokee Investigations," I answered, one octave lower than normal, slightly annoyed. *Toughness is all.*

"Who is that?" Gretchen asked, feigning surprise.

"Who's asking, doll?" I said, doing my best Bogie, which wasn't half bad.

"Your girl Friday, you dumb lug."

"My girl Friday deserted me."

"She'll be back in the office Monday morning," Gretchen said.

"Well, I hope she'll be well rested."

"Oh, she will be."

"Good to hear," I said.

"I understand Mary and Lacy are leaving town," she said.

"You get around."

"Try to stay out of trouble until I get back," Gretchen said.

Then the line went dead. I had no idea whether she had hung up or we were disconnected, but she didn't call back.

17

Sunday morning, I took Lacy and Mary to Tri-Cities Airport. We were there early enough to check their bags and still have time for breakfast in the airport restaurant. They were excited. I was less excited. In fact, I wasn't at all excited. To be honest, I was depressed.

"What are you going to do while we're gone?" Lacy asked.

I hope to catch a bad guy, I thought.

"Par-tee!" I said.

"I'll bet," Lacy said. "You'll hang out at the office and the diner, go to the gym, eat takeout food, and watch TV."

"That's exactly what you'll do," Mary said, though she knew I had other things on my mind.

"What can I say? I'm boring."

"You're not boring," Lacy said. "But you are predictable."

Mary smiled and nodded.

◆　◆　◆　◆

At the security checkpoint, I kissed Mary a bit longer and more passionately than I should have.

"Get a room," Lacy said. She gave me a quick hug and was gone.

"You sure know how to give a girl a good sendoff," Mary whispered in my ear.

"Wait 'til you get back," I said so only she could hear. "I do really well with a welcome-home."

"I look forward to it."

She gave me a quick kiss, then turned and went through security and didn't look back. As I watched them walk toward their gate, I felt an extreme sense of loss.

Grow up, Youngblood, I told myself. *It's only a week.*

I left security and went to the observation deck and stayed there until their flight was airborne. I didn't leave until the tiny dot that was the Boeing 737 faded over the horizon. I was alone and not liking it.

On my way out of the airport, my cell phone rang. I flipped it open. Lacy teased me all the time about upgrading. Someday soon, I wouldn't have a choice.

"Want to meet me at the club for dinner?" Roy asked.

I knew his call was no coincidence. Mary had put him up to it. Roy and I never had dinner at the club.

"Sounds good," I said. "Give T. Elbert a call and ask him to join us. He doesn't get out much."

"I'll do it," Roy said. "What time?"

"Seven."

"See you there," Roy said.

◆   ◆   ◆   ◆

Late that night, I sat at the kitchen counter with a newly opened bottle of Amber Bock, cleaning my Glock Nine. The Glock didn't need cleaning. I was delaying my inevitable journey up the stairs to an empty bed. Jake and Junior lay nearby on the floor, sensing something was not quite right. Roy and T. Elbert had lifted my spirits at dinner, but not without some good-natured teasing that was at least R-rated and that they found extremely funny.

Mary had called on my way back to the condo to say she and Lacy had arrived safe and sound and were going out to eat with Susan at some trendy restaurant. I heard laughter in the background.

As I took another drink, wallowing in my aloneness, I heard the distant rumble of thunder. The day had been hot and humid, and thunderstorms were always in the forecast in July and August. I put the Glock away, picked up my beer, and went toward the balcony at the back of the condo. Jake and Junior followed. I slid the heavy glass door and left it open. The wind was picking up, and the night was cooling. Bad weather was headed our way. I sat with my beer in anticipation of the storm. Junior lay beside me. Jake paced nervously. He did not like storms.

I took a drink and turned my thoughts to other things. Amos Smith had called earlier from McGhee Tyson Airport in Knoxville.

"I'm boarding," he said. "Thanks for this opportunity."

"Have a good trip, and come back with some answers," I said. "It's important."

"Don't worry," Amos said. "I'll get answers. The dudes who made the jacket are still in business. I checked them out on the Internet."

Amos was now somewhere over the Atlantic Ocean. I hoped I had not sent him on a wild goose chase. My obsession to know everything was likely to bring me grief I would not have found if I just minded my own business. My father used to quote two worn out clichés: "Knowledge is power" and "Forewarned is forearmed." I agreed with both.

The killer of two mid-thirties women seemed to have a connection to me. As I drank my beer, I memory-scanned my past, trying to come up with anything that might help. I was still working on it when I went to the fridge and got another beer. The dogs followed me to the kitchen and back to the balcony. Fifteen minutes and another beer later, I still had no ideas. I was starting to get buzzed.

Distant lightning briefly illuminated the woods behind the condos. I thought I saw a figure moving higher up through the woods. Another flash, and the figure, if it was there at all, was gone. *Probably my imagination working overtime*, I thought. Another flash, then a boom. The time between lightning and thunder was diminishing. The storm was getting closer and louder. Jake went inside. Junior seemed not to notice. I stroked the back of his neck. The wind increased. A few seconds later, the rain arrived, not a little at a time but all at once. The overhang above the balcony kept me reasonably dry. The wind picked up, the trees rocked back and forth, and the rain came down in sheets. I was entranced.

I had always loved storms. I sat marveling at the intensity. The swirling wind was creating a heavy mist, and I was getting damp. I moved my chair back toward the door and at the same time positioned another chair to put my feet in. Junior moved with me and lay down when I was settled. Jake was nowhere in sight.

The thunder and lightning moved off and left a steady rain to lull me into a state of relaxation very near sleep. I drank the rest of my beer listening to the rain and wind until finally I heard nothing.

18

I awoke with a headache and a bad taste in my mouth. Sometime during the night, I had managed to find my bed. I gargled to get rid of the taste and then took the dogs out. I came back, made coffee, and took a hot shower. With the headache under control, I dressed and said goodbye to the dogs. I went through a Dunkin' Donuts drive-through and picked up a medium coffee and a toasted poppy seed bagel with cream cheese.

When I arrived at the office, Gretchen was already in, looking very much like she had been on a two-week tropical vacation. Her hair was sun-streaked, her skin tanned, her face beaming.

"Welcome back," I said, stopping in front of her desk.

"You don't look so good," Gretchen said. "Rough night?"

"The storm kept me up."

"Uh-huh," Gretchen said, not buying a word of it.

"Hold my calls," I said, moving toward my office. "When I finish eating, we'll go over some things."

"Feel better," Gretchen said as I shut my office door.

◆　　◆　　◆　　◆

I caught Gretchen up on the events of the past two weeks and gave her plenty of work to keep her busy for the foreseeable future. Soon after she returned to her desk, the phone rang and my intercom buzzed.

"Big Bob on line one," Gretchen said.

I picked up, knowing it could not be good news. "What's happening?" I asked.

"Too damn much," Big Bob said. "Johnson City got a confirmation on their dead body. It's the UConn woman. She was a nurse, last seen at a nurses' convention in Lexington, Kentucky."

So the Georgia typeface was not a clue, I thought.

I knew by the urgency in the big man's voice that there had to be more. "What else?"

"Another body."

"Where?"

"Greeneville," Big Bob said. "Dumped just like the others. No ID. I'd bet a hundred dollars she's a nurse, too."

"No bet," I said. "When did they find her?"

"Last night."

"How did you find out so fast?"

"I know their chief of police, and he knew about our body and Johnson City's," Big Bob said. "We've got a serial killer on the loose, Blood. It's time for you to call your friends at the FBI."

♦   ♦   ♦   ♦

I called his private number.

"Youngblood," he answered. "Long time no talk."

"How are you doing, Dave?"

"I'm still here," he said. "They're making it harder and harder for me to retire."

FBI agent David Steele had been my chief instructor at Quantico when, fresh out of college, Scott Glass and I had joined the bureau. I knew within two weeks that the FBI was not going to work for me, but I hung on through the initial training phase for Scott's sake. I finally came to my senses and resigned, knowing I was not cut out to take orders from government suits. I headed for Wall Street to take orders from financial suits while Scott made the FBI his career. At Quantico, my relationship with David Steele had been rocky, but we reconnected when I was working what came to be known nationally as the Tattoo Killers case or the Three Devils case. We formed an unfriendly alliance that grew friendlier as the case progressed. I hadn't seen Dave since the day he was in my office with Jared Gray, assistant director of the CIA. But that's another story.

"You're becoming a legend," I teased.

The FBI didn't like to see high-profile agents take early retirement. David Steele had at least ten good years left.

"I'd rather be a retired ex-agent," he said.

"Not going to happen," I said. "I have another case for you—a serial killer murdering nurses and dumping them in East Tennessee."

"Tell me about it," he said, fully engaged.

I gave him a brief overview.

"I'll call Mountain Center, Johnson City, and Greeneville and have the files emailed to me," David Steele said. "After I review them, I'll request that we open an official investigation. I'd like you to consult on this. I'm an agent down right now."

"Be glad to, as long as I can work another thing I've already started," I said.

"I'll take any time you can give me."

"I may somehow be connected to this serial killer," I said.

"How so?"

"Read the files, and then we'll talk. I want you to form your own opinion."

"Good thinking," David Steele said. "I'll be in touch."

19

Tuesday morning, David Steele sat in one of the two large chairs in front of my desk with three files in his lap. He had the Johnson City file open.

"That was a good stretch, coming up with the UConn woman's name," he said. "Take me through your thinking on that."

I told him about the lists I'd made and my feeling that I was somehow connected to the killer. When I finished, he sat and stared out my second-story window.

"So you think this is personal?"

"On some level," I said. "He may know me, or maybe he's just heard of me. But for some reason, he wants me involved."

"Well, he got his wish," David Steele said. "I need you to take the point on this. I'm slammed with other cases, and your consultant status is current, so that shouldn't be a problem with the bureau. I'll need you to update me on your progress."

"Is that an order, drill instructor?"

"You bet it is, Youngblood. It's hard to get giving orders out of my system."

"Not a problem, Dave. Glad to help."

"If you need anything, let me know."

"I want to look at all the victims' personal effects," I said. "Can you set that up with Johnson City and Greeneville? I'll need photos of every-thing—clothes, shoes, contents of their purses or whatever else they were carrying."

"All the evidence from the crime scenes will be in Knoxville this after-noon," David Steele said. "I'm picking up Mountain Center's evidence box after I leave here. We'll label and photograph everything, and I'll send you a file by email. I'll also include all the crime-scene photos."

"I assume Greeneville ran prints on their victim. I know Mountain Center and Johnson City did."

"They did," he said. "No hits on the Greeneville victim. We'll expand the database search and see if we get anything. I'll send everything to the lab as soon as I take pictures of the evidence. We'll see if we can come up with something they might have missed."

"Now that the first two victims have been identified, you should find out about their credit-card accounts and see if any of their cards have been used."

David Steele smiled. "This isn't our first rodeo. We're doing that, but I appreciate your double-checking."

"Sorry, but you did say I'll be the lead on this, so I need to know everything you're doing."

"Point taken," David Steele said. "If we get a credit-card hit, we'll let you know. Our lab will look not only for prints but any residue or fibers that might be clues to the killer or where the victims were killed. If we find anything, we'll let you know that, too. We'll take care of all the technical stuff. I need you thinking outside the box. That's what you're good at. We need some leads, some direction, anything."

♦　　　♦　　　♦　　　♦

After I left the office late that afternoon, I rounded up Jake and Junior and headed to the lake house. Without Mary and Lacy, the condo was like a room with no furniture, hollow and depressing. I had to get out of there. The lake house was home, and I felt comfortable there like nowhere else.

I had fenced in a large area of the side yard so the dogs could run without getting loose. When we arrived, I set them free there, and they took off like birds fleeing a cage. I knew Jake's enthusiasm would be short-lived, and Junior's not so much.

Later, as the sun sank over the mountains on the far side of the lake, I sat on the deck with my laptop in front of me, eating Chinese takeout I had picked up before leaving Mountain Center—sesame shrimp, house-fried rice, and two spring rolls. Three bottles of Sam Adams light sat near the food. One was empty, another half full. The bottle in waiting would not have to wait long.

The dogs lay near me, exhausted from their side-yard romp. I ate and looked at the crime-scene photos and pictures of the victims' personal effects. I briefly wondered how I could look at dead females and eat without being bothered. In truth, the photos *did* bother me; they just didn't dampen my appetite. I let the thought go and continued eating.

David Steele had sent me a Zip file. Inside were six folders, two from each location. One folder contained the crime-scene photos and the other photos of the personal effects: clothing, undergarments, shoes, jewelry, and purse contents. I was amazed at what could be found in a woman's purse.

The ringing of my cell phone broke my concentration.

"The ever-intrepid Donald Youngblood speaking," I answered, knowing the identity of the caller.

"Hey, Cowboy," Mary said in that sexy voice that stirred my inner being. "What are you up to?"

"I'm at the lake house having a party with a couple of topless hotties," I said.

"Liar."

"Okay, but they are topless, and they were hot, but they're cooling off fast. In fact, they're downright dogs."

Mary laughed. "So you couldn't stand being in the condo by yourself."

"Something like that."

"God, I miss you," Mary said. "It's ridiculous."

"I know the feeling."

"Anything interesting going on?"

I told her about the third body and my involvement in the case with David Steele and the FBI. When I finally managed to steer her away from the case and to her visit, I heard about the Golden Gate Bridge, the Pacific Coast Highway, the giant redwoods, Alcatraz, Fisherman's Wharf, Lombard Street, and Mary and Lacy's other destinations.

A half-hour later, we said good night. I felt better having heard her voice and knowing she was just a phone call away.

An hour after dark, I shut down my laptop, and the dogs and I turned in for the night. I went to bed thinking there was a clue somewhere in those files that I was missing.

Turns out, I was right.

20

The next day, I decided to break up my routine. The dogs and I stayed at the lake house. I had no idea why I didn't feel like going to the office. Maybe it was knowing that the blond Wonder Woman was not in town.

I called Gretchen. "Until further notice, I'm working from the lake house. Give out my cell-phone number only when you think it's necessary."

I expected a wisecrack. I didn't get one.

"Are you okay, Don?"

"I guess so," I said.

"Missing your girls, huh?"

"Big time."

"When do you think you'll be back in?"

"Maybe tomorrow, maybe not," I said. "I just don't know."

◆　　◆　　◆　　◆

Later that morning, I prepared breakfast. I cut up a potato and made the Youngblood version of home fries, with lots of paprika, some rosemary, and a dash of salt and pepper. I fried hot sausage patties and scrambled eggs with shredded cheddar cheese and fresh basil. I grilled two slices of Jack Spratt's delicious sprouted wheat bread, baked in Bountiful, Utah, which Scott Glass had introduced me to on my last visit. I took a mug of steaming coffee and my plate of food and ate on the lower deck. Afterward, I cleaned up, looking for other things to do and finding none.

Near noon, the dogs and I took the houseboat out on the lake. I use the term *houseboat* loosely. It was really a glorified barge my dad had built while I was growing up. A wooden deck sitting on pontoons, the houseboat was approximately twenty feet long and ten feet wide and had twin engines on the rear. Half of it was covered to offer shade on hot days. The uncovered part we called the sun deck. It made the houseboat sound like more than it was. All the decking, recently painted by Lacy and me, was light gray. Three-foot railings with heavy-duty wire mesh surrounded the houseboat except for two door-sized openings on either side for diving off and climbing back on. Each opening had a short folding ladder. The houseboat wasn't fancy, but it was sturdy and clean and was a tether to my childhood that I cherished.

I found a shady spot and fished for a while, hooking four largemouth bass, which I later released. Meanwhile, I snacked, drank beer, and listened to a soft-rock station on my ancient portable radio. Later, I motored to a warmer spot and went swimming. Jake joined me immediately. Junior paced before finally deciding to join the fun, after some coaxing. I came out on several occasions and dove back in. When the dogs appeared to be struggling, I hauled them back on board and went in one last time. Neither Jake nor Junior joined me. They shook off all the water they could and lay down in the sun.

That night, as I drifted into a dream-free sleep, I still had the feeling I was missing a clue from the crime-scene and evidence photos. *I need to look at those again*, I thought.

21

The next day, I realized I could not make a steady diet of killing time at the lake house. Twenty-four hours was long enough to feel sorry for myself. *You're supposed to be a tough guy, Youngblood*, I thought.

I left the dogs with food and water in the fenced-in side yard and went to the office early. I read my message slips from Gretchen, checked email, locked up, and headed down the back alley to the Mountain Center Diner. I went through the rear entrance to my table, where Roy Husky sat reading the local paper.

"Anything interesting in there?" I asked as I sat.

"Not a thing," Roy said. "How are you making out without your ladies?"

"Surviving." I restrained myself from adding *barely*.

Doris appeared at our table, pad and pencil in hand. "Haven't seen you in a few days, Mr. Youngblood."

"I've been out of town," I said. Well, that was literally true. The lake house was out of town.

Doris seemed placated by that news and took our orders without further comment.

"What's new with you?" I asked Roy.

"Nothing much since Sunday night. Bruiser is supposed to start Monday. We're gearing up for the new contract, but there are still some glitches to work out. I'm up to my ass in alligators, and somebody forgot to drain the swamp. What about you?"

"Well, Sunday night is kind of a blur," I said. "Since then, I've just been trying to figure some things out."

Roy smiled but kept his own counsel. We moved on to safer topics: sports and politics. Roy and I were generally like-minded in our political views.

Breakfast arrived. As we ate, Roy filled me in on some of the mundane news in the *Mountain Center Press*.

"T. Elbert was asking about you yesterday," he said. "Said to tell you Sunday night did not take the place of a porch visit."

I grimaced. I hadn't been on T. Elbert's front porch in over two weeks, a long stretch, based on my usual visits.

"Thanks for reminding me," I said. "I've been so distracted by this serial killer thing and the Saddle Boot thing that my daily routine has been shot to hell."

"What serial killer thing?"

"Between us?"

Roy nodded.

"I'm working with the FBI again."

He shook his head. "That can't be good."

I told him about the three dead women and the notes.

"You do have a special talent for drawing bad guys," Roy said.

Don't remind me, I thought.

◆　　◆　　◆　　◆

Later that morning, I was back in the office reviewing the crime-scene and evidence photos, which I had printed and laid out on the conference table.

"What's all this?" Gretchen asked as she closed the outer office door.

I told her about the three murders.

"Take a look and tell me if you see anything out of the ordinary," I said.

She spent a long time studying the pictures.

"I don't know much about the crime-scene stuff," she said. "But I'm seeing about what I'd expect in the purse contents."

I gathered the photos and took them into my office. "Hold my calls," I told Gretchen as I shut the door.

I sat and started shuffling through the evidence photos, concentrating on the purse contents. I saw fingernail clippers, nail files, ChapStick, lipstick, lip gloss, tissues, key rings filled with keys and bar-code cards for various stores, a couple of small spray cans of mace, a referee's whistle, nasal spray, pill boxes, breath mints, and billfolds. The billfolds contained cash but no credit cards, pictures, or driver's licenses.

I had a thought—a longshot at best. I picked up my phone and called David Steele.

"It's your favorite consultant," I said when he answered.

"Did you call for a compliment, or do you have something?"

"I had a thought. Do you have the evidence from the three murders?"

"Yes," he said. "The boxes just came back from the lab. We got a few prints, but they're either from the victims or persons unknown, and none of the unknowns are in the system or show up more than once."

"I need to have a look," I said. "Can I come down?"

"I need to be in Morristown later today," David Steele said. "Buy me dinner and I'll make a personal delivery."

"You've got a deal."

•   •   •   •

Late that afternoon, the three evidence boxes sat on my conference-room table. Drinking a fresh cup of coffee brewed on my Keurig, David Steele sat and watched me sift through the contents. I put on rubber gloves and methodically went through each box. I was particularly interested in the car keys. Each of the rings held four to six keys and seven to ten plastic bar-code cards. I removed the cards from the rings and laid them out in three separate groupings, being careful to place them in the order I took them off. I saw grocery-store cards, pharmacy cards, Office Depot, Sears, Ace Hardware, AAA, AutoZone, and Hallmark. I was hoping to find a match. I found one: they all had AAA cards. I didn't think that was a clue but didn't know for sure.

Then I noticed something. On every key chain was a plastic charm. None were alike. One key ring contained a miniature typewriter, one a miniature sailboat, and the third a small guitar. The sailboat and type-writer were a shiny silver color. The guitar was more of a pewter color.

"Did you notice these plastic charms?"

"I really didn't pay much attention to the key rings," David Steele said, standing to take a closer look. "You think the charms are more than a coincidence?"

"Maybe," I said. "Our killer seems to be into clues and riddles. At this point, I'm willing to consider anything."

"They all had AAA."

"I noticed."

I took the charms off the key rings and laid them in the appropriate groupings. Then I took pictures of each group. When I finished, I put everything back the way I had found it.

"I need someone to run down all these swipe cards and make sure they actually belonged to the victims," I said. "Start with the AAA cards."

"That's a good thought," David Steele said.

I spent another half-hour going through the boxes but didn't find anything that piqued my interest. I put everything back in the boxes and replaced the lids.

"Come on," I said. "I'll take you to the Mountain Center Country Club for dinner."

"Lucky me," David Steele said. "I finally get to see how the rich guys live."

22

Although I almost never visited T. Elbert on a Friday, I was long overdue for a trip to his front porch. As my private investigation enterprise had grown over the years, my visits had become fewer and fewer. There was a time when I had visited every Wednesday like clockwork. But times had changed, and the dynamics of my life changed with them. T. Elbert was a smart man; he understood, but that did not stop me from feeling guilty. Thankfully, Roy Husky took up some of the slack.

I picked up coffee and bagels at a Dunkin' Donuts drive-through and headed for Olivia Drive. He was waiting on the porch in one of his rocking chairs. The morning was pleasantly cool for summer but I knew it would be hot later in the day. Ceiling fans were turning lazily, pleasantly stirring the cool air above our heads. I set the coffee and bagels on a table between the two rockers and sat. I had sent T. Elbert an email, so he knew I was coming.

"Thanks for the delivery," he said, reaching for the corrugated tray that held the coffee. If he noticed the letter-sized manila envelope underneath the tray, he made no comment.

"My pleasure," I said, folding back the flap on my cup lid and taking a drink.

"How's temporary bachelorhood?"

"Not so hot. I miss my ladies."

T. Elbert unwrapped a toasted poppy seed bagel with cream cheese, took a bite, and nodded approval. I had already started on a toasted sesame seed bagel. I wiped cream cheese from the corner of my mouth.

"What's new?" he asked, taking a drink of his black coffee.

"I'm working with the FBI again," I said nonchalantly.

T. Elbert's head popped up, his eyes like lasers acquiring a target. "What?"

I looked at him, smiled, and took a drink. I had caught him off guard but now had his full attention.

"Damn it, Donald. I want to hear all of it, every detail."

So, as I usually did with T. Elbert, I dragged the story out as long as I could. I paused at critical parts to take a bite of bagel or a drink of coffee. T. Elbert listened patiently, processing all of it.

"Another serial killer," he said when I was finished. "You do have a talent for drawing the bad ones."

"So it seems," I said, sliding the envelope from beneath the tray and handing it to him. "Evidence photos from all three victims. Take a look and see if you come up with anything I didn't."

"I'll do it. I appreciate being in on this."

Asking T. Elbert to look at the photos turned out to be a good move on my part.

◆　　◆　　◆　　◆

The morning was quiet. Gretchen arrived at her usual time and poked her head in my office.

"Good morning."

Usually, Gretchen went to her desk and buzzed me on the intercom to say she was in. Since returning from vacation, she was much more animated. I knew something was up.

"Good morning to you, too," I said. "Pour yourself a cup of coffee and come on back."

A minute later, Gretchen was sitting in front of my desk with a cup of coffee and her notepad. I went over her assignments for the day. She smiled as she took notes. Something was definitely up.

"You're in a good mood."

"I am," she said.

"I surmise you no longer think all men are rats."

"One is most certainly not."

"So you met this guy on vacation."

"I did," Gretchen said.

"Long-distance relationships are tough."

"He lives in Nashville. Not too far and not too close."

"What does he do?"

"He's an aide to the governor," she said.

"I know the governor."

"I know you do," Gretchen said. "Chase heard the governor mention your name during the Three Devils case."

"Chase?" I stifled a laugh.

"One cannot help what one's parents name them. I certainly wouldn't have chosen Gretchen."

"So use your middle name."

Gretchen gave me a look. "Let's not go there. My middle name makes Gretchen sound like a movie star. I'd better get busy." She got up and headed toward the door.

"You're going to see Chase this weekend, aren't you?"

She stopped in the doorway and smiled. "Maybe," she said coyly. Then she disappeared into the outer office.

◆   ◆   ◆   ◆

Later that morning, the phone rang and my intercom buzzed.

"Amos Smith," Gretchen said.

"Amos," I said, pressing the line-one button on my console.

"*Buon giorno*," Amos said.

"Good morning to you, too. Although it must be afternoon where you are."

"Indeed it is," Amos said slowly. "I'm going to dinner soon with a lovely Italian lady."

"So you called to brag?"

Amos laughed. "Well, maybe a little. I called to tell you I have what you need. I'll come up next week, and you can buy me one of those great breakfasts at the Mountain Center Diner."

"You could just tell me now."

"Way too much to tell over the phone," Amos said. "I took notes, which are back at the hotel. Besides, I want to do a show and tell. Hey, here comes my date. Got to run, Youngblood. I'll call you when I get back. *Arrivederci!*"

Amos was gone.

It sounded like he was having more fun than I was.

◆   ◆   ◆   ◆

Right after I hung up with Amos the phone rang again. A few seconds later, Gretchen's voice came over the intercom announcing a call from David Steele.

"What's going on, Dave?"

"Checking to see if you have anything new," he said.

"Not much. I gave the photo file to T. Elbert to see if he could spot anything."

"The retired TBI agent in the wheelchair," he said.

"That would be him. Although the retired part is something of a mystery. He may still be on the payroll."

"Guess another pair of eyes can't hurt."

"Not if they're his," I said. "What did you find out about the bar-code cards?"

"Nothing. They all had AAA, and all the bar-code cards belonged to the victims. We seem to be at a dead end, Youngblood."

"That happens a lot in our business," I said.

"It does."

"I'm surprised the press hasn't made the serial killer connection yet," I said.

"We're doing a better job of compartmentalizing those things than we used to," Dave Steele said. "Only a few people know about this case. We've tracked down leaks on other cases in the last few years, and agents have been severely reprimanded and put on notice. Word gets around. Everyone is clamming up."

"Well, let's hope the trend continues. I'll be back to you if T. Elbert comes up with anything or something else breaks."

I needed a solid lead and was hoping it would come soon.

As it turned out, I didn't have to wait long.

◆   ◆   ◆   ◆

Late that afternoon, I drove to the lake house, collected the dogs, and went to the condo. I seemed to have gotten over my initial loneliness. I wondered if that was good or bad. I ordered pizza from Best Italian, prepared myself a Caesar salad, and opened a Sam Adams Light. I ate in front of my computer and caught up with the world of sports. My baseball team from childhood was the Cincinnati Reds. They had not been good for a number of years but now were residing in first place in the National League's Central Division and looking like a playoff contender. I pored over their statistics while enjoying my feast. Life was good, at least in my sports world.

23

I spent an uneventful weekend at the lake house doing odd jobs on Saturday and taking the houseboat out on the lake with the dogs on Sunday. I talked to Mary and Lacy on the phone. Since they were staying another week, they obviously didn't miss me as much as I missed them. How could they possibly want another week away from me?

Late Sunday evening, I took the dogs for a walk, then came back and checked email one last time before I turned in. I had an email from T. Elbert:

Come see me Monday morning. I might have found something. No need to bring coffee. I'll make coffee.

T. Elbert making coffee—that was a really good sign.

◆　　◆　　◆　　◆

Monday morning when I arrived, T. Elbert was not on his porch. The front door was open. I opened the storm door and went inside. The house was cool.

"Anybody home?" I shouted.

"Back here," T. Elbert shouted back. "Pour yourself a cup of coffee and come on back."

I walked through the living room and dining room into the kitchen and fixed myself a cup of coffee with cream and sugar. I took a sip and muttered approval, then returned to the dining room, made a left down a short hall, and then a left into T. Elbert's bedroom office. The room contained a bedroom suite and had enough space left over for a sprawling old oak desk that faced the doorway. A computer, a printer, and a fax machine sat on the desk. T. Elbert was staring intently at his computer screen.

"Come here and look at this."

I went around his desk and leaned over his shoulder. On his screen was a Cracker Jack website. He was scrolling through a list of Cracker Jack toys, charms, and prizes.

"So far, I've found two of the three charms: the sailboat and the typewriter. They're old, from the fifties."

"That's good work, special agent."

T. Elbert beamed. "This research certainly brought back memories. When I was a kid, I loved getting a box of Cracker Jack. I liked the peanuts and popcorn, but the real treat was the prize inside the box. They put good prizes in back then. Now, they're just worthless pieces of paper."

"Simple economics," I said. "They're cutting costs to improve the bottom line."

"Screw the bottom line. They shouldn't mess with tradition."

"You should write the president of the company," I said.

"I may do that."

Every now and then, T. Elbert went on a rant about one thing or another. I knew to let it run its course. We drank coffee and said nothing for a while.

"You know what you should do now?" T. Elbert asked, as if leading me to a conclusion.

"I do," I said. "Check the backgrounds of the three victims to see if they have any ties to Cracker Jack collecting."

"That's what I'd do," he said. "But I'll bet they don't."

"No bet," I said. "But if we can tie those charms to a buyer or a collector, it might lead to our killer."

"That would be like finding the proverbial needle in the haystack," T. Elbert said.

"You're right. But if I start poking around, I might get lucky or stir something up."

"Let me think about it," T. Elbert said. "I want to help you with this."

"Be my guest. The more, the merrier."

"Now get out of here and let me work," he said. I could tell he was revved up.

"Yes, sir."

I left.

T. Elbert barely noticed.

◆   ◆   ◆   ◆

I was in the office an hour before Gretchen was due to arrive. I checked email, then went online and looked in on the market. The Dow continued to swing back and forth around thirteen thousand. It would be interesting to see what happened after the presidential election. Could fourteen thousand be attainable? Could it actually get to fifteen thousand? Would the market crash? Who knew?

The phone rang. Caller ID was blocked. Since I was working a couple of cases, I had to answer.

"Cherokee Investigations," I answered blandly, expecting a telemarketing pitch.

"Youngblood," the familiar voice said. "I'm not trying to be a pest, just checking in."

"I was going to call you," I said. "T. Elbert came up with something."

"What?"

I told him about the Cracker Jack charms.

"Christ have mercy," Dave said. "If the press gets hold of this, I can hear it now: the Cracker Jack Killer."

"Yeah, I thought about that. We need to keep the Cracker Jack charms on a need-to-know basis only."

"Agreed. So what's next?"

"I'll try to find out who sold them to whom," I said. "They're old, so they didn't recently come out of a box. Maybe you can get someone to check websites that sell Cracker Jack toys and charms."

"Good thought," David Steele said.

"Also have someone check to see if the victims were collectors. I doubt it, but it's worth a shot. And see if any of the charms are connected to the victims somehow. See if they sailed or played guitar or wrote."

David Steele chuckled as he listened to me ramble. "I've got a better idea. I'm going to assign a junior agent to you. He can do the grunt work."

"I thought all your agents were too busy to work this case."

"They are," he said. "This agent was just assigned to me. I don't have time to deal with him right now, so try to keep him busy. If you need any legwork, let him do it. Serial killer cases are always high priority, so anything you need him to do, he'll do it. His name is Buckley Clarke."

"Buckley?" First Chase and now Buckley. Couldn't parents name their kids anything traditional?

"What can I say? I think it's an old family thing."

"Okay," I said. "Have him come see me."

Maybe he can stain the deck at the lake house, I thought.

◆　　◆　　◆　　◆

It was midafternoon, and Special Agent Buckley Clarke sat in one of the oversized chairs in front of my desk.

"I didn't expect you so soon," I said.

"I think Agent Steele was anxious to get me out of the office," Buckley Clarke said. "I'm looking forward to working with you on this case. Agent Steele speaks highly of you. He said you broke the Tattoo Killers case."

"Did he tell you I left the FBI after basic training at Quantico?"

"What he told me was that you chose not to pursue a promising career in the FBI. I think he mentioned something about issues with authority. He also said you were, and I quote, 'a damn fine investigator,' and that I can learn a lot from you."

"How nice. He wouldn't say that face to face in a million years."

Buckley smiled. I could easily hate him. He was blond haired and blue eyed and had an easy smile and a disarming manner. He was also six feet tall and slim and had movie-star looks.

I brought him up to speed on the Cracker Jack Killer.

"I shouldn't have to tell you this is confidential," I said.

"But you're telling me anyway."

"I am. We do not want the press getting hold of this information."

"Why don't we refer to him as CJK?" Buckley said. "That way, if anyone overhears us, they won't know what we're talking about. They'll think it's someone's initials."

"Okay," I said. "I like it. I'll tell Agent Steele it was your idea."

Buckley seemed pleased.

"Here's what I want you to do."

He eagerly took notes as I gave him his first assignment. I must admit that I, too, felt a little excited.

Get over yourself, Youngblood.

24

Late Tuesday morning, I sat at my table in the Mountain Center Diner with Amos Smith, who was regaling me with tales from his trip to Italy. The leather jacket was in a carry bag draped over the back of a vacant chair. The diner was practically empty, the breakfast crowd gone and the lunch crowd yet to show up.

"I'm going back," he said.

"To Italy?"

"Yes."

Well, there can be only one reason to go back so soon, I thought.

"To see a woman," I said.

"How did you know?"

"I'm a detective. We know things. Besides, it wasn't much of a stretch."

Amos smiled and took the last bite of his omelet. "I'm renting a villa for a year."

"A year. It must be serious."

Amos smiled. "Might be."

We had enjoyed breakfast as I let Amos ramble on without getting to the business at hand. Doris cleared our table and brought fresh mugs of coffee.

"Time for show and tell," Amos said.

He opened his laptop, booted up, and clicked on a picture file named Italy. A sub file was named Forzini. It included pictures of a storefront, pictures inside the store, pictures of the employees, and pictures of the jacket-making process.

"Thorough," I said. "I'm surprised they gave you so much access."

"I told them I was an American freelance journalist doing a story on Italian handmade leather jackets."

"Do you also work for National News Network?" I asked.

Amos smiled again. "I do."

"So did you find out who ordered our jacket in question?"

"I did."

"And how did you accomplish that?"

"Well ..." Amos paused for effect. "When they asked me how I found out about Forzini Brothers, I showed them the jacket and told them I had purchased it on eBay. They were none too happy that an owner of one of their handcrafted jackets would sell it online and were very willing to share the name and address of the buyer."

"Smart," I said.

"I was trying to earn back your investment in the trip."

He handed me a page from his personal notepad. In Amos Smith's neat handwriting, it read,

John Cross Durbinfield
Durbinfield Estate
East Hampton
Long Island, NY 11937

CJS
RWB

"Durbinfield, as in *the Durbinfields*?"

"Exactly," Amos said.

Well, that certainly explained the expensive leather jacket. The Durbinfields were one of the most powerful and wealthy families in finance. I wondered if John Cross Durbinfield was a prodigal son who had disdained the family name and set out on his own as Johnny Cross. Or had he been tossed out of the family because he was a black sheep? If Johnny Cross was indeed Lacy's father, things might get complicated. Lacy might be heir to a real fortune, not just my measly millions.

"What are these other two sets of initials?"

"Three jackets were ordered," Amos said. "All were identical, except for the initials."

"That's good work, Amos."

"I'm glad I could find what you were looking for," he said. "You'll never know how much that trip meant to me."

He opened a file named Sophia and clicked on the first picture—a beautiful dark-skinned woman.

"This is Sophia. Her father was Indian, from India, and her mother was Italian."

"Nice," I said.

"She is a little younger than me. She has been a widow for three years now."

"She seems like a good reason to go back."

"She is that."

"When are you leaving?"

"A few weeks," Amos said. "I'm trying to lease my house."

"Well, keep in touch. I've gotten used to your being around."

"Not to worry," Amos said. "I'll be a phone call away if you need anything."

◆   ◆   ◆   ◆

"I need you to do some research," I said to Gretchen.

"Do we have another case?" she asked excitedly.

"We do," I said, thinking of John Cross Durbinfield, whose leather jacket with the golden stitched dragon now hung in my office closet.

"Does this involve the FBI?"

"No."

"Good," Gretchen said. "What do you need?"

"Find out all you can on John Cross Durbinfield."

"Durbinfield? As in the obscenely rich Durbinfields?"

"That would be them," I said. "There should be tons of info on the family. See how much you can find out about John Cross. The old man is dead, and I think his widow, Elizabeth, is chairman of the board of Durbinfield Financial. I'm guessing John Cross would have been her son, unless he was a cousin or something."

"Okay."

"Make this top priority. Anything you're doing that can wait, let it wait."

"You bet," Gretchen said. "I'm starting now."

◆   ◆   ◆   ◆

Late that afternoon, I drove to the condo. Both dogs eagerly jumped in the back of the Pathfinder as soon as I lifted the tailgate. They knew that wherever we were going, they'd get to run.

I drove to the lake house, settled the dogs in the side yard, and unloaded a few things I had brought from the condo, including my laptop. I changed into shorts, a T-shirt, and trail-running shoes. I ran up the driveway and down to the main road and went right for about half a mile to the lake park entrance and down to the picnic parking area. From there, I accessed a four-mile loop trail that wound through the woods and worked its way back along the lake to the parking area. I was careful of the rocks and roots on the trail. The last thing I needed was a sprained ankle.

The weather was hot and humid. By the time I did the return trip down the driveway to the lake house, I was soaked in sweat. The dogs watched as I ran around the opposite side of the house and down to the dock. I stripped down to my Under Armour briefs and dove off the dock into the mercifully cool lake.

◆　　◆　　◆　　◆

"Where are you?" Mary asked.

"On the lower deck at the lake house."

"You can't seem to make up your mind where you want to be."

"Only because you're not here. I'm starting to feel like a monk."

Mary laughed. "That feeling will go away very soon after I'm back. I've already made arrangements for Lacy to spend the night with Hannah."

"Clever girl," I said. "I like the way you think."

"You better," Mary said. "I need my man. I've had enough of chick talk and perfect weather to last me awhile. I need to get back to normal."

"How's Lacy doing?"

"Great. Susan introduced her to some girls her age, and she's made a new friend, Candy. But come Sunday, she'll be ready to go. She knows this isn't the real world."

"Candy?"

"What can I say? It's California."

I also talked to Lacy, who was attentive but had things to do, so our conversation was short. Lacy gave the phone back to Mary, and I took a few minutes to tell her about John Cross Durbinfield.

"Durbinfield?" Mary said. "My God!"

"Not quite," I said. "But certainly gods of finance."

"What's your next move?"

"Find out all I can about John Cross Durbinfield."

"That could get interesting," Mary said.

"It could."

"What's going on with the serial killer case?"

"You mean CJK," I said.

"CJK?"

I recounted my meeting with T. Elbert and my phone call with David Steele and told her about Buckley Clarke. "Buckley came up with the CJK part."

"That had to make T. Elbert feel good," Mary said. "Making the Cracker Jack connection."

"It did indeed."

I heard shouting in the background. It sounded like Lacy.

"Got to go," Mary said. "Watch yourself, Cowboy. Things could get dangerous."

Yes, I thought, *things could.*

25

"I have some information on John Cross Durbinfield," Gretchen said.

"That was fast."

"In case you haven't noticed, when I get hold of an interesting project, I am very driven."

I laughed.

"I've noticed. How late did you stay up?"

"Midnight," Gretchen said.

"I owe you a day off."

"I'll take it."

"What have you got?"

"Well, for starters, John Cross Durbinfield is actually John Cross Durbinfield III. Cross is his great-grandmother's maiden name. He went to Franklin Pierce Academy in Pierce, New Hampshire, a prep school for old-money smart kids. He graduated in 1986. The interesting thing is that I couldn't find anything on him after his graduation from Franklin Pierce."

He got tired of the good life and took off, I thought.

"What else?"

"The Durbinfields have an estate in East Hampton, Long Island."

Gretchen handed me a picture of the Durbinfield mansion. It reminded me of the Biltmore Estate in Asheville, North Carolina—more hotel than house, more staff than family, money gone wild.

"Nice little shack," I said.

"I cannot even imagine that kind of wealth," Gretchen said.

"You could if you were born into it."

"I printed some magazine articles regarding the Durbinfields for you to look at when you get time," Gretchen said, handing me a file. "And one other thing. He was an artist. There's an article in the file that says he won an art award his senior year. It sounded pretty prestigious."

"Okay, thanks."

"Buckley Clarke called and wanted to know if he could come by this afternoon," Gretchen said, standing to leave. "I'll be working on monthly summaries today, unless you have anything else for me."

"Nothing I can think of. Call Buckley and tell him to come around three."

"Will do."

Gretchen turned and walked out of my office, closing the door behind her and leaving me alone with a single thought: *What do I do now?*

◆   ◆   ◆   ◆

Buckley Clarke sat across from me looking dapper and anything but an FBI agent in dark brown pants, a cream-colored shirt, and a yellow silk tie.

He's going to give other agents a complex, I thought.

"Nice suit," I said.

"I like clothes," he said.

Buckley had removed his jacket and draped it across the back of the other chair facing my desk. He seemed relaxed. He removed a file from his briefcase.

"I spent the last two days on the phone," he said.

I waited.

"Victim number one, the nurse at Sloan-Kettering, went missing from a nurses' convention in Washington, D.C. She had the sailboat charm on her key chain. I talked with NYPD and got the name of some of her friends and coworkers, and as far as any of them knew, she did not have a connection to sailing and was not a Cracker Jack charm collector."

I knew victim number one was Ashley Hill. I didn't know the names of the other two victims and didn't want to know.

"Husband or boyfriend?"

"No husband, and as far as anyone knew, she was not dating," Buckley said.

"Go on."

"Victim number two was a nurse from Hartford, Connecticut. She went missing from a nurses' convention in Lexington, Kentucky. I talked with Hartford PD. She was married, so I talked with her husband. He's past the shock phase and into the really pissed-off phase. Once I calmed him down, he was helpful and seemed pleased that the FBI was trying to find his wife's killer. She was the one with the typewriter charm. She was not a writer and wasn't interested in writing, as far as her husband knew. He couldn't recollect ever seeing the charm on her key chain. His alibi is airtight, so we're not looking at him as a suspect."

I nodded.

Buckley paused to look at his file.

"Victim number three was from Cleveland, Ohio, and was last seen at a nurses' convention in Cincinnati. She was recently divorced and not seeing anyone, as far as her close friends knew. The ex-husband is doing a tour in Afghanistan, so that rules him out as a suspect. Her friends said the divorce was amicable. There was a guitar charm on her key chain, and as far as anyone knew, she did not play guitar. Her mother did tell me she played piano when she was young."

"That's good work, Buckley."

"Thanks. What now?"

Good question. I had no idea.

"Where are you staying?" I asked.

"I have an apartment in Knoxville," Buckley said. "I'll drive back whenever you say we're done for the day."

"We're done," I said. "Meet me here in the morning around nine-thirty."

"Will do," he said, writing in his notepad.

◆   ◆   ◆   ◆

Before I left the office, I called David Steele.

"You need Buckley for anything?" I asked.

"Not right now," he said. "What's up?"

I told him.

"So we have an invisible killer, no leads, and you're grasping at straws."

"Sounds familiar, doesn't it?"

"Yeah, but you seem to have a knack for picking the right straw. So go ahead and do what you want to do, and I'll justify the cost."

"Thanks," I said.

There was dead air for a moment, and I thought I had lost Dave.

"Are you there?"

"Yeah, I was thinking," he said. "And I don't even want to say this out loud, but I'm going to anyway."

I waited.

"Are you surprised we haven't had another body or note? I mean, we're overdue for one if he keeps to the same schedule."

I hadn't thought about it and didn't want to.

"Maybe three is it," I said. "Maybe he died of a heart attack or got hit by a bus or tried to kill the wrong nurse."

"It would be great to be that lucky," David Steele said. "But until then, keep working it and see what you can find."

26

At nine-thirty sharp the following morning, Buckley Clarke sat across from my desk, notepad open and pen at the ready. I admired his discipline. I was blessed with a good memory and rarely wrote anything down. I sometimes recorded notes in a case file, but much of the information concerning my past cases was in my head.

"I want you to visit the living quarters of our three victims," I said.

Buckley wrote on his pad. "Sorry, but I need to ask if you have approval for this."

"Agent Steele has approved the travel. You can check with him if it makes you comfortable."

"Not necessary," he said. "You have no reason to lie to me."

"Can't think of one."

Buckley smiled. "What am I looking for?"

"A connection," I said. "Take a camera and spend some time at each victim's abode. Don't get in a hurry. Take lots of picture, open drawers, look at photo albums. You can get a sense of someone by seeing where they live. When you're finished, write down what you feel you've learned about that victim. Take all day if you need to."

Buckley was furiously writing, trying to keep up with my oratory. I paused to let him catch up. He finished and looked up.

"Do them in order. First victim's home is the first place you visit."

"Why?"

"I don't know," I said. "It just feels right. There might be some kind of time line you can pick up on that maybe you wouldn't if you didn't do them in order. I'm grasping at straws here."

"It's a good thought. What else?"

"As I said, don't get in a hurry. Be patient, go slow. If there's a connection, you'll find it."

I didn't think there was a connection. But if I was wrong, it might crack the case wide open.

"Do you have any questions?"

Buckley studied his notes. "No."

"Go," I said.

He went.

◆　　◆　　◆　　◆

That afternoon, I took a brief look at the market, but my heart wasn't in it. I was torn between my two cases. CJK was life and death; JCD was not. However, CJK seemed to be at a standstill, and I had a burning desire to solve the mystery surrounding Johnny Cross.

I called Roy Husky. His assistant answered. Roy with an assistant—I had to adjust. I waited.

"Hey, Gumshoe," Roy said when he finally came on the line. "What's so important that you have to bother the vice president of Fleet Industries?"

"Thought you might be bored, just sitting there and twiddling your thumbs and all."

"I wish," Roy said. "What's up?"

"Is Jim Doak available for a quick trip tomorrow?"

"Hang on."

I heard the sounds of a keyboard.

"Jim and his jet are free," Roy said. "What time?"

"Morning. Tell Jim wheels up at eight o'clock."

"Where are you headed?"

"Pierce, New Hampshire."

"What's in Pierce, New Hampshire?"

"An exclusive prep school for the very rich."

"Still chasing down the Saddle Boot thing?" Roy asked.

"I am," I said.

◆　　◆　　◆　　◆

I was sitting on the lower deck watching the sun slowly descend over the hills on the far side of the lake. Jake and Junior lay on either side of me. I was drinking my second Amber Bock. The night was perfect except for the fact that Mary was three thousand miles away. Her voice in my cell phone sounded like she was next door. Hearing her was comforting, but I wanted all of her—to see her, to touch her.

"Just three more nights," she said. "Hang in there."

"You cannot do this again," I said.

"I know."

"Lacy starts school next week."

"I'm aware of that."

"Next time, Susan comes here."

"Right," Mary said.

"I'll pay for the trip."

"Sure you will." Mary paused. "What happened to that confirmed bachelor who was used to living alone and didn't know if he could adjust to being married and living with two females?"

What did happen to him? I wondered.

"He fell in love," I said.

"How do you do that?"

"Do what?"

"Come up with the perfect answer at just the right time."

"It's an art form. I've spent years cultivating it."

Mary laughed. "How are the dogs?"

She was steering away from my loneliness. I was glad to take a different path.

"They're right here, and they're fine," I said. "How's Lacy?"

We talked that way for a while, then finally said good night. When we hung up, I felt empty and incomplete. I watched the sun disappear, finished my Amber Bock, took the dogs in, and went to bed at an unprecedented nine o'clock.

27

"Buckle in, Don," Jim Doak said over the intercom.

I had being flying off and on with Jim Doak on the same Fleet Industries jet for about five years. I hadn't liked flying commercial before, and now I hated it. Flying around the country on a private jet will do that to you.

I watched the countryside grow smaller and smaller as we climbed to our cruising altitude. I faced forward in a comfortable leather bucket seat, a small table within easy access. My overnight bag was in an overhead compartment above me, though I didn't plan on spending the night.

My laptop was logged on to the Franklin Pierce Academy website. I was trying to learn as much as I could about the academy so I could decide on my approach. A private detective would raise red flags. A parent looking for a prep school for his teenage daughter would be okay, except that Lacy was a senior and was due to start school next week. I supposed I'd have to find a phone booth, turn around twice, and come out as Alexander Youngblood, National News Network freelance journalist, an alias created by Amos Smith. A journalist doing a story would likely get more attention and more answers than a parent looking.

I called Amos to give him a heads-up.

"I'm going undercover with the National News Network ID you made for me last year," I told him. "I just wanted to tell you in case you get a hit on the website or an email."

"Does this have to do with the leather jacket?"

"Yes."

He paused. I waited.

"I'll go on this morning and add something current," Amos said.

"Make it look like I'm working on a feature about private prep schools," I said. "Something like, 'Coming Soon: The Value of a Private-School Education.'"

"That sounds fine. I'll do some embellishment, but the private-school thing will be the main theme."

"Thanks, Amos."

"My pleasure, as always."

◆   ◆   ◆   ◆

We landed at Laconia Municipal Airport, a small, independent, non-commercial facility in Laconia, New Hampshire. I rented a Cadillac Escalade from Avis and drove north. Franklin Pierce Academy was located on the northeast shore of Lake Winnipesaukee, a 72-square-mile lake with 182 miles of shoreline. The school was not easy to find. A modest, tasteful sign marked an entrance obscured by shrubs and trees that needed to be trimmed. I drove past it, turned around, drove back and made a left between double columns of stacked stone. I drove through woods for approximately a quarter-mile, and then the landscape opened up. Buildings were scattered around the neatly groomed grounds. In the distance,

I spied the lake. I drove to what appeared to be the main building and parked. Only then did I notice the small sign: *Administration Building.*

I located my National News Network ID, clipped it to my dark blue blazer, and, briefcase in hand, bounded up the stairs and pushed through the front door, a freelance journalist eager for a story. The receptionist gave me a pleasant smile. The nameplate in front of her told me she was Cornelia Barnes.

"May I help you?"

"I hope so." I handed her a card. "I know it's short notice, but I'm doing an article on exclusive prep schools, and I want to include Franklin Pierce Academy. Is anyone available who could give me some background?"

"Well," she said, looking at her computer, "President Rich usually talks to the press, but his calendar looks full for the rest of the week. I'm afraid you'll have to schedule an appointment."

Scheduling an appointment was the last thing I wanted. I didn't need some nosy academic searching out the nonexistent National News Network. The school had to want me now.

"I wish I could, but I have a deadline. I guess I'll just have to go to my backup plan and interview the folks at Northwood Academy. I'll send President Rich a note and let him know I tried to see him." I turned to leave.

At the mention of a local competitor and my threat of contacting President Rich, her demeanor changed.

"No, wait," she said hurriedly. "Let me see what I can do. Please have a seat. I'll be right back."

She walked briskly down a hall at the back of her station and disappeared to the right. I sat on a nearby couch and waited. Two minutes later, she was back.

"President Rich will talk with you. He said to give him fifteen minutes to wrap up a meeting."

"Thank you, Cornelia."

She blushed, I think.

◆   ◆   ◆   ◆

Franklin Pierce Academy president Philbin Rich was a tall, silver-haired man, probably in his sixties, who reeked of self-importance.

"Philbin Rich," he said as we shook hands. I waited for "You can call me Phil," but it was not forthcoming.

"Alexander Youngblood," I said. I got even by not asking him to call me Alex.

"I understand you're doing a story on exclusive prep schools," he said.

"I am," I said, flipping open my notebook. "I'm interested in things I cannot find online. And I'd very much like to talk with a few teachers to get their perspective."

He seemed a little deflated. I was betting he had a Franklin Pierce Academy history lesson ready to go.

I primed his pump with a few suggestions. "How about recent additions? Buildings, teachers, computers, new courses, that sort of thing. Really current stuff."

He brightened. "Well, of course."

I spent the next half-hour taking worthless notes. Philbin Rich was in love with the sound of his own voice. I was finally saved by Cornelia, who announced over the intercom that *Phil* was late for his next appointment. I was dismissed, but not before getting the names of three faculty members to interview, including the head of the Art Department—a teacher I specifically asked for.

◆   ◆   ◆   ◆

My first and, I hoped, only interview was with Juanita Jones, a tall, slender woman with an angular face who was about the same age and hair color as Philbin Rich. I wondered if it was a requirement of the position. She talked, and I took notes. She was genuinely excited about her students and teaching at Franklin Pierce. She had been at the academy for twenty-two years.

"Do you display the work of your students?"

"Only the outstanding work," she said. "We have a gallery. If your work makes it to the gallery, that's quite an accomplishment. It makes for some keen competition."

"Could I see the gallery?"

"Certainly," she said. "Come this way."

I followed her out of her office and down the hall to the gallery entrance. Oil paintings, watercolors, and drawings in both ink and pencil hung on the walls. All were expensively framed. Sculpted pieces rested on small tables and pedestals.

I stopped by a striking portrait of a female face drawn in red and blue ink. "This is most unusual. Vivien Leigh?"

"Very good, Mr. Youngblood," Juanita Jones said. "You have an excellent eye."

She led me to a smaller room with a discreet *Awards Room* sign by the entrance.

"All of this work has won an award of some kind," she said.

I went slowly around the room until I spotted it. It was titled *View from the Dorm* and signed **J. Cross**.

"This is very good," I said. And it was. The watercolor painting depicted a view out a dorm window of Lake Winnipesaukee—a fall scene on a clear day, students mingling in the foreground, sailboats far out on the lake in the background.

"Yes, we're very proud of this one," she said. "It won the prestigious James Gary Award for best watercolor of the year in 1986."

"Interesting," I said, as if processing a thought. "Do you know how I can get in touch with the artist? I may want to do a side story on this painting."

"No, I don't," she said, sounding disappointed. "The J. stands for John, and Cross was his middle name. His last name was Durbinfield."

"As in *the* Durbinfields?" I asked, looking appropriately amazed.

"One and the same. Not likely they'd want to talk to the press."

"How about a close friend or girlfriend?"

"Rose Dalton," she said immediately. "Rose and Johnny were close. She might know where he is, and as luck would have it, she stays in touch. She has a gallery in Soho and is always inquiring about up-and-comers. I can give you the name and address of her gallery."

◆   ◆   ◆   ◆

I left Franklin Pierce Academy without interviewing another teacher. I had the best lead I could hope for, and I intended to run with it.

I called Jim Doak. "Got time for a side trip?"

"Sure," he said. "I have nothing on my schedule until Monday morning, unless something last-minute comes up. Where are we going?"

"White Plains, if you can arrange it. Teterboro would be my second choice."

"What time will you be back at the jet?"

"In about an hour."

"See you then," Jim said.

◆   ◆   ◆   ◆

We landed at Westchester County Airport outside White Plains, New York, late in the day. I rented a Chevy Traverse from Hertz, drove to a nearby Ritz-Carlton, and checked into an executive suite. I unpacked my overnight bag, took off my travel clothes, and replaced them with a T-shirt, shorts, white socks, and sneakers. I went to an empty workout room and stayed an hour. Back in my suite, I showered, dressed, and booted up my laptop to check email and the Dow. I later ordered two beers and a grilled salmon dinner from room service, channel-surfed, and then watched part of a Reds game. They were playing the Mets. I was getting tired. So were the Mets. The Reds were thumping them.

I called Mary and told her about my day.

"Where are you going with this?" she asked.

"I don't know. Knowing is better than not knowing."

"Not always," Mary said.

28

Early the next morning, I drove into Manhattan. Since it was a Saturday, I didn't have to worry about rush-hour traffic. I went down the West Side Highway to Soho, getting off on West Houston and heading east. Traffic was light, the day cloudless, the temperature cooler than expected for mid-August.

Soho, an abbreviated reference to the district's location meaning south of Houston Street, was as widely known for its unique buildings with cast-iron facades as it was for its art community. I located Rose Dalton's gallery, the Savannah Rose Gallery, on Spring Street and found parking a block away. I had Googled it on my laptop and found that it opened at nine o'clock. I had an hour to kill. I took a table by the window in a nearby coffee shop, ordered breakfast, and read the paper. Part of me missed New York. The city had an ever-present energy I found intoxicating.

At nine o'clock, I folded my paper, took my last drink of coffee, left a generous tip for my overly attentive waitress, and paid the bill. I walked out of the coffee shop and down Spring Street toward the gallery.

The woman who greeted me when I entered was a classy, slender, sandy-haired beauty in her mid-forties. She stood about five-six. Her blue eyes were bright and knowing.

"Welcome to the Savannah Rose Gallery," she said. "Is there anything in particular I can help you with?"

I dropped the bomb quickly, trying to take advantage of the shock factor. "I wonder if you have any watercolors by an artist named Johnny Cross."

Her demeanor did not change. "John Cross Durbinfield, alias Johnny Cross," she said. "I haven't heard that name in years. I did have some of his works years ago, but they sold as quickly as they came in."

"I understand you attended school with him in New Hampshire."

"Juanita Jones said a reporter might come by asking about Johnny," she said. "I guess you're he."

"Alex Youngblood," I said, extending my hand.

"Savannah Rose," she said, grasping my hand firmly. "Formerly Rose Dalton, as you know."

"Yes, Miss Jones told me. When is the last time you saw Johnny Cross?"

She looked around the gallery at the few early browsers and held up one finger. "Kelsey," she said to a young woman behind the nearby counter. "Watch things for a while. I'll be in my office."

I followed her through an open door at the back of the gallery to a large, tastefully decorated office. We sat on a couch with a coffee table in front of us.

"Would you like something to drink?"

"No thanks," I said. "I just had breakfast and all the coffee I could drink."

She nodded and took a breath. "The last time I saw Johnny Cross was when he and two buddies, wearing those cool leather jackets with the gold dragon on the back, rode off on their motorcycles in the summer of '86. Johnny said they were headed south to ride a stretch of highway called 'the Tail of the Dragon.' It's in North Carolina, I believe, or maybe Tennessee. I think it inspired their jackets. Johnny was always talking about riding it."

"I drove it once," I said. "Never again. More curves that I care to remember."

"Doesn't sound like a lot of fun."

"It wasn't. At least not in a car. It's one of those things you do so you can say you've done it. Might be more fun on a motorcycle."

"Well, they certainly thought so," Savannah said.

"Were they part of a gang?"

"No, nothing like that, unless you consider three a gang. They called themselves 'the Three Dragons.' I remember thinking, *There go the Three Dragons, doomed by birthrights hanging like invisible millstones around their necks.* All of them were rich kids trying to run away from family money and all the responsibility that went with it."

"What happened to them?"

"The other two died before they turned thirty. One was killed on his motorcycle, and the other died of a drug overdose. I haven't heard from Johnny in years, so I suspect he's probably also dead."

"What makes you think so?"

"Johnny and I were close in school. We weren't lovers or anything like that, just good friends. I knew he was planning to bolt that summer. He had opened an account and started saving money his sophomore year—traveling money, he called it. He received a generous allowance from his grandmother and always put at least half of it away. He wanted to see the country, work odd jobs, and paint. From time to time, he would send me a painting, and I'd sell it and deposit the money into his account. He was really gifted. His paintings sold the minute they came in. They were so popular that I held private auctions with sealed bids. I stopped receiving paintings in 1996. Because he moved around so much, his account statement came to me. The last activity on the account was in 1997."

"Anybody else know about the account?"

She paused and stared at me. "You know," she said, "you're way too easy to talk to. I maybe shouldn't be telling you all this."

"Whatever you tell me is confidential. Nothing will be printed without your approval. You have my word."

She stared at me as if processing a thought. "You're not a reporter, are you?"

Savannah Rose Dalton was no dummy. If I was going to get any more information, I had to drop my undercover persona.

"Whatever you tell me is between us," she said. "You have my word."

I smiled. It wasn't the first time I'd been maneuvered into a corner by a smart woman.

"I'm a private investigator," I said.

"Is Johnny dead?"

"Probably. Somebody who wore one of those jackets is dead. As far as I know, the body has not been identified. It's probably Johnny Cross, but it's remotely possible it was somebody claiming to be Johnny Cross."

"But you don't think so."

"No, I don't."

"And why do you think it's Johnny?"

"Someone told me," I said. "Someone I believe."

"How long ago did he die?"

"In 1997," I said.

A sad look crossed her face. "I'm sorry to hear that, but I'm not surprised."

"You said his grandmother sent him money. Is she still alive?"

"I don't know, but I doubt it," she said. "She wasn't well when we were in school."

"What about his parents?"

"His father died when Johnny was young. His mother was alive and well the last I heard from her. She contacted me from time to time to see if I'd heard from Johnny. I would always say I hadn't. That's the way Johnny wanted it. They did not get along."

I stood. I had come to the point of not wanting to pursue Johnny Cross any further. Savannah walked with me to the front of the gallery.

"Thanks for your time," I said.

"I'm glad you came," Savannah said. "Can I ask you a question, Mr. Youngblood?"

"Sure."

"Why are you interested in Johnny Cross?"

I let the question hang for a few seconds.

"Someone who believes he might be dead is interested in his background," I said.

"I see," she said. "The family?"

"No, not the family."

"That's fortunate. You'll do well not to get mixed up with the Durbin-fields, especially Elizabeth Durbinfield."

"I don't plan to," I said. "By the way, did Johnny have any siblings?"

"An older brother, Andrew. He graduated from the Harvard Business School and went to work for Durbinfield Financial and eventually took over."

"How much older?"

"I'm not sure, but at least six or seven years. He'd already graduated Harvard when we were at Franklin Pierce."

"Did they get along?"

"I guess so," she said. "We didn't talk about Andrew. All Johnny ever said was that Andrew was much older and that they were different."

I knew Elizabeth Durbinfield was chairman of the board at Durbin-field Financial and that Andrew Durbinfield was listed as president and CEO. I wondered who really ran the empire.

29

Sunday afternoon, I was at the security checkpoint in Tri-Cities Air-port waiting for Mary and Lacy. Without them, the last two weeks had seemed like two months.

Their flight landed and taxied to the assigned gate. In the distance, I saw passengers spilling into the concourse. Two blond heads appeared. I took a deep breath, anxiously watching as they approached the security checkpoint, smiling widely as they came.

Lacy came through first and gave me a hug. "We missed you," she said. "It's good to be back."

"I missed you, too."

Mary hung back, giving Lacy some alone time with her father. But it didn't last. She came to my arms and hugged me fiercely.

"God, I missed you," she said.

"Control yourselves," Lacy scolded.

"Let's get out of here," Mary said.

◆   ◆   ◆   ◆

I took some of the less-traveled back roads and listened to tales of California, mostly from Lacy.

"It was so cool, Don," she said from the backseat. "Have you ever been there?"

"Years ago, I went to San Francisco. I liked it, but I didn't think I could take a steady diet of it."

"You're right," Lacy said. "I'm glad to be home."

"Me, too," said Mary, squeezing my thigh.

When we arrived at the lake house, Hannah and her mother were waiting to take Lacy to Mountain Center, as prearranged by Mary.

"I'll stop by the condo and get my Pathfinder and some other stuff," Lacy said. "I don't need my suitcase." She gave me a hug.

"First day of senior year tomorrow," I said. "Enjoy every minute."

"I will."

Then she gave Mary a hug and whispered something in her ear.

Mary laughed. "Go on," she said. "Get out of here."

We watched them go up the gravel drive and out of sight.

"What did she say?" I asked.

"That's between us girls," Mary said. "Now, get in the house."

◆   ◆   ◆   ◆

We were in bed, catching our breath after round one of some vigorous lovemaking. At least I hoped it was only round one. The sheet covered us to the waist. We had rolled on our sides to face each other, smiling. Smiles that said we had something few others did: the perfect mate.

"Was that worth the wait, Cowboy?"

"That's probably the dumbest question I've ever heard," I said.

Mary laughed. "I'll take that as a yes."

"It goes way beyond yes."

"It does," Mary said. "Now, tell me about *your* trip."

I took my time recounting my yesterday and the day before. From time to time, I lost my train of thought. A beautiful, half-naked woman lying next to me could do that.

"So what's next?"

"For the time being," I said, "nothing. I know enough that if Lacy ever asks, I have something to tell her. Right now, she doesn't want to know. Someday, she might."

"I think that's a good decision." She moved closer, kissed me, and slid one hand under the sheet. "Feels like you're up for another go."

I laughed. "It does, doesn't it?"

Much later, we had dinner.

30

Monday morning, Mary and I loaded Jake and Junior and drove to our condo in Mountain Center. We deposited the dogs and left for work in separate vehicles. I went to my office and Mary to Mountain Center police headquarters.

I looked at the pile of notes on my desk, the result of my being away for two days. Pink slips from Gretchen were neatly piled in the middle, impossible to avoid. The only one that interested me was a call from Buckley asking to meet that afternoon. The other notes were mostly from Gretchen about stock purchases she had made on the requests of clients. Office mail was stacked neatly in my inbox. Most of it looked like junk. I made a mental note to check it later. I went through the pink slips again, more carefully this time, to see who was calling about what.

Mortgage rates were the lowest they'd been in years, which meant money was cheap. It also meant savings accounts and certificates of deposits paid so little that they weren't worth the trouble. Clients were looking for other places to park their cash and make a decent return. I had developed a list of low-risk stocks that paid reasonable dividends and sent it to all those entrusting me with their investments. They were spoiled. Some years, they had made up to 45 percent. Now, they were disappointed at making only 3 to 5 percent, though that was a good return, based on the economic outlook.

I went online and looked at the market. The Dow had pushed over thirteen thousand, a number that did not reflect the overall economy. My list of stocks was doing well, showing steady growth and forecasting solid dividends. I made a note to add two more stocks to my list and to place another three on my watch list.

I was checking email when I heard the outer office door open and close. Seconds later, my intercom spoke.

"I'm in," Gretchen said.

"Get settled and come in when you're ready," I replied.

◆   ◆   ◆   ◆

My intercom buzzed promptly at three that afternoon.

"Buckley Clarke to see you," Gretchen said.

"Send him in."

Buckley came in and stood there for a few seconds, unsure of the protocol. He was dressed in a dark suit with a white shirt and a black and silver striped tie.

"Sit," I said. "Get comfortable."

"Sure," he said. "Why didn't I think of that?" Buckley removed his suit coat and draped it over the other chair.

"What have you got?" I asked.

"A lot of information."

"Did you find a connection?"

"With the exception that they were all nurses, I couldn't find one single thing. As far as I can tell, they never met, never attended the same nurses' conventions, and never crossed paths. Other than nursing, I couldn't even find a common interest."

"Well, it was worth a shot."

"It's all in the file," Buckley said, handing me a folder. "I had to do a report for Agent Steele. I met with him this morning."

"Thanks. I'll take a look at it."

"Where do we go from here?"

"I don't know," I said. "If you have any ideas, I'm all ears."

"I'll think about it," he said. "Right now, we're at a dead end."

◆   ◆   ◆   ◆

After Buckley Clarke left, I went back online to see if I had any new email. I saw one from T. Elbert:

> **Drop by tomorrow if you can and give**
> **me an update on the Cracker Jack case.**
> **Also, I might have a lead for you to follow.**

I wrote T. Elbert back and told him I'd be there with coffee and assorted goodies. We could certainly use a new lead.

◆   ◆   ◆   ◆

Late in the day, the phone rang. I have a mental list of things I refer to as "Youngblood's Universal Truths." A sampling: *If you're in a hurry to get someplace, you'll always be behind a slow person*, or *No matter what time it is, when you're ready to leave the office, the phone will ring*. Caller ID was blocked.

"Cherokee Investigations," I answered, slightly annoyed.

"Sounds like you're on your way out," David Steele said.

"Of course I'm on my way out. I want to go home, open a swell bottle of wine, and have a drink with my lovely wife."

"Swell?"

"Forgive me," I said. "I was recently at an exclusive prep school in New Hampshire. Guess I caught something."

David Steele laughed. "Mountain Center will cure you of that soon enough."

"Without a doubt," I said. "What's up?"

"Did you read Buckley's report?"

"Not yet. He briefed me a couple of hours ago."

"It's a good piece of work," he said. "The kid is thorough."

"Anything stand out?"

"No, and that brings me to the point of this call. I need Buckley on something else, unless we get a new lead. CJK seems to be dormant for now—no kills and no notes."

"If something breaks on my end, I'll let you know. But I don't think CJK is going away." I didn't want to mention T. Elbert's possible new lead until I found out what is was.

"Maybe not," David Steele said. "But until he comes out of hiding or we develop a new lead, all we can do is wait."

◆　　◆　　◆　　◆

That night, we ordered Chinese takeout and sat at the kitchen bar. Mary and I grilled Lacy about the first day of school.

She went into great detail: "It was fine."

"Fine?" I said. "That's all you got?"

She nodded.

"Come on," I said. "Throw us a bone. Anything."

Lacy laughed. "I have two classes with Biker."

"How nice," I said with a hint of sarcasm. I liked Biker just fine but sometimes pretended I didn't, just to tease Lacy.

As we ate, Mary and I slowly pulled bits and pieces of information from Lacy, who eventually got bored and went to her room.

"What's the latest with CJK?" Mary asked.

I told her about Buckley's report.

"Any ideas?" I asked.

"Yes," Mary said, arching an eyebrow. "But they have nothing to do with CJK."

"Tonight?"

"Tomorrow."

She obviously knew something I didn't.

31

We were on T. Elbert's front porch eating bagels and drinking Dunkin' Donuts coffee. I had told him all I knew about CJK.

"The Cracker Jack Killer," T. Elbert said slowly with emphasis. "If the press gets hold of that, they'll have a field day."

"Only a handful of people know about the Cracker Jack angle," I said. "I think we can keep that under wraps. What surprises me is that the press hasn't connected the dots on the three killings."

"Small-town newspapers have limited staff these days," T. Elbert said. "It's all they can do to survive. Local TV is what you have to watch out for."

Regardless of all the information leaked to or uncovered by the press, I knew that some criminal cases managed to fly under the media radar. I could only hope CJK would be one of them. I didn't want to be in the news again. The Three Devils case had been enough fame for a lifetime.

"Tell me about this possible lead."

"I think you're going to like this one."

He paused, took a bite of bagel and a drink of coffee, and smiled at me. I waited.

"A Cracker Jack convention takes place annually at different locations around the country," T. Elbert said. "And this year's happens to be less than a week away. I'm thinking maybe our killer bought the charms from a collector. It might be worth going to the convention and snooping around. You could get lucky."

"Maybe I'll send Buckley. Where is it?"

He smiled widely and said slowly, "Las Vegas."

Naturally, I thought.

◆　　◆　　◆　　◆

I was in the office by nine o'clock. I got settled in and called Wanda Jones.

"Is Bruiser still in Vegas?"

"Yes," Wanda said.

"For how long?"

"Don't know."

"What do you mean you don't know?" I asked, maybe a little abruptly.

"I mean I don't know."

I waited.

"The government thing for Fleet is on hold," Wanda said finally. "Some bureaucratic bullshit. Anyway, Bruiser's boss wants him to stay as long as possible and train his replacement, and Joseph Fleet agreed there isn't much to do here, so I don't know when he'll be here permanently."

"Is the wedding still on?"

"Of course it's still on, Don. Are you trying to piss me off?"

"No, of course not. I just want things to work out for two people I care about."

Wanda sighed. "We're fine. Bruiser is flying in almost every week-end on Friday, we screw ourselves silly over the weekend, and he flies out Monday."

"Jeez, Wanda. Too much information."

She laughed. "Just letting you know we're fine."

"When is he due in again?"

"A week from Friday."

So he'll be in Vegas for the Cracker Jack convention, I thought. I kept that to myself.

"Call us," I said. "We'll get together for a drink or a meal, if you're not too tired."

"I'm hanging up now," Wanda said—rather cheerfully, I thought.

◆   ◆   ◆   ◆

The mail that had piled up while I was in New Hampshire and Soho was still sitting on my desk, waiting to be opened. I went through it piece by piece. Most of it was junk mail, along with a few bills. Near the bottom of the pile was a curious plain white envelope addressed to Cherokee Investigations. It had a Washington, D.C. postmark and no return address. The slight bulge in the center of the envelope put me on the defensive. *I don't like the looks of this.*

I took a pair of surgical gloves from the middle right drawer of my desk, put them on, and carefully slit the top with a letter opener. I removed a single white sheet of folded paper. Holding it as far from my body as possible, I carefully unfolded it. It didn't explode. There were no puffs of white powder. A simple note was typed in the center fold:

I have to be away for a while, but I'll be back.

Taped in the bottom fold was a tiny plastic pistol that resembled a .38 Police Special. I would have bet the condo it was a Cracker Jack charm.

◆   ◆   ◆   ◆

"You got what in the mail?" David Steele asked—somewhat unbelieving, I thought.

"A note from CJK."

"What does it say?"

I read it.

"What the hell? Is he taking a vacation?"

"Beats me," I said. "But it explains why we haven't had any more dead women recently."

"But why send a note?"

"Who knows? He's crazy. Maybe he wants to let us know he's still out there."

"Maybe he wants to be sure you keep looking for him. You don't know who he is, but he definitely knows who you are. It's personal on his end."

"Well, he can be sure I won't stop looking."

"I'll send Buckley tomorrow to pick up the note and see if we can get any prints off it."

"Not likely," I said. "But when you send Buckley, send those charms with him. I may need them for a little show and tell."

"What have you got going?" Dave asked.

I told him about the Cracker Jack convention in Vegas.

"I want to show those charms around and see if I can turn up anything."

"That's a long shot," he said.

"I'm pretty good with long shots. Besides, it's all I've got."

"Well, be careful. Vegas can be a dangerous place."

"Yes," I said. "I know that from past experience."

◆   ◆   ◆   ◆

Late in the afternoon, after Gretchen left, I called Roy Husky at his office number. His assistant informed me Mr. Husky was on the other line and that she would have him call me back as soon as possible. I smiled to myself as I thought about how far Roy had come since I met him. Given our backgrounds, our friendship was unlikely. But life has a way of playing tricks that defy odds and reason.

Outside my office window, I noticed the sun had disappeared and the day was darkening. The banner outside the Dunkin' Donuts blew briskly in an ever-freshening wind. A storm was coming. I brought up a Doppler radar site on my computer that showed thunderstorms rolling in from the west. I turned on my portable weather radio and listened to the forecast of severe storms for the Mountain Center area until six. The droll, dispassionate voice warned of high winds, rain, and possible flooding in low-lying areas but made no mention of hail or tornadoes.

As I started to close down the office, my phone rang. At least I was expecting a call this time and caller ID let me know who the caller was.

"Mr. Vice President," I said.

"What's up, Gumshoe?"

"Is one of the jets available later this week?"

"No," Roy said. "Booked solid, I checked before I called you back. Where are you going?"

"Vegas."

"Need backup?"

"Not likely."

"Well, be careful," Roy said. "And stay out of parking garages."

"Definitely."

"Storm coming," Roy said.

"I know."

◆   ◆   ◆   ◆

I had almost finished my shutdown routine when the phone rang again.

"You see what's happening outside," Mary said.

"I do. Where are you?"

"At the condo."

"Early day," I said.

"Yes," Mary said. "Lacy is having dinner at Hannah's."

"Uh-huh."

"And I'm in the bedroom, and the candles are lit, and soft music is playing."

I took a deep breath. "What do you have on?"

"Toenail polish."

I was at a loss for words.

"How fast can you be here?"

"Pretty damn fast," I said.

Thank God for Hannah and her mother.

◆   ◆   ◆   ◆

An hour later, we were a naked tangle of legs and arms under the quilt on our king-sized bed. Outside, the thunder rolled, the wind blew, and the rain came down in sheets. Inside our bedroom, the music was still playing and the candles still burning. I was floating in a drug-like state that I wanted to continue as long as possible.

"You okay?" Mary asked, snatching me back from wherever I was.

"I'm way beyond okay."

"Me, too."

"I'm going to Vegas," I said nonchalantly. *Timing is all.*

"Vegas?" Mary raised herself on an elbow and stared at me. "Why? I thought you were never going back to Vegas."

I told her about the Cracker Jack convention.

"At this point, it's the only lead I've got."

"Well, be careful."

"It's a Cracker Jack convention," I said. "How threatening can it be?"

"If anyone can find trouble at a Cracker Jack convention," Mary said, "it would be you."

32

Las Vegas hadn't visibly changed much since I last visited—and nearly died in the hospital from a parking garage beating administered by three thugs of bad boy Victor Vargas.

I took a flight from Tri-Cities Airport to Atlanta and then direct to Las Vegas in first class. Altogether, the trip was not an unpleasant experience, even though Jim Doak and the Fleet Industries jet had spoiled me. I rented a Lincoln Navigator from Hertz, made the short trip to the Renaissance Hotel on Paradise Road, retrieved my suitcase and computer backpack, turned the SUV over to a valet, and headed for the lobby.

At the front desk, I was greeted by a familiar face.

"Welcome back, Mr. Youngblood." The hustling bellhop from a few years back was now a front desk manager.

"Lance," I said. "Good to see you again. You've come far in a short time."

"Got my degree in hotel management and a promotion," he said proudly.

"Congratulations."

"I've booked you in the same top-floor suite you had the last time," he said, taking on a more professional demeanor.

"I appreciate that."

"How many keys would you like?"

"One."

He nodded and programmed the key.

"Do you need help with your luggage?"

"I think I can handle it."

"Anything you need," Lance said, handing me a folder that held the key, "just let me know."

"Will do."

I turned and wheeled my suitcase toward the elevators.

◆　　◆　　◆　　◆

The Velvet Slipper looked the same as last time—the same desert earth tones, the same dark wood, the same horseshoe bar, even the same bartender, who was working the other end of the bar. He spotted me and casually headed my way.

"What'll you have?" he asked. He was young and good looking and probably played well to the female crowd.

"Do you have an amber ale on tap?"

"Sure do. Evolution Amber Ale, brewed in Park City, Utah."

"Can I get a sample in a shot glass?"

"No need," he said. "First one's on me."

He was back in a minute and set a pint glass in front of me.

"If you don't like it, I'll dump it and we'll find you something else."

"Nice," I said, taking my first taste.

"You're Bruiser's friend, right?" he asked, placing a bowl of mixed nuts in front of me.

"I am."

"Donald Youngblood, right?"

"Right," I said, taking another drink.

"I heard about the Vargas thing. I liked the way you handled that."

"Might be some people in town who didn't."

"I doubt it."

"Just the same," I said, "the fewer people who know I'm in town, the better."

"You were never here," he said, smiling. "Let me know if you need anything."

He moved to the far end of the bar to wait on another customer. I waited for Bruiser. If he was here, he'd spot me sooner or later. I sipped my amber ale and noticed a tall, good-looking, well-endowed redhead moving toward me. She smiled at the bartender as she went by. He gave her an almost imperceptible shake of his head, and she abruptly veered off behind me and kept going.

I had just about finished my beer when a highly attractive brunette sat beside me. The bartender hadn't seen her to warn her away.

"Buy me a drink?"

Normally, I would have told her to buzz off, but she was really something to look at, and I was curious.

"Sure. What'll you have?"

"A glass of Chardonnay would be perfect."

As the bartender started back toward me, I caught his eye. "A glass of your best Chardonnay," I said. "And hit me again."

He nodded.

"I'm Nikki," the woman said. She was almost as tall as Mary, slender, and well dressed. I guessed her age at around thirty-five.

"Don," I said.

"Pleased to meet you, Don." She smiled. She had great teeth.

"Working girl?" I asked. No need to beat around the bush. I had no intention of letting this go any farther than a drink.

She laughed. "If you mean do I have a job, then yes, I'm a working girl. If you mean am I a prostitute, then no."

"No offense," I said. "In Vegas, it's hard to tell a working girl from a soccer mom."

"A sense of humor," Nikki said. "I like that." She took a drink. "Is that wedding ring for real or just a prop?"

"For real."

"Too bad," she said, and took another drink.

"So what do you do for a living, Nikki?"

"I'm a financial analyst."

"How did you end up in Vegas?"

"Husband hunting," she said. "Trying to land a rich one."

"If that's the case, you need to get out of Vegas," I said. "Rich men don't come here looking for wives."

"I'm starting to realize that," she said. "Where do you recommend I go?"

"New York City. If you're really interested, I have some connections."

"Do you have a card?"

I handed her one of my Cherokee Investigations cards.

"Private investigator," she said. "So how do you have connections in the New York financial market?"

"I used to work on Wall Street," I said. "It got boring."

She took another look at my card. "Donald Youngblood. Haven't I heard of you?"

"Maybe."

"I'll send you my résumé," she said, finishing her Chardonnay. "Thanks for the drink."

"My pleasure."

I watched her walk away, stylish and graceful. It was not an unpleasant sight. I knew an old letch in New York who would be more than a little interested in hiring her.

◆　　◆　　◆　　◆

As I was nursing my second beer, I spotted Bruiser's reflection in the bar's mirror. He was smiling and moving my way. I turned on my barstool before he reached me.

"What brings you to town?" he asked, taking a seat beside me.

"Wanda sent me to check up on you."

He laughed. "Mary threw you out is more likely."

"Nope. Mary, Lacy, and I are just fine."

"You're working a case," Bruiser said. "That's the only reason you'd come back here."

"For the FBI."

Before I could say anything else, the bartender was back.

"Another?"

"Sure," I said. *Three beers*, I thought. *Vegas is a bad influence.*

"Mr. Bracken?"

"The usual," Bruiser said. "These are on the house."

"Sure thing," the bartender said.

He walked away down the length of the bar, and Bruiser moved closer and lowered his voice.

"Tell me."

"Inner circle only," I said.

"Sure."

I told him about CJK and the Cracker Jack convention. Meanwhile, our drinks arrived. I was halfway through my third pint of Evolution Amber Ale when I finished the story.

"What are you hoping to find?" Bruiser asked.

"Someone who remembers selling the four charms, and who they sold them to."

"Long shot," Bruiser said.

"What better place to hit a long shot that Vegas?"

"Maybe so, but be careful. Victor Vargas had some cousins who took over when you rid the world of him. If they find out you're around, they might want some payback."

"So if they want payback, why wouldn't they come looking for me in Tennessee?"

"It's not high on their list of priorities. They know you killed Victor in a fair fight, and that he came looking for you. As far as they're concerned, there's no family honor to uphold. However, if they find out you're in town, it could go sideways. I'm just saying watch your back, and call me if you need me."

"What are their names?"

"Don't know," Bruiser said. "Everyone just calls them 'the Cousins.' They drive around in a cherry red Cadillac Escalade."

"How many of those in town?"

"More than one," Bruiser smiled. "But if you see one, pay attention."

33

The next morning, I drove out Paradise Road toward the convention center across from the Springhill Suites. I found a parking spot and went inside. It didn't take me long to locate the Cracker Jack convention in a large hall on the second floor. The place was buzzing. A sea of tables in row after row displayed an unending collection of Cracker Jack prizes and charms. Collectors were there to buy and sell and especially to show off their collections. I picked up pieces of conversations as I walked around: bargaining, negotiating, bragging. I strolled the aisles and browsed, fascinated by what had come out of Cracker Jack boxes in the last hundred-plus years, remembering my own excitement as a kid opening a box. It was more about the prizes that the caramel-coated popcorn and peanuts. I pulled out my notebook and pencil—Alexander Youngblood, ace reporter.

Many items were priced. The range was from five dollars to well up in the thousands. Most of the crowd was older than I was.

An attractive, fit-looking blond woman maybe ten years my senior sat behind a table filled with charms and prizes. I stopped and looked at her collection. *Marge*, her nametag read.

"Nice," I said.

"Thank you. Are you a collector?"

"No, I'm a freelance writer doing research on Cracker Jack charms."

I flipped my notebook open, made a note, and flipped it closed—very professional. I was ready with my phony National News Network ID, but she didn't bite.

"We mostly call them prizes," she said. "If I can answer any questions, just let me know." Marge was pleasant, like a second-grade teacher talking to a student who didn't quite get it.

I pulled four charms out of the pocket of my dark brown sports coat. Each was in its own plastic baggie. The three that had been left on the key rings of the dead women, and one that had been sent to me.

"I found these in an old cigar box in my parents' house," I said. "Are these Cracker Jack charms? Prizes, I mean."

She smiled. Her student was learning. "Yes, they are. They're from the nineteen fifties."

"What are they worth?"

She smiled again. "They're worth whatever someone is willing to sell them for and someone else is willing to pay. Establishing value is tricky. It's not like coin collecting. If I offered you, say, twenty-five dollars apiece for these and you accepted, then we would have established a value. That's how it works."

"I see," I said—and being an economics major, I did see. "Know who might have duplicates of these?"

"Sidney Green might," she said. "He has the most extensive collection here. You'll find him in the far corner over there." She pointed. "He has three tables of prizes."

✦   ✦   ✦   ✦

I found Sidney Green sitting behind the middle of his three tables, in the process of making a sale. He was a rotund man with a cherub face and a twinkle in his eye. Sidney obviously enjoyed what he was doing. When the transaction was completed, the buyer moved on. I paused at his corner table and pretended to study his wares.

"Well, my good fellow," Sidney said, "see anything you like?"

"All of it," I said.

"Ah, a true connoisseur." His laugh was infectious and made me like him at once.

"Do you keep duplicates?" I asked.

"When I can," he said. "I'm in the business of buying and selling."

I showed him the four charms. "Ever see these?"

"Sure. I've had them all at one time or another."

"Ever sell these four as a set?"

"A most curious question, sir," Sidney said. "Where is this leading?"

I had his attention now, but I had to throw him a juicy morsel or I'd lose it.

"I'm a freelance reporter working a story," I said. "This set of charms may be linked to a criminal case. If I can find who sold them, I might be able to find who bought them."

He rubbed his chin and stared off into the distance, seemingly lost in thought, but I could almost see the wheels turning in his head. Sidney Green was foremost an entrepreneur.

"And I suppose there would most assuredly be a finder's fee."

"Most assuredly."

"Probably one hundred dollars," Sidney mused.

"You're a quick study."

"How may I get in touch with you?" he asked.

◆　　◆　　◆　　◆

When I left my parking space at the convention center, I spotted a cherry red Cadillac Escalade parked across the street. I pretended not to notice, then snuck another peek. The windows were darkly tinted, so it was impossible to tell if anyone was inside. I pulled into traffic and headed toward the Velvet Slipper, paying particular attention to my rearview mirror. When I spotted the Escalade a few cars back, I speed-dialed Bruiser on my cell phone.

"I seem to have picked up a tail," I said.

"A cherry red Escalade?"

"All nice and shiny."

"How do you want to play it?"

"I'll lead them into the parking garage across the street from the Velvet Slipper," I said.

"*The* parking garage?" He sounded surprised. My last encounter with thugs there had not ended well.

"It owes me one," I said.

He laughed. "It does that. Park on the second level on the end opposite the elevators. If they're smart, they'll park between you and the elevators. I'll be waiting in the shadows, and I'll be armed, should there be gunplay."

"On my way," I said.

◆   ◆   ◆   ◆

Ten minutes later, I made a left into the parking garage, took a ticket, watched as the gate went up, and drove through. The Escalade waited a few seconds, then followed at a discreet distance. I swung up the ramp to Level 2, made a left, drove by rows of open parking spots, and made another left past the elevators. I drove to a corner spot and parked facing in where the ramp started up to the third level. In my rearview mirror, I watched as the Escalade did as Bruiser had predicted, pulling into a spot close to the elevators. I waited. No one got out.

Showtime, I thought as I exited the Navigator and headed toward the elevators. I felt somewhat safe in the knowledge that my Glock Nine rested snugly in its holster on my left hip, hidden by my jacket.

I was twenty feet from the Navigator when the Escalade's doors opened and two Hispanic men emerged. One was slender and nearly my height. The other was a few inches shorter, a stocky man powerfully built. Neither looked friendly. I kept walking. They positioned themselves in front of the elevators, legs spread, arms folded.

"*Buenos días, amigos*," I said.

"Not for you it isn't," the slender man said. He had a Spanish accent, but his English was good.

"Why is that?"

"We are cousins of Victor Vargas," the slender man said.

"Ah," I said. "Frick and Frack."

It was a wasted insult.

"We're going to mess you up some," the slender man said. "In memory of Victor."

"How sentimental of you. Two against one—not really fair."

"Fuck fair."

"I see you've learned English quite well," I said. "Does your friend here talk at all?"

"I talk with my fists," the stocky man said.

"How nice. The language of thugs."

No one smiled. I guessed the humor was lost in translation. They started moving toward me.

"Hey, dirt bags," Bruiser said, stepping out from behind a concrete support column. Not politically correct, but effective.

The Cousins were startled. They had that deer-in-the-headlights look, caught between Bruiser and me. We moved in. The slender man threw a quick left jab that landed square on my nose and hurt like hell. I was leaning away from the punch, or the damage would have been worse. Having succeeded with the first one, he came back with another, but I was ready. I moved my head an instant before contact, grabbed his arm as it went by, slipped inside the punch, turned him slightly to my left, and delivered a hard left knee to his solar plexus. He grunted as he went to his knees. I followed up with a hard right hand to the side of his face, which sent pain shooting up my right arm. He went down hard and smacked the concrete with the side of his face I hadn't hit. I flipped him on his back, straddled him, and drew back my right fist for the finishing blow.

He quickly spread his hands and said, "*No mas.*"

I stood and removed my Glock. "Stay down and keep quiet or I'll blow your brains out."

The thought of his brains all over the parking garage must have done the trick. He looked terrified. "*Si.*"

The stocky man was also down and wasn't moving—so much for talking with his fists. Bruiser spoke his language a little too well. Out of the corner of my eye, I had seen the man throw a seemingly devastating punch to Bruiser's midsection. It was as if his fist hit a wall. Bruiser had thrown a left hook in return and knocked him cold.

"I'm calling the cops," Bruiser said. "You're bleeding. I'll tell them to send an EMT."

"Ask for Detective Ed Rodriguez," I said.

My nose was throbbing.

◆   ◆   ◆   ◆

"I thought you were never coming back to Vegas," Ed Rodriguez said.

A few years back, I had been beaten unconscious in the same parking garage, and Detective Rodriguez had investigated the so-called mugging. I had danced around the truth until my case was over and then told him most of the story.

"Couldn't resist," I said. "You know, for old times' sake."

"Returning to the scene of the crime, so to speak," he said.

"Ironic, isn't it?"

"I'm guessing irony has nothing to do with it."

Rodriguez, four uniform cops, and an EMT were on the scene. The Cousins were in cuffs and being hauled off to jail by two of the uniforms. It took the EMT some time to revive the stocky man, who had a major lump on the side of his face. The EMT then cleaned up my nose while Rodriguez talked to Bruiser. My upper lip was swollen. I put an ice pack on it when I wasn't talking.

"Unlike that guy's jaw," the EMT said, referring to the stocky man, "your nose isn't broken. Keep ice on it for twenty minutes, then off for twenty minutes. Do that for a few hours, and it should feel pretty good by tomorrow morning."

"I didn't hit him that hard," Bruiser protested, overhearing the broken-jaw remark.

Rodriguez laughed. "Any harder and you would have killed the scum-bag, and good riddance." He turned to me. "You want to tell me why you're really here?"

I showed him my FBI creds.

"Impressive. You've come a long way, Youngblood."

"I'm working a case for the FBI that began in my hometown," I said. "That's all I can tell you right now."

"Yeah, yeah, I know," he said. "Later, you'll tell me the rest of the story."

"Scout's honor."

"Okay, we're done here," Rodriguez said to the remaining uniforms and the EMT. They moved toward the elevators before he turned back to me. "I'm going to book those two for assault, carrying without a permit, and whatever else I can think of. They'll probably cut a deal, so it's unlikely you'll have to testify."

"I will if I have to," I said.

"How long are you in town, Youngblood?" Rodriguez asked.

I heard a ding and watched over his shoulder as the uniforms ushered the Cousins into the elevator. The doors closed, and they were gone.

"Another day or two."

"Good," Rodriguez said. "The sooner you're gone, the easier my job will be."

I ignored the dig. "Do me a favor if you can."

"Anything for you," he said, trying to appear annoyed.

"Squeeze those guys and see if you can find out how they knew I was in town."

"I'd like to know that myself. I'll let you know if I find out anything. In the meantime, try to stay out of trouble."

Of course, I knew he was kidding. *Me, stay out of trouble?*

◆ ◆ ◆ ◆

"You're there less than forty-eight hours, and you're back in the same parking garage getting beat up again," Mary said angrily. "You haven't got a lick of sense."

I had just finished a nice room-service dinner and called Mary—a call I was starting to regret.

"Calm down. I caught one punch on the nose. I'm fine, the Cousins are in jail, and I might have a lead."

"Sorry," she said. "Jesus, Don. You draw trouble like a magnet draws metal."

"That's me," I said. "Good ole magnetic Don Youngblood."

Mary laughed, and I knew things were okay.

"Tell me about your last two days. Like T. Elbert, I want details."

I told her everything I could think of.

"Try not to attract any more trouble. And get your butt home. I'm missing you."

"One more day and I'm out of here."

"Promise?"

"Promise. And I always keep my promises."

"Good boy," Mary said.

34

We met at Café 325 in the Las Vegas Marriott, conveniently located almost equidistant from the Springhill Suites and the Renaissance Hotel, making it a relatively short walk for both of us. Sidney had picked the spot when he called earlier that morning. "Of course, you'll pay for breakfast," he said.

They were there when I arrived, sitting side by side at an out-of-the-way table in a nearly empty dining room. I sat across from them.

"Mr. Youngblood," Sidney said, "meet Peter Lewis."

Peter and I shook hands. He was short and squat and had a wide face and dark eyes that seemed ready to pop out of his head. In stark contrast to Sidney, he wore a worried look on his face.

A waiter took our order. Sidney was hungry, Peter not so much. I ordered crunchy French toast with strawberries and bananas.

We exchanged small talk. Sidney seemed as relaxed as a bluetick hound lying in the sun on a hot day in July. Peter seemed like a Chihuahua in the middle of a Las Vegas freeway at rush hour.

"Peter has something to tell you," Sidney said with great satisfaction. "Go ahead, Peter, don't be shy. Mr. Youngblood doesn't bite."

Peter smiled weakly. "Some months ago, I had a request on my blog," he began in a low, conspiratorial tone. "I have a Cracker Jack blog called 'Kernels and Nuts.' Anyway, a visitor to my blog asked where he could get the larger Cracker Jack charms from the fifties. He said he was working on a special project and must have four charms, but one absolutely had to be the revolver. I had the revolver and five or six others, so I wrote him back and told him to make me an offer. He wrote back and offered two hundred dollars for the four. Of course, I accepted. I told him I'd send them out as soon as I received the money. A few days later, I got a money order in the mail with a note. The note said to send the revolver and three other charms, he didn't care which three, to a P.O. box. So I did. He wrote me on my blog that he had received them and thanked me, and that's the last I ever heard from him. Am I in trouble?"

"No," I said, "of course not."

Peter seemed to relax a little.

Our food arrived, and we dug right in.

"Did you save the note?" I asked.

Peter winced. "I'm afraid I didn't."

I took a bite of my French toast and forked in some strawberries and bananas.

"What about the P.O. box address?"

"Sorry," Peter said, shaking his head. "There was no way for me to know it might be important."

"Not your fault," I said. "Do you remember the name on the P.O. box address?"

Peter smiled. "Smith."

"First name?"

"The initial T.," he said. "T. Smith."

"Smith," I repeated.

"Probably not his real name," Sidney said.

"Probably not," I said.

We ate in silence until Sidney shared a story about his latest acquisition. It was lost on me, but Peter seemed impressed. I left cash for the check, and we rose to leave.

"You have something for me?" Sidney asked pleasantly.

"I do," I said, handing him an envelope with five twenty-dollar bills inside that included a phony National News Network business card.

He took a peek. "A pleasure doing business with you, sir."

"If this guy ever contacts either of you again," I said, "get in touch with me. You have my email address."

"Most assuredly," Sidney said.

Peter was silent.

◆   ◆   ◆   ◆

By the time I finished with Sidney and Peter, it was too late to book a flight back to Tri-Cities Airport and arrive at a reasonable hour. I decided to stay one more night. That meant I had time to kill. Since I do not have a time-killing personality, I needed something to do. I went back to my suite at the Renaissance and made a list of people I needed to call or owed a phone call.

I called Gretchen first. Nothing was going on at the office she couldn't handle—her words exactly.

Next, I called David Steele and told him about my conversation with Peter Lewis.

"That's good work, Youngblood," he said. "I'll have someone check out the blog and see if there's any way we can find the origin of that particular inquiry."

Then I called Sister Sarah Agnes Woods, nun, friend, confidant, and all-around smart cookie, who ran a rehab center called Silverthorn in the backwoods of Connecticut. I had known Sister Sarah from the beginning and supported Silverthorn with donations and investment counseling.

She had degrees in psychology and psychiatry and a unique understanding of the human psyche.

"You're where?" she asked incredulously, knowing what had happened the last time I was in Las Vegas.

"Vegas," I repeated.

"You don't have a lick of sense," she said, exasperated.

"You and Mary seem to think alike on that one."

"No big surprise," she said. "Mary's a smart woman."

After a lengthy conversation with Sarah Agnes, mostly about Silverthorn and the unnamed celebrities residing there, I called Raul Rivera. Raul was an old college friend from Colombia who had his fingers in many pies and who had been instrumental in helping me put an end to my first big case.

"How goes life in paradise?"—always my opening line when I phoned Raul.

"Donnie! Life in paradise is very good. Long time since I have heard from you. Is everything okay?"

"Everything is fine, Raul. Tell me what's new in your life."

We stayed on the line for twenty minutes. Raul did most of the talking. Somewhere in the middle of our conversation, he told me about his lady *du jour*. His latest love, he said, was *the one*. This was maybe the tenth beautiful woman Raul had professed to me was *the one*.

"How long have you been dating?"

"About a month," Raul said. "Her name is Danielle."

"A month. A little early to be declaring her *the one*, isn't it?"

"Ah, Donnie," Raul said, trying to sound disappointed. "You are such a pragmatist. You need to be more of a romantic. The heart does not judge love in days and nights."

After we hung up, I could only shake my head at Raul's whimsy. He was smart and tough, but a hopeless romantic. I hoped it would not be his downfall.

◆   ◆   ◆   ◆

Late in the afternoon, Detective Rodriquez called.

"Detective," I said. "How nice of you to ring."

"Yeah, Mr. Hospitality, that's me. How's the nose and lip?"

"Look almost normal," I said. "Only hurt when I smile."

"So don't smile."

"I won't. Try not to be funny."

He chuckled. "I wanted to give you an update. The Cousins are out on bail. Not surprising, but I thought you should know."

"Think they'll come looking for me again?"

"No," he said. "They had their shot. They'll leave you alone."

"What about Bruiser?"

He laughed. "No way. Bruiser is a bit of a celebrity with lots of well-connected friends. Going after Bruiser could get them killed."

"I didn't realize Bruiser has so much juice."

"The casino business is a close-knit circle. They take care of their own."

"Glad to hear it," I said. "Got anything else for me?"

"Yeah. I squeezed the cousin with the broken jaw and found out they were tipped off by someone at the airport who had access to passenger information on incoming flights. Your name was on a short list of people they wanted to know about if they showed up in Vegas."

"Nice to be remembered."

"They won't forget you anytime soon," Ed Rodriguez said. "When are you leaving town?"

"Early tomorrow morning."

"Safe travels, Youngblood," he said. "Take care of yourself."

◆   ◆   ◆   ◆

That evening, I met Dr. Sam Chang for dinner at the Envy Steakhouse in the Renaissance Hotel. A small, pleasant man, Sam Chang had been the doctor at Las Vegas's Sunrise Hospital who was in charge of putting me back together after the parking garage incident a few years back. If he noticed my slightly swollen upper lip, he kept it to himself.

I had given him a few investment tips since I saw him last. All had proven profitable, including one involving a drug company whose stock had risen over 25 percent. Still, I wanted to do more.

We shared an excellent bottle of old-vine red zinfandel and engaged in small talk that didn't include why I was in town. When the waitress came, we both ordered filet mignon, medium-rare.

"How's the head?" Dr. Chang asked.

"Seems fine. Although there are times Mary wonders about that."

He chuckled and took a drink of wine. His movements were precise and unhurried. "You made national news awhile back."

I smiled. "Don't remind me. It was more attention than I wanted—somewhat embarrassing."

"It made me a minor celebrity around the hospital. I was the doctor who treated the famous private detective."

"And did a damn fine job of it," I said, raising my glass.

We both took a drink. Our steaks arrived. I seldom ate red meat, devouring a good steak only every month or two. The filet mignon was excellent.

"I'd like to make a contribution to the hospital or to your private practice," I said. "Maybe a piece of equipment or some latest technology you might need."

"That's a nice gesture," he said, "but why do you feel it's necessary?"

"I'm a humanitarian."

"And you have more money than you know what to do with."

"That, too."

"Let me think about it," he said. "What are my parameters?"

"Let's say a hundred grand."

"A hundred-thousand-dollar shopping spree," he said. "This is going to be fun."

35

The next morning, a Saturday, I took the earliest flight I could out of Vegas, booking myself first-class on a seven o'clock Delta flight to Atlanta. I felt a certain sense of relief when the plane took wing.

Losing three hours traveling east, I arrived in Atlanta at 1:50 P.M. and took a 3:00 puddle-jumper to Tri-Cities Airport. On the ground a little after 4:00, I retrieved my Pathfinder from long-term parking and was at the lake house an hour later. No one was there to greet me.

I went through the kitchen and grabbed my binoculars before going out the back door to the upper deck. I spotted them on the lake, anchored about a hundred yards out. I walked down to the lower deck for a closer look. Mary, Lacy, and Hannah were decked out in skimpy bikinis, sunbathing. Jake and Junior were lying in the shade beneath the covered section. I stood there with the binoculars, admiring my wife. Then Lacy spotted me and waved vigorously. Then Mary waved, then Hannah. Jake and Junior remained oblivious.

Lacy started one of the twin engines, and the barge slowly moved toward me, carrying on its gray deck the two most important people in my life.

As soon as the barge nudged the dock, Lacy jumped off and ran to me. "We're glad you're home," she said. "You've got to tell me all about Las Vegas."

Lacy had been to Vegas once in search of her runaway mother. We had found her mother, who decided she didn't want to be a mother anymore. A series of subsequent events had resulted in my marriage with Mary and our adopting Lacy.

"Later," I said. "There's not a lot to tell."

"How's the nose?"

I looked at Mary. She shrugged.

"The nose is fine," I said. "No more questions."

I received a hug and a quick kiss from Mary. "Welcome home."

"Good to be here," I said. I wanted to add *blabbermouth*, but I didn't. I had to get used to the fact that Mary and Lacy shared everything. I was sure they shared a great deal that I didn't know about.

"Hannah and I are leaving now," Lacy said. "I'm spending the night with her after our double date."

"Call us when you get there," Mary said.

"And be careful," I said.

"Stop worrying," Lacy said. "I'm a good driver."

"It's not you we worry about," Mary said.

"Come on, Hannah," Lacy said. "Let's get out of here before we get a full-blown lecture."

But there was no resentment when she said it, and I knew she liked it that we cared so much. We watched them go through the back door. Seconds later, we heard the fading sound of tires on gravel as my old Pathfinder rolled up our driveway.

"What's for dinner?"

Mary smiled. "Me, Cowboy."

"Yippee ki-yay," I said. "I'm starving."

◆   ◆   ◆   ◆

"What's really for dinner?" I asked an hour later.

"I figured we'd be eating late, so I planned tortellini with Alfredo sauce, garlic toast, and Caesar salad, which, of course, you will make. Sound okay?"

"Sounds great. Now, I really am starved."

"So let's eat," Mary said.

She got up, pulled on a T-shirt and a pair of shorts, and headed out of the bedroom. I watched every movement, again congratulating myself on how lucky I was.

❖　　❖　　❖　　❖

We ate dinner by candlelight at a small table I set up in front of the fire-place in the great room. The weather was turning, and though it wasn't cold enough to justify a fire, I lit one anyway. Rather, I turned on the gas logs to a low flame. *Ambiance is all.*

We shared a bottle of Chardonnay and engaged in unhurried conversation about what had happened to each of us since I left.

"What's your major news flash?"

"We had a lockdown and a locker search at the high school," Mary said. "We got a tip about some drugs, but we had to make it look routine, so we searched a hundred lockers at random."

"And the locker you got the tip about was one of them."

"Naturally."

"Anybody we know?"

"No," Mary said. "Of course, the kid had no idea how the drugs got there."

"Of course," I said. "Got any proof?"

"We ran prints on the baggie. They're a match."

"Were the kid's prints in the system?"

"No," Mary said. "We took them off a soda can."

"Sounds like entrapment."

"Don't think so," Mary said. "He asked for the soda, then left the can behind when he was bailed out. He had no reasonable right to privacy, and we had probable cause. We just wanted enough leverage to squeeze his source out of him. He lawyered up, but I think he'll deal."

"You sound like a lawyer."

"I almost have to be," Mary said. "One false move and your perp walks."

"What kind of drugs did you find?"

"Angel dust."

"Bad stuff," I said.

"Terrible. It affects every kid a little differently."

I shared out the last of the Chardonnay, and we both took a drink.

"Tell me about the CJK case," Mary said. "What's your gut saying?"

I told her about my meeting with Sidney Green and Peter Lewis.

"I don't think CJK is going to kill again," I said. "I think that if he was, he would have bought more charms from Peter. I think he bought the pistol specifically for me. I don't know why yet, but I intend to find out. As far as killing nurses, maybe he was in a hospital and had a bad experience."

"Maybe he dated a nurse and it ended badly."

"Not a bad thought," I said. "Now you sound like a cop."

Mary smiled. We drank more wine. It was almost gone.

"What is it with you and threes?" Mary said. "First the three devils dancing tattoo, and now three dead nurses."

Something clicked in the back of my mind. "You may be on to something. What if this has something to do with the Three Devils case?"

◆   ◆   ◆   ◆

That night, I lay in bed thinking about a possible connection between CJK and the Tattoo Killers. Mary was sound asleep beside me, her breathing soft and measured, bringing a sense of peace to my confusing world. There was a time when I had feared to love. Now, I feared not loving. What would I ever do if I lost this woman? I pushed the thought away.

If a connection existed between the two cases, it had to be between CJK and Matthew Sherman, whom I had called "the head devil" until I knew his real name. I had managed to track down Matt Sherman's father, Bret, in an assisted-living center outside Louisville, Kentucky. At the time of our first meeting, Bret was in the early stages of Alzheimer's. That particular day, he was lucid enough to tell me that Matthew had been institutionalized. He hadn't specified whether prison or mental hospital, and I hadn't pressed the issue, since his son was already dead.

It wasn't much, but it was a thread of a lead I would follow until it ran out. Still, there was something else, something I was missing. I was sure of it. And I thought I might know where to begin looking.

36

Sunday was a day of relaxing. We ate breakfast and then took the barge out and puttered around on the lake while listening to the Titans play at Pittsburgh in their opening game of the NFL season. They shocked the experts and won.

We did not talk about local crime, angel dust, JCD, or CJK. We simply enjoyed an uncomplicated day.

I reflected on that as I sat at my desk early Monday morning. Among my many emails was one from Las Vegas Nikki with her résumé attached:

In case you were serious about New York,
here is my résumé. Thanks for the drink.
Nikki Anderson

I downloaded and printed the résumé. It stated that Nikki had graduated from Stanford with honors. Her work career looked impressive. I forwarded it to my old boss:

You would definitely want to interview this one, you old letch.
Don

Then I wrote Nikki back:

I was serious and have forwarded your résumé to my old boss in
New York. Let me know if you hear anything. I'm betting your will.
Don

I was still going through email when the phone rang.

"Meet me at the diner in half an hour," the voice said. "We haven't talked in a while, and there's something I have to tell you."

"Bad news?"

"No."

"See you there," I said.

◆   ◆   ◆   ◆

A half-hour later, I went down the back stairs, up the alley, and through the back entrance of the Mountain Center Diner, ignoring, as always, the **Employees Only** sign. He was already at my table, steam rising from a mug of coffee in front of him. We nodded at each other as I sat. Before I could get a word in, Doris was there with another mug.

"Ready to order?" she asked.

"The usual," I said, the usual being a feta cheese omelet with home fries and rye toast.

"Billy?"

"Pancakes and bacon," Billy said. "Full stack. Double order of bacon."

Doris smiled and bustled away.

"You driving over for breakfast," I said. "What's the occasion?"

"I'm closing the office in Cherokee."

Billy was never one for beating around the bush.

"I'm not surprised."

"Charlie wants me full time," Billy said.

Charlie was Charlie Running Horse, sheriff of Swain County, North Carolina.

"I'm not surprised at that either. How soon?"

"Two weeks. I'm wrapping up a few small cases and then shutting the doors."

Billy's moving on was inevitable. I had known the day would come, I just didn't know when. I was mentally prepared. I felt a combination of excitement and sadness—excitement for Billy's continuing evolution and sadness in knowing that part of our relationship was ending.

He seemed to read my thoughts. "Nothing has changed between us."

"I know."

"Never will," Billy said.

"I know."

"I'll always be there when you need me. Any time, any place."

"I know that, too," I said. "Enough already."

Billy smiled and pointed at me. He'd been pushing for a reaction—and gotten one.

I glared at him. "Stop doing that."

"Too much fun."

Our food arrived, and we ate in comfortable silence.

"It's been awhile since we talked," Billy said. "Tell me what you found out about the jacket."

I told him about sending Amos Smith to Italy, about finding out who Johnny Cross really was, and about my trips to Franklin Pierce Academy and the Savannah Rose Gallery. He processed all of it without comment and continued to dispose of his breakfast.

"Ever ride the Tail of the Dragon?"

"Sure," Billy said. "You can't own a Harley and not ride the Dragon's Tail."

I laughed. "I should have known."

"How about you?" Billy asked.

"Once."

"On a bike?"

"Car."

"Why?" Billy asked, as if it was the dumbest thing he'd ever heard.

"I was a teenager," I said. "I was trying to impress a girl."

"It figures. Did it work?"

"She got sick."

Billy laughed, a long rumble like distant thunder. I ate home fries, took a drink of coffee, and waited for him to calm down.

He was still smiling when I said, "Think I should tell Lacy about all this?"

Billy shook his head. "Don't answer questions that haven't been asked."

"My thoughts exactly," I said. "But it's good to have confirmation."

"Someday, you might feel compelled to tell her. You'll know when the time comes."

"You are very wise," I teased.

"I am," Billy said, not smiling.

Doris cleared our plates and refilled our mugs. I moved away from the subject of Johnny Cross.

"I'm working a case with the FBI."

Billy eyebrow's elevated. "Tell me about that."

I gave him the long version, omitting nothing.

"What do you think?" I asked when I finished.

"I think you need to be careful. I think it's personal between you and this killer, and I think it will come to a showdown. Make sure I'm there when it does."

"Happy to," I said.

◆   ◆   ◆   ◆

Back at the office, I called David Steele.

"I'm reporting in."

"You never just report in," he said. "More than likely, you want something and you're using *reporting in* as a means to segue into it."

"Are all FBI agents so cynical?"

"A large majority," he said. "Tell me what you got."

"I forgot to mention one thing about the Vegas trip that has nothing to do with CJK," I said.

"Let's hear it."

I told him about my encounter with the Cousins, about Bruiser's involvement, and about Detective Ed Rodriguez.

"I'd hate to get hit by Bruiser Bracken," David Steele said. "That had to hurt."

"Sure looked like it did."

"You think the Cousins will leave you alone?"

"Detective Rodriguez seems to think so."

"Want me to put some heat on them?"

"Probably best to let it lie," I said. "What's Buckley been up to lately?"

David Steele laughed. "You're stalling, Youngblood. What do you really want?"

No way to slide in, so I jumped. "Do you still have the file on the Tattoo Killers case?"

There was silence on the other end of the line. I knew the question would raise a red flag. David Steele was processing, and he was a quick study.

"You think CJK is connected to Lucifer?"

Lucifer, often referred to as "the head devil," was the FBI's code name for the ringleader in the Tattoo Killers case. He and his young following marked their victims with tattoos of a devil dancing around a fire. The corresponding file in my office bore the label, "Walker Case—Three Devils Dancing."

I knew that Lucifer was Matthew Sherman. I had discovered that after the case was over and decided it was best for all concerned if I kept it a secret. The FBI had no knowledge of Matthew Sherman. If David Steele found that I knew the real identity of Lucifer, he would not be pleased. The FBI didn't like loose ends. But since the case was closed, it was a minor loose end—one the bureau didn't have time to pursue.

"Maybe," I said. "I just want a look at the file."

"Why, Youngblood? What are you not telling me?"

"I don't know. All I've got is a gut feeling."

More silence.

"I'll have Buckley bring it to your office this afternoon," David Steele said. "He'll stay with you and the file until you're finished. You can make notes, but don't copy anything."

"Okay."

"And if you see any connection, you will share it with me," he said, as if ordering a probationary recruit.

I resisted the temptation to be a smartass and took the humble route. "I will. I promise."

"Youngblood . . ." David Steele paused. "Nothing, I'll talk to you later."

I knew I was due for a lecture, but I guessed he'd decided it was a waste of time.

◆   ◆   ◆   ◆

Late that afternoon, Buckley sat patiently in the oversized chair closer to the window as I read the Tattoo Killers file. It contained a lot of material, and I was surprised and more than a little proud at how much credit I had been given in closing the case.

Toward the end of the file, the thing nagging me jumped right off the page and startled me so much that I felt the air being sucked out of my lungs. The name Matthew Sherman had used as an alias: Trevor Smith. CJK had used T. Smith to order the Cracker Jack charms. It could not be a coincidence. It was a message for me.

I looked at Buckley to see if he had noticed my reaction. He hadn't. He was working on his iPad.

"Buckley."

He looked up.

"I'm done," I said, handing him the folder.

"Find anything?"

"I'm not sure."

But I was sure, and I had to decide whether or not to share my secret with David Steele.

◆   ◆   ◆   ◆

Late in the day, I got a phone call I had hoped I would never receive.

"Mr. Youngblood, this is Sheriff Dave Phillips from Saddle Boot, West Virginia. Remember me?"

"I do, sheriff," I said. "How long's it been?" *Vagueness is all.* I knew exactly how long it had been.

"Not sure," he said. "Three or four years, I guess." Sheriff Phillips also knew exactly how long it had been. This was not a social call.

"What can I do for you, sheriff?"

"I need to talk to you about a dead body," he said.

"The same dead body Agent Brown told me about?"

"That's the one."

"Why call me?"

"I think you might know something about it," he said.

"What makes you think that?"

"I'll tell you when we talk," the sheriff said.

"So talk," I said, getting tired of the charade.

"I'd like to make it face to face," he said. "Kind of an exchange of information."

"An exchange would mean you know something you think I'd be interested in."

"I think so," he said. "Why don't you come up to Saddle Boot and we'll discuss it?"

"I don't think so, sheriff. I'm pretty busy right now."

I had no intention of going into Sheriff Phillips's jurisdiction. He probably didn't have any reason to hold me, but why take chances? What I knew was hearsay and wouldn't be admissible in a court of law, even if anyone were alive to stand trial.

"Worth a try," he said. "How about I come see you?"

"Off the record?"

"Sure. A friendly chat, just you and me."

"Come ahead," I said.

"Tomorrow okay?"

"I'll be here all day."

◆   ◆   ◆   ◆

That night, Mary and I were in bed reading when I told her about my phone call from Sheriff Dave Phillips. I would have informed her sooner, but Lacy was always within earshot and had big ears, hearing everything she wasn't supposed to.

"He's pretty smart for a county cop," Mary said.

"He's been around the block a time or three. I expect he can add two and two."

"I think he added a lot more than two and two if he came to the conclusion you know something. What led him to you?"

"I don't know. Guess I'll find out tomorrow."

I slid my hand underneath her panties and started working my way down. Suddenly, a grip like a vice tightened around my wrist.

"What do you think you're doing?"

"It's been two days," I said.

"Poor baby."

"We could be really quiet."

"Not likely. But I could meet you here for lunch tomorrow."

"Deal," I said.

"What if Sheriff Phillips shows up at lunchtime?"

"Then you'll arrest him," I said.

"On what charge?"

"How about disturbing the piece?"

"Oh! That's really bad."

But she was laughing when she said it.

37

"Would you like coffee?" Gretchen asked.

She had just escorted Sheriff Dave Phillips into my office and seen that he was comfortably seated in one of the oversized chairs in front of my desk.

"That would be great," he said.

"Cream and sugar?"

"Black is fine," he said.

Gretchen shot me a look that said, *Why can't you take it black?* She liked to tease me about it. A big, bad private eye should *not* take cream and sugar in his coffee.

"I'll be back in a minute," Gretchen said.

She was back in about thirty seconds, during which time Sheriff Phillips completed a quick visual survey of my office. He was a tall man, and still as lean as the last time I had seen him, though his hair was grayer. The years on the job were etched in the lines of his face.

"So this is what a private detective's office looks like," he said.

Since I had never been introduced to him as a private investigator, he was letting me know he had done some research. Of course, it was on my office door, but I suspected he already knew.

"We prefer to be called private investigators," I said.

"Sorry," he said, doing his best to play the humble card. "I don't get out much."

"Let's get to it. You came a long way."

"Okay," he said. "You know we found a body. The method of concealing it made it hard to determine how long the victim had been dead. But I now know that, since the body has been identified."

He looked for a reaction from me. Although the news was a surprise, I remained bland and motionless. He continued.

"Remember I told you and Agent Brown that Betty Malone used to date a drifter name John? Well, it was Johnny Cross who she dated, and it was his body we found."

I did my best to act like I was hearing about how to make grass grow, and I thought I pulled it off pretty well. If he knew the dead body was Johnny Cross, then I wondered if he knew it was actually John Cross Durbinfield.

"How did you identify the body? Was he in the system?"

"Not exactly," he said.

"What does 'not exactly' mean?"

"Before I go any farther," he said, "I have a question. Did you know the dead body was Johnny Cross?"

"Why would you ask me that?"

"I find it curious that the Malone place sold soon after we found the body not far from the property," he said. "I don't like coincidences. So I did some digging. It seems that a Mr. Roy Husky purchased the place—for a very fair price, I might add, considering it wasn't on the market."

I acted disinterested. Sheriff Phillips paid no attention to my disinterest. He went on.

"Mr. Husky's address was listed as Amelia Island, Florida. When I cross-checked it, the same address came up for a Mr. Joseph Fleet. It seems that Mr. Fleet owns Fleet Industries, which happens to be headquartered in Mountain Center. I also find it interesting that Roy Husky is a vice president at Fleet Industries. You probably know both of those gentlemen."

"Probably," I said.

"Too big a coincidence. So, back to my original question, did you know the dead body was Johnny Cross?"

"We're off the record, right?"

"Yes."

"I knew your dead body might be Johnny Cross. I wasn't absolutely sure until you told me. How did you get an identification?"

"After we struck out in the criminal database, my deputy, Christine, went online to a DNA registry and found a Cross family," he said. "She posted Johnny Cross's DNA profile. Early morning a couple of days later, two suits showed up with a court order to claim the remains. I tried to stonewall under the guise that the body was part of an ongoing murder investigation. That afternoon, I got a call from the governor. Can you believe it, the governor! The Cross family must have some juice. So I released the body."

"No choice," I said.

He nodded and took a deep breath. "How did you know it might be Johnny Cross?"

"Will Malone told me."

"Will Malone?"

I nodded.

"How'd he know?"

"He buried Johnny Cross."

"Buried him?" he said, more than a little surprise in his voice.

I nodded again.

"Who killed him?"

"Betty Malone," I said. "As least that's what Will told me, and I believed him."

"Tell me all of it."

I told him the entire story. *In for a penny, in for a pound,* I thought.

"Well," Sheriff Phillips said, "it fits with our forensic evidence. Why did Roy Husky buy the farm?"

"Wanted a farm. I knew it was for sale."

"How did you know that?"

"Thelma Malone told me."

"You get around, don't you, Mr. Youngblood?"

"When I have to," I said.

"I think Roy Husky bought the farm so you-all could remove any trace of Johnny Cross," he said.

I shrugged. "Why would we do that?"

"I don't know."

I was silent and feigned disinterest.

"Might interest you to know that a private detective—excuse me, private investigator—showed up asking questions a couple days after the body was taken," Sheriff Phillips said.

"What kind of questions?"

"He was trying to find out everything he could about Johnny Cross. You can bet somebody told him about Betty Malone. Who in the devil was this Johnny Cross that he's drawing so much attention years after his death?"

"Cross was his middle name."

"Oh?" Sheriff Phillips said.

"His last name was Durbinfield."

"Durbinfield? As in *the Durbinfields*?"

I nodded.

Sheriff Dave slowly let out a long, deep sigh. "No wonder I got a call from the governor."

We sat in silence a minute as Sheriff Dave processed all I had told him.

"Did you ever find Tracy?"

I nodded. "Dead."

"Sorry to hear that," he said. "How?"

"Drug overdose."

He shook his head. "Accident or on purpose?"

"We'll never be sure," I said.

We were silent a moment.

"Is that your wife and daughter?" Sheriff Phillips asked, nodding toward a picture of Mary, Lacy, and me that sat on my bookcase in front of the window.

"It is."

"Your daughter looks a lot like Tracy Malone."

"Be best for all concerned if you keep that observation to yourself," I said.

"No need to broadcast it," he said. "I think I'm beginning to get a grasp of the situation."

Fifteen minutes before noon, Sheriff Dave Phillips finally left my office, thank goodness. I had a noon appointment I didn't want to miss.

Sheriff Dave and I had come to an agreement. He would close the file on Johnny Cross as an unsolved murder, by reason that there were no viable suspects. He didn't see any reason to pursue the murder, since Betty Malone was long dead.

For him, the Johnny Cross case was over. For me, it was just beginning.

38

I sat at my desk early Wednesday morning, trying to decide what direction to take in the CJK case. Since I had never told the FBI that Lucifer was actually Matthew Sherman, the bureau hadn't known to run him through its criminal database, the NCIC. I needed to find out if he was in the system. If he was, I might be able to connect Matthew Sherman to CJK.

I thought about it for a while. The way I saw it, I had two choices. I could get hacker *extraordinaire* Stanley Johns to hack the FBI's system for the cost of a pizza and a few sodas, or I could come clean with David Steele, a conversation I did not look forward to. I decided not to risk Stanley's going to prison in the unlikely event he got caught. I called David Steele's unlisted number.

"Reporting in again, Youngblood?"

Slowly and with emphasis, I said, "Not exactly."

"You've got something?"

"Yes."

"Tell me."

"In person," I said.

"Why?"

"It's a two-part report. The first part, you're going to like; the second part, not so much."

"You're buying me lunch at the Mountain Center Diner," he ordered, the long-ago FBI instructor resurfacing.

"My pleasure," I said, knowing he couldn't assault me in front of the noontime lunch crowd.

◆　　◆　　◆　　◆

We had finished eating, talking only about personal stuff—his potential retirement, now on hold; sports; my married life and teenage daughter.

We both had ordered club sandwiches with fries and left not a crumb. Doris removed our plates.

"Good sandwich and great fries," David Steele said.

Doris beamed. "We hand-cut our fries every day from fresh Idaho potatoes. Can I get you-all some coffee?"

"Sure," I said, delaying the inevitable.

"Sounds good," David Steele said. Then he leveled his gaze on me. "Let's hear it."

"The part that's going to piss you off or the part you're going to like?"

"Piss me off first," he said. "Then maybe the other part will calm me down."

"Remember that during the Tattoo Killers case we referred to the head devil as Lucifer?"

"I do. So?"

"Then we found out he was using an alias that traced back about twenty years."

"Yeah. So where's this going?"

"So I know who Lucifer really was."

I waited for an explosion. There wasn't one.

"I hope you found this out after the case was closed," he said.

"I did."

"And you decided not to tell me," he said. Now, he was getting annoyed.

"Yes."

"Why?"

I told him the story of Bret, Sammy, and Matthew Sherman. About how the loss of young Sammy to leukemia at an early age had driven the older brother crazy and eventually turned him into the orchestrator of teenage serial killers. David Steele listened without interruption.

"So you didn't tell me because you thought the FBI might question Bret Sherman, and he would find out about Matthew's death."

I nodded. "I didn't see the need."

"Well," David Steele said, taking a drink of coffee, "I would have left the man alone. Of course, that doesn't mean somebody higher up would have let it lie. So as far as I'm concerned, you did what I would have done. No harm, no foul. Let's keep that between you and me."

The longer I knew him, David Steele seemed to play less and less by the book than in the good ole days when he was a tight-assed instructor at Quantico.

"Now, tell me the good stuff," he said.

"Remember the alias Lucifer used?"

He thought for a minute. "I deal with a lot of cases, and that was just a footnote to the file after the case was over. I'm afraid I don't remember. What was it?"

"Trevor Smith," I said.

"So?"

I stared at him and waited for him to process it.

"Damn!" he said. "T. Smith. CJK ordered the charms as T. Smith. CJK knew Matthew Sherman?"

"It would be a mighty big coincidence if he didn't."

David Steele stared out across the diner with a worried look on his face.

"He's coming after you, Youngblood. You need to lie low."

"No way," I said. "He wants an end game, and I intend to give him one. I'm going to find him before he makes his last play."

◆   ◆   ◆   ◆

An hour later, Buckley Clarke sat across from me in my office, ready to take orders.

"I hear we might have a break," he said.

"How much do you know?"

"Nothing," Buckley said. "Agent Steele called me on my cell and said, and I quote, 'Get your ass to Youngblood's office as fast as you can, and do what he says,' end quote. What are my orders?"

"Have you read the Tattoo Killers file?"

"Three times."

"Remember the name Trevor Smith?"

"The alias Lucifer used. It went back a number of years, and then nothing."

"Right," I said.

"What do you know that I don't?"

"I know that Trevor Smith was born Matthew Sherman in Lexington, Kentucky."

"How do you know that?"

"It's not important," I said. "What is important is that when CJK ordered the charms from Peter Lewis, he used the name—"

"T. Smith," Buckley said before I could finish. "Christ have mercy, that cannot be a coincidence. CJK knew Lucifer."

"It appears so," I said. "And he wants a final showdown with me. We need to find him before that happens. Here's what I want you to do."

39

I heard him coming before I saw him. The sound of his leather heels on the marble floor outside my office door was unmistakable. He opened the door and came in. I heard the sound of coffee being made in my Keurig. He came into the inner office carrying a mug, tossed his Cowboy hat on the chair next to the window, sat in the chair closer to my office door, and took a drink.

"I've got to get one of those machines," he said.

"To what do I owe this pleasure?"

"I thought you'd like to know a private detective is in town asking questions about Lacy Malone," Big Bob said. "So far, he doesn't seem to be having any luck. But sooner or later, he's going to connect the dots."

Lacy had dropped the Malone name when the adoption was final. She was officially Lauren Lacy Youngblood. If a private detective was checking records, he'd come up empty. But if he asked enough people, he'd find out that Lacy Youngblood used to be Lacy Malone. I had no doubt the Durbinfields were investigating the death of Johnny Cross.

"Thanks for the heads-up," I said.

"What's this about?" the big man asked.

"It's about someone who was killed eighteen years ago."

"Murder?"

"Maybe."

He drank his coffee and looked out the window, thinking. It didn't take him long to put it together.

"Lacy's father?"

"Maybe," I said.

"You want to give me a few more details?" he asked, getting annoyed. "Damn it, Blood, do I have to drag everything out of you? Can't you just tell me what the hell is going on?"

So I told him the story of Johnny Cross and Tracy Malone, who might have been rapist and victim or star-crossed lovers, depending on who was to be believed.

"So Lacy's grandmother killed a Durbinfield, who was most likely Lacy's father," he said. "That's a secret worth burying."

"I thought so, too," I said. "But this secret is literally no longer buried."

"Be nice to find out how much this private eye knows. Maybe he's just questioning people who knew Johnny Cross."

"Except that Lacy has never heard of Johnny Cross."

"You sure about that?" Big Bob asked.

I paused to consider it. "Not one-hundred percent."

Maybe I should find out, I thought.

The only information Lacy had shared with me about her father was that her mother might have known who he was but never told her. If that was true, then the possibility of Lacy's finding out who her father was went to the grave with Tracy Malone. I could not rule out the possibility that John Cross Durbinfield was not Lacy's father.

"Maybe I should run this guy out of Mountain Center," Big Bob said.

"I appreciate the thought, but I need to know what he knows. Sooner or later, he'll either leave town or show up in my office."

He didn't leave town. And it was sooner rather than later.

◆   ◆   ◆   ◆

That afternoon, I kept my office door shut while I concentrated on some stock market research I had been putting off. Interest rates on savings accounts and CDs continued to be so low as to be nonexistent. More and more, my clients were pulling their cash out of banks and begging me to make them a measly 3 to 5 percent return. Stocks had become one of the best games in town.

A gentle rap on the door to my inner sanctum interrupted me. Gretchen came in and closed the door behind her.

"A Mr. Philip Vance is here," she said softly. "He says he's a private investigator from New York. I told him you were busy, but he asked me to tell you it concerns a murder investigation you might be aware of."

"Send him in."

◆   ◆   ◆   ◆

Philip Vance was about my size and had salt-and-pepper hair cut short. I had no doubt the ladies found his chiseled looks attractive. He wore a friendly smile and a charcoal gray pinstripe suit with a white silk tie centered on a pale gray shirt. He looked in shape. He sat in the same chair Big Bob had occupied a few hours earlier.

"Thanks for seeing me," he said.

"Professional courtesy. What can I do for you?"

"I'm investigating the death of a man known as Johnny Cross who knew Tracy Malone," he said. "I understand Tracy is also deceased, and that you adopted her daughter, Lacy."

Well, it didn't take him long to find that out, I thought. The Durbin-fields apparently hired the best.

"That's true," I said. *Cooperation is all.*

"I would very much like to interview Lacy to find out if her mother ever mentioned Johnny Cross."

"I can find that out for you," I said pleasantly.

He hesitated. "I'd rather ask her myself."

"Philip, that's not going to happen," I said, no longer pleasant.

He smiled. "Call me Phil."

I smiled back. "Phil, that's not going to happen."

The smiled faded. "Why not?" he asked, trying hard to act surprised and innocent at the same time.

"Because Lacy lost her mother in a very unfortunate way and has started a new life, and I don't want her reminded of her past," I said firmly.

He paused as if thinking about it. "I understand."

He sounded sincere. I relaxed a little.

"I'll ask Lacy if she's ever heard of Johnny Cross and get back to you," I said. "Give me your cell-phone number."

"Sure," he said, handing me a business card. "Thanks."

But he no longer seemed interested.

◆   ◆   ◆   ◆

That night, Lacy, Mary, and I had takeout from a local barbecue res-taurant. We sat at the bar and shared the feast before beginning serious conversation.

"Did your mother or grandmother ever mention a man by the name of Johnny Cross?" I asked, looking at Lacy.

I had shared the essence of my visit from Phil Vance with Mary and had prepared her for my question, which I put forth as casually as possible.

"I don't think so," Lacy said. "Why?"

Go with the truth, Youngblood, I thought.

"A private detective was in my office today. He's investigating the death of Johnny Cross in West Virginia and was told your mother or grandmother might have known him there. Since he can't ask your mother or grandmother, he wanted to talk to you, so I told him I'd ask you."

"Never heard of him," Lacy said. "How'd he die?"

"The private detective didn't say." I tore a rib off my rack.

"How is basketball practice going?" Mary asked, shifting the conversation.

"Really well," Lacy said, and went into every detail of that afternoon's two-hour practice, Johnny Cross apparently forgotten.

40

The next morning, I decided to go to the Mountain Center Diner for breakfast. It was Friday, and the place was hopping. Few tables were unoccupied, mine, of course, being one of them. Phil Vance was alone at a table for two at the window facing the street, drinking coffee. He saw me and motioned me to his table. I motioned back to mine and kept going, hoping he wouldn't join me. He was undeterred. In the time it took me to sit, he was at my table.

"They reserve tables here?" he asked, noticing my sign.

"Not exactly."

"Ah, I see." He smiled.

Doris materialized.

"The usual," I said before she could get a word out.

She looked at Phil Vance.

"What's the usual?" he asked.

"A feta cheese omelet with rye toast, home fries, and coffee," she said.

"That'll work for me, too." Phil Vance turned back to me. "I take it you frequent this establishment."

"Home away from home," I said.

"You're probably a local legend," he said. He obviously knew about the Tattoo Killers case.

"Small town. Get your name on the national news just once and you're set for life."

He nodded. "So did you get a chance to speak with your daughter?"

"I did."

He waited.

"She's never heard of Johnny Cross."

"I didn't expect so," he said. "But I had to ask."

"Who hired you?"

I didn't expect an answer and certainly didn't expect the truth, but I got a surprise.

"Elizabeth Durbinfield," he said. "Johnny Cross was a Durbinfield, her son. But I suspect you already know that. I also suspect you know more than you'll tell me."

Our food arrived. We ate in silence.

"I'm not trying to jam you up," he said, taking a break from his breakfast. "Elizabeth Durbinfield is just seeking closure. If you know something that could help with that, it would be much appreciated."

I said nothing. We continued eating. Phil Vance ate faster than I did. Then again, he was from New York.

"From what I can piece together," he said, "John Cross Durbinfield might have been your daughter's biological father."

I tried not to show any reaction. "Interesting theory. How did you make that jump?"

"I know he had a relationship with Lacy's mother. I know the family left town soon after he disappeared. And I know Tracy gave birth about nine months later. Add it all up, and it certainly is a possibility."

"Or a coincidence," I said. "Tracy could just as easily have gotten pregnant by one of her high-school classmates."

"A DNA test would prove or disprove that."

"Again, Phil," I said, "that's not going to happen."

"Why not?"

"Invasion of privacy."

"She could be heir to a fortune," he said.

"Money is not an issue."

"Yes, I know you're well off, but still."

"Forget about it," I said. "Lacy has a nice, uncomplicated life here. I want to keep it that way."

"Elizabeth Durbinfield could get a court order."

"I doubt it," I said. "There is no compelling reason for a judge to grant one."

"You're probably right," he said. "No offense. Just doing my job."

"None taken." I finished my breakfast. "When do you leave?"

"Later today," he said.

"Breakfast is on me."

"Professional courtesy?"

"You catch on fast," I said. "If I get up your way, you can return the gesture."

"It would be my pleasure." He handed me his card. "Call me if you get to the Big Apple."

His card was elegant, understated, and obviously expensive.

"Did you know there's a series of books and movies based on a New York City detective named Philo Vance?" I asked.

"Yes, I've heard that," he said. "Back in the twenties and thirties, I think."

Doris bustled over and refilled our mugs, then hurried away, a coffeepot in each hand.

"Elizabeth Durbinfield doesn't like to take no for an answer," Phil Vance said. "Whatever it's worth, I'm on your side. I think she should leave you alone. As soon as I get back and file a report, I'm out of this. Sometimes, the rich shouldn't get their way. But I expect it won't be over for you."

"I didn't think it would be," I said.

41

Early Monday morning, Roy and I sat on T. Elbert's front porch with the usual fare. I had spent a relaxing weekend and was ready to face the week. Saturday, Roy, T. Elbert, Billy, and I had gone to see Lacy play basketball as the Mountain Center Lady Bears scrimmaged a pretty good Knoxville team. Mary had been called in to work to investigate a series of break-ins and could not go to the scrimmage. The Lady Bears won by ten points, and Lacy had led all scorers with twenty-one, including five three-pointers. Saturday night, Lacy had stayed at Hannah's, leaving Mary and me alone. We took full advantage of the empty house. Sunday, Mary, Lacy, Hannah, and I had spent the day on the lake. Life was good.

"Lacy looked great in that scrimmage," T. Elbert said. "She's a player."

"She is that," Roy said. "Is she interested in playing college ball?"

"We haven't talked much about it," I said. "But I don't think she is. Sometimes, I think she's playing basketball just because Billy and I played."

We sat in silence, watching the cars go by on Olivia Drive. Most were exceeding the speed limit, probably running late for work.

"Tell us about this Vegas trip," Roy said.

I told how I was working with the FBI, tracking down a lead. I was vague with the details. I didn't mention CJK. I trusted Roy completely, but the fewer people who knew about CJK, the better.

"Ouch," Roy said when I described Bruiser's jaw-breaking punch.

"Hurts me to think about it," I said.

"Well, at least you got back in one piece," Roy said.

I finished my account, then polished off my sesame seed bagel and coffee.

"I'm tracking down another lead that may be promising," I said. "I'll let you know."

Roy remained silent. Like Billy, he was content with not knowing things he didn't need to know. T. Elbert, most of the time, wanted to know everything. I indulged him when I could.

"What's going on with your government project?" I asked Roy.

"Tying up some loose ends. We should be good to go in a week or two. As soon as we're ready, we'll be bringing Bruiser in."

"What's next for you?" T. Elbert asked me.

I had no way of knowing at the time, but the answer to that question turned out to be a lot more than I wanted to deal with.

"I'll await developments," I said.

◆   ◆   ◆   ◆

That afternoon, Agent Buckley Clarke sat across from me.

"I cannot believe how many Trevor Smiths and Matthew Shermans I found in different databases, and I'm not even finished," Buckley said. "Nearly 250. We're searching for the proverbial needle in the haystack. And these databases may not go back as far as we need them to. And in a lot of cases, they rely on information from the individuals themselves. So I narrowed the search by date of birth and whittled the list down to about three dozen names so far. There will probably be more."

"Does your criminal database information show how long they were incarcerated and when they were released?"

"In some cases but not all," Buckley said.

"Okay, based on information from his father, we think Matthew Sherman was in a correctional facility. He was released at some point and soon afterward assumed the identity of Trevor Smith. He was around twenty-five years old. So any trouble he got in after that was probably under his alias."

"Unless he used both his true identity and his alias."

"Maybe," I said. "But I didn't find any evidence of Matthew Sherman, and neither did the FBI. If he was using both identities, it will make it harder to track his movements."

"Maybe he had a safe house somewhere."

"No way to know."

"Nothing we can do except keep narrowing the field," Buckley said. "If we find them alive, we cross them off the list."

"Keep at it," I said. "I have to think this one through."

I was still in the office at five o'clock that afternoon, long after Buckley's departure. I had a strong feeling that if I could tie Matthew Sherman to CJK, I could find CJK. The clock was ticking, and I had a sense of panic because I was missing something. I had not considered that Matthew Sherman might have used both identities, but it made sense.

◆   ◆   ◆   ◆

I lay in bed reading *The Big Sleep* by Raymond Chandler, a classic private detective novel written in 1939. Philip Marlowe wasn't having any better luck with his case than I was with mine. I was hoping he might give me some inspiration.

Mary was asleep in relative darkness, since my reading lamp cast light on my book and not much else. I caught myself staring at the pages but not reading. I was thinking how to connect Matthew Sherman to CJK. I had to make certain assumptions. CJK knew Matthew Sherman, and I was betting they had met in prison or maybe at a mental institution. The questions were where and when.

Buckley had said something that piqued my curiosity. What if Matthew Sherman had a safe house? Or maybe Bret Sherman still had a house somewhere. If I could find it, maybe I could discover some clues as to the identity of CJK. It was a long shot, but long shots had paid off for me in the past.

I marked my book, cut off my light, and drifted into a restless sleep filled with dreams that were as nonsensical as they were fragmented.

42

The next day, I took the dogs to the office, arriving before anyone else was on the floor. We came up the back stairs and started down the hall toward my office. The only audible sound was the click of dog nails on the marble floor. Jake and Junior raced down the hall, nearly sliding into my office door as they attempted to stop on the slick surface. They spun in excitement, waiting for me to unlock the door. As soon as I opened it, they bolted through, performed their customary inspection, and gave me the all-clear by lying down on their beds for an early-morning snooze. Office security is hard work.

◆   ◆   ◆   ◆

"How hard would it be to track down land records in Kentucky and adjoining states to see if Bret or Matthew Sherman owned property?" I asked Buckley. I had called him as soon as I made coffee.

"A real long shot," Buckley said. "We would have to go county by county, and I don't think property ownership records carry dates of birth. What are you thinking?"

"I'm thinking that your safe house idea might be worth looking into."

"Do you want me to quit what I'm doing and start on property records?"

"How much more time do you think you need?"

"Two days, maybe three."

"Finish what you're working on," I said. "I'll approach this from a different direction."

◆   ◆   ◆   ◆

I left the dogs in the office and took the elevator down to the first-floor lobby. I chatted a few minutes with Sam Watson and walked across the street to Dunkin' Donuts. Everyone knew my penchant for Dunkin' Donuts coffee and kidded me about how lucky I was that one just happened to open across the street. The joke was on them; it wasn't luck at all.

I ordered a medium coffee with cream and sugar, a toasted poppy seed bagel with cream cheese, and a medium black coffee for Sam, who had declined my offer of a bagel or donut by referencing his expanding waistline.

Back in the office, I made quick work of my abbreviated breakfast and then played one of my long shots in the form of a phone call to the Maple Oaks Retirement Community. After a few transfers, I was finally able to speak to Nurse Nancy, who always seemed to know Bret Sherman's current condition.

"Sure, I remember you, Mr. Youngblood," Nancy said. "You're the only visitor Mr. Sherman has had in years."

"How's he doing?"

"Fading," Nancy said. "He's gone for longer periods of time now, then he comes back for a few days."

"How about today?"

"He's somewhere else. Has been for a couple of weeks. No telling when, or if, he'll ever come back. You never know when they'll be gone for good."

"If he comes back, let me know immediately," I said. "I'd like to visit him one more time."

"I'll do that, Mr. Youngblood," Nancy said.

43

Wednesday morning, I got a major surprise. I heard a tap on my office door about an hour after Gretchen arrived. She slipped in, closed the door, and locked it.

"What's wrong?"

She walked to the front of my desk, put both hands on it, and leaned toward me. "There's a woman with two bodyguards out there. She wants to see you immediately. The bodyguards look less than friendly."

"Did she give you her name?"

"No," Gretchen said. "She said you'd know who she is."

"Tell her I'll see her, but the bodyguards have to wait in the hall."

Gretchen nodded and turned for the door.

"No, wait. I'll tell her myself."

I followed Gretchen to the outer office. A tall, slender, stately woman stood near the door with two hulks behind her. She had stylish gray hair and was impeccably dressed in a long tweed skirt, a delicate-looking white blouse, black boots, and a black leather jacket. I was sure her clothes were the most expensive available. The hulks were a little taller than me and had crew-cut hair. One was blond and the other a little less so. They vaguely resembled each other. They wore dark suits and looked in good physical condition. Ex-military, no doubt.

"Elizabeth Durbinfield, I presume," I said, my tone and demeanor neutral.

"You presume correctly," she said, neither friendly nor hostile. "May we talk?"

"Please join me in my office," I said with a wave of my hand. "And ask your employees to stand sentry in the hall. If they remain in the office, Gretchen might get too excited. We'll leave the hall door open in case they have to run to your aid."

I witnessed what I thought was a faint smile.

"I was told you have a quick wit. It's rewarding to know that I was not misinformed."

She turned and gave a slight nod to the hulks, who backed out the doorway; I half-expected them to bow. Elizabeth Durbinfield walked past me into my office and sat in the chair closer to the window. I followed and closed my door, but not all the way. She scanned her surroundings with neither approval nor disapproval, taking it all in.

Then I got an even bigger surprise.

"I'd like to hire you."

I tried hard not to show a reaction. "To do what?"

"To find out who murdered my son."

I stared out my window. I had been hired to do many things, but never to find out something I already knew.

"Why me?" I asked, stalling.

"Don't be modest," Elizabeth Durbinfield said. "You're nationally known. You're rich, you're not motivated by money but by justice, and you have connections with the FBI."

"I think I'm going to blush."

"And then there's that rapier wit," she said, smiling.

The real reason for her visit was still lurking in the background. I decided to drag it out in the open.

"I thought you wanted my daughter's DNA," I said.

"We can have that discussion another time."

"We can have it now," I said. "You cannot have my daughter's DNA."

"Very well," she said, seemingly undeterred. "Will you, as they say on TV, take my case?"

"I'll think about it. I've got a lot going on right now. I'm consulting on a very sensitive case."

"With the FBI," she said.

"How did you know that?"

"An educated guess," she said. "You have worked with them before."

"It might be a while before I can help you," I said.

"I understand, but I do hope you'll do it." She turned and looked out my window, as if considering her options. Her gaze fell on the picture of Lacy, Mary, and me. "Your wife and daughter?"

"Yes."

"They're very pretty. One would never know your daughter is adopted." I was glad she didn't add "and maybe my granddaughter."

"It's not a secret."

"Apparently not," she said, standing.

I stood.

"I've never seen the Biltmore Estate," she said. "So I'm going to Asheville, North Carolina, for a couple of days for a private tour. I'll be at the Renaissance Hotel. Please remember, I've recently discovered my son is dead. I need to know what happened. I need closure on this. Good day, Mr. Youngblood."

She turned and walked out of my office, past Gretchen, and into the hall, shutting the outer door behind her. I stood at Gretchen's desk trying to process what had just happened.

"Well, that was weird," Gretchen said, as she came into my office.

"It certainly was," I said.

◆　　◆　　◆　　◆

That night, Biker came over for dinner. We ordered pizza. After dinner, Biker and Lacy went down the few steps to the den to watch television. Mary and I stayed at the kitchen bar to finish our drinks and talk.

"What was Elizabeth Durbinfield like?" Mary asked.

"She emitted a strong scent of entitlement," I said. "Like royalty."

"Nice of her to visit the common folk."

"She's trying to get on the right side of me, thinking I'll agree to let Lacy give her a DNA sample."

"And you will not agree to that because in all probability Lacy is her granddaughter, in which case you're afraid we'd probably never see a minute's peace from her interfering in Lacy's life."

"Precisely," I said.

"What about her son, Johnny Cross? Don't you think she deserves to know what happened?"

"Do you?"

"As a mother, I certainly do," Mary said. "You need to forget that you don't like her and concentrate on what you'd do if she was just a nobody. What can it hurt if she knows most of the truth?"

"Most?"

"You can leave out the possible rape part. It's not something a mother would want to hear about her son."

I took a drink of Amber Bock and stared at the wall.

"There's nobody she can prosecute and no witnesses to the crime who are still alive," Mary said. "It's all hearsay. If you tell her, she might leave us alone."

"I'll think about it," I said.

44

Early Thursday morning, I was in an almost-empty Mountain Center Diner getting ready to order breakfast when Roy Husky walked in. He came to my table carrying a *Wall Street Journal*. I was a bad influence.

"First time in months we've been on the same page," Roy said. "I've haven't seen you in here in ages."

"I was in three times last week," I said. "Before that, I can't remember when. I always tell Doris I was traveling."

Right on cue, Doris appeared to pour coffee for Roy and take our orders.

"I had a special guest in my office yesterday," I said as soon as Doris went toward the kitchen.

I paused for effect. Roy made a rolling motion with his hand for me to spit it out.

"Elizabeth Durbinfield."

"The chairman of the board of Durbinfield Financial?"

"That's the one."

"Rubbing elbows with the little people, is she?" Roy said. "What did she want?"

"To hire me to find out who killed Johnny Cross."

Roy nearly choked on his coffee. "You're kidding."

"Nope."

"What did you say?"

"That I'd think about it."

"What are you going to do?"

"I don't know. Mary thinks I should tell her."

"Well, he was her son," Roy said. "And you do know what happened to him. You need to get shed of this thing."

◆　　◆　　◆　　◆

I spent most of the morning thinking about what Mary and Roy had said and trying to justify *not* telling Elizabeth Durbinfield about the death of her son. Then I went to Moto's Gym for an hour and a half. The workout relieved some of my frustration but got me no closer to making a decision. Then I made one. Well, kind of. If Elizabeth Durbinfield showed up in my office again, I would make the decision at that point.

Maybe she would just forget about it and go back to Long Island. Wishful thinking.

In midafternoon, the phone rang. Gretchen was out for a few minutes. I picked up.

"Mr. Youngblood, it's Biker. We may have a problem."

"What is it?"

"Two guys are hanging around waiting to talk with Lacy."

"Big dudes, blondish, short hair?"

"That's them," Biker said. "You know who they are?"

"I do. What are they doing now?"

"They started asking around about Lacy. Someone must have told them Lacy was at basketball practice, because they went to the gym. So I followed them. They hung around, then went back to their SUV. They're driving a silver Chevy Tahoe, and they're parked near Lacy. I'm guessing they're waiting for her to come out of practice."

"Where are you?"

"I'm sitting on my bike talking to Alfred and acting cool, like I'm just hanging out. I've got a good view of them."

"Okay, stay put. I'm on my way."

I hurried down the back stairs and into my Pathfinder like the building was on fire. I drove at Mach 1 to Mountain Center High School, calling Big Bob as I went.

"I'm on my way," he said. "Don't shoot anyone."

"I won't if you'll tell your troops not to pull me over."

"Put the pedal to the medal, Blood," Big Bob said. "You're covered."

◆   ◆   ◆   ◆

As I pulled into the parking lot, I took it all in. I saw the silver Tahoe. I saw Biker on his Harley talking to Alfred. I saw Lacy coming from the gym with Hannah. And I saw the hulks get out of the Tahoe and wait as Lacy, unsuspecting, came toward them.

My tires squealed as I pulled in behind the Tahoe, effectively blocking its exit. I got out, adrenaline surging. I heard sirens in the background.

"You two need to get your butts back in your SUV now," I said, moving toward them. They were wearing black slacks and white polo shirts with *Elite Security* embroidered in black over a pocket on the left side.

"I don't think so," the blonder hulk said.

He karate-kicked me in my left side with his right foot, causing me to careen into an adjacent pickup truck. My ribs hurt like I'd been stabbed with a hot knife. He followed with a kick with his left leg, but I was ready. Ignoring the fire in my ribs, I stepped inside the kick, grabbed his leg, and hit him hard in the face with a left hook. Then I kicked his right leg at the knee, and he went down. I hit him with another left and drew blood. I was cocking my left arm for one more when the other hulk grabbed me from behind. He had both my arms locked behind my back as he pulled me off his partner and slammed me into the pickup. The right side of my face caught the worst of it, connecting with the front door frame where it met the window. I felt the anger building inside me, ready to erupt like a volcano.

I leaned back, got both knees up with my feet against the driver's door, and pushed with everything I had. We exploded backward. I heard a scream as his hold on me disappeared. I later learned I had pushed him into the rearview mirror of the Tahoe.

As he reached for his back, I spun and hit him in the gut with a left and followed it with a crushing right to the face. His head bounced off the passenger-side door, then hit the running board as he went face down onto the pavement. He didn't move. I wanted to hit him again and again. I wanted to scream, "Get up, I'm not finished with you!" But the anger subsided, and the world around me came back into focus. Biker was towering over the other hulk, advising him to stay where he was or expect more punishment.

"Get cuffs on him," I heard Big Bob growl behind me. "And call an ambulance for this one." He pointed to the man on the ground in front of me.

I turned to face him. "Nice of you to show up. How much did you see?"

"Most of it." He smiled. "You did okay, Blood."

I heard the squeal of tires and saw an unmarked car with a flasher moving quickly toward us. I knew immediately that Mountain Center police detective Mary Youngblood was on the scene. She skidded to a stop, got out, and rushed toward me.

Everyone started talking at once.

"What happened?" Lacy asked, running to me.

"Don, are you okay?" Mary asked. "You're bleeding."

"What's this about?" Big Bob asked.

"Who are those guys?" Biker asked.

"I need to sit down," I said. "My ribs are killing me."

◆   ◆   ◆   ◆

We sat on a nearby bench, Mary on one side and Big Bob on the other. Mary dabbed at a cut above my right eye with a napkin she had retrieved from her car. Lacy and Biker stood a few feet away. I heard and then saw an ambulance pull into the parking lot to collect the fallen man, who still was not moving.

"I have no idea," I heard Biker say.

I was having trouble breathing. "Lacy," I said.

"Yes, Don," she said, coming toward me.

"There's an instant ice pack under the driver's seat on my Pathfinder. Get it please."

"Sure."

She walked away to find it.

"I need to get him to the hospital," Mary said to Big Bob. "I'll fill you in later."

"Go," he said. "I'm going to book those two on assault as soon as they get out of the hospital."

Lacy popped the ice pack spreading the chemicals inside and gave it to me. It was already cold. Then she helped me into Mary's cruiser, shut the door and got in the backseat. Mary laid rubber as we left the school parking lot. Biker followed on his Harley.

◆　　◆　　◆　　◆

Dr. Evan Smith was on call. He saw Mary and Lacy bring me in and immediately told the admitting nurse he would be handling my injuries. This was the same Dr. Smith who attended to me when Matthew Sherman, alias Lucifer, had tried to abduct me from my office building and ended up bouncing my head off the marble floor in the hall—the same Dr. Smith who painstakingly treated Mary when she took a bullet from Oscar Morales in her Kevlar vest during a meth-lab raid.

He looked longingly at Mary. Or that's what I thought, at least.

"Hello," he said.

"Hi," Mary said, a little too friendly for my taste.

Get a grip, I scolded myself. *You are not a jealous person.*

"What happened?"

"He doesn't play well with others," Mary said. "Short version, he took a karate kick to the ribs."

"Wouldn't have been two against one, would it?" Dr. Smith asked.

"The other two are already here?" Mary asked.

"In cuffs, and a lot worse for wear than Don here."

Mary helped me into an examining room, and Dr. Smith followed. Biker and Lacy were told to take seats in the waiting room. I put down the ice pack and removed my shirt. Dr. Smith gently touched the place I was kicked. I moaned.

"Let's get you to x-ray," he said.

◆　　◆　　◆　　◆

We were back in the admitting room. The x-ray process had proven tedious and uncomfortable. Mary had sent Lacy to the hospital pharmacy to fill prescriptions for ibuprofen and oxycodone/acetaminophen.

"The x-rays show hairline fractures to the seventh and tenth ribs," Dr. Smith said. "Not much you can do except take it easy and take the pain meds."

"I know the drill," I said. "I had a rib injury a few years ago."

"Yes, I saw that on the x-rays." He looked at Mary. "Take him home and put him in bed."

"I'll do that," Mary said.

And that's exactly what she did—unfortunately, without benefits.

45

I awoke Friday morning from a drug-induced sleep full of dreams I couldn't quite remember. I tried to sit up. I couldn't. The muscles around my rib cage screamed opposition and refused to function. I rolled out of bed to my knees and finally stood. I heard voices in the kitchen—Mary, Lacy, and Biker. Like a hundred-year-old man without a cane, I carefully shuffled down the hall and down the stairs. I was so quiet they didn't hear me coming. I spied myself in the hall mirror. I had a black eye on the right side of my face, and my upper lip was puffy on the same side.

When I stepped off the last stair onto the landing, Mary saw me.

"You shouldn't be up."

"Good morning to you, too."

"Why didn't you stay in bed?"

I forced a smile. It hurt. "Remember the last time I had my ribs tuned up? I want to get ahead of this. Besides, it's not as bad as last time." *Just barely*, I thought.

I struggled onto a barstool and found a relatively comfortable position.

"Coffee," I said.

Mary complied. "Lacy is staying home in case you need anything."

It would have been pointless to argue, so I didn't. "Thanks," I said, looking at Lacy.

"You were great yesterday," Lacy said, placing her hand on my arm.

"Doesn't feel that way," I said, managing a weak smile.

"You were awesome," Biker said. "It was over so fast. I've never seen anything like it."

I could imagine the buzz when Biker arrived at Mountain Center High School.

"Thanks for the heads-up and for having my back," I said.

"I didn't have the chance to do much," Biker said.

"Doesn't matter. It's the thought that counts."

"I've got to go to work," Mary said. "Biker, you get to school."

"Yes, ma'am," Biker said.

◆　　◆　　◆　　◆

As soon as Mary left, I sent Lacy to the Mountain Center Diner for bacon, egg, and cheese biscuits. The bumps and bruises hadn't curbed my appetite; I was starved. The diner's biscuits were legendary. Oversized baking-soda biscuits from a recipe passed down in Doris's family, they were the best I had ever eaten. Every now and then, I would indulge myself in the diner's biscuits and gravy and feel like a stuffed turkey the rest of the day.

"Everyone wanted to know how you're doing," Lacy said when she returned with the biscuits. "And they wanted to know what the fight was about."

I took a bite from a biscuit. "They were Florida fans," I said.

"I'll bet."

"Remember what Mary and I always tell you about need-to-know?"

Lacy nodded. "The fewer people who know about your business, the better."

"Smart girl," I said, taking a drink of coffee.

"Tell me sometime?"

"Sure," I said.

Thankfully, she didn't pursue the matter any further.

●　　●　　●　　●

I spent most of the rest of the day propped up in bed working on my laptop. The Dow was over thirteen thousand and looking strong. I bought, I sold, and I researched. Bargains were hard to find. I had scooped them up months ago.

Late that day, my cell phone rang. No caller ID.

"Youngblood," I said.

"David Steele. I called the office, but Gretchen said you were working from home."

"That's a nice way of saying I look too scary to come to the office."

"What happened?"

I told him.

"It's not connected to CJK," I said.

"Speaking of which, Buckley isn't having much luck identifying a viable suspect. Everyone on his list keeps turning up alive. I need him on something else for a day of two."

Which probably means all week, I thought.

"I'll call him next week," I said. "I should start to look better in a few days."

46

At midmorning on Saturday, I sat in a padded lounge chair on the lower deck at the lake house enjoying a mild breeze and moderate temperatures. I had managed to find a decently comfortable position, but my rib cage ached constantly, my face hurt, and my hand was sore. The second day after any injury was always the worst. The umbrella over the table kept me in the shade. I had spent a restless night. My eyelids were heavy. The breeze lulled me into a doze. If I could have stayed that way the balance of the day, I would have been happy. But happiness was not in the cards.

The sound of tires on my gravel drive snapped me out of it. I heard a car door slam. A minute later, the big man came around the side yard and climbed the stairs to the lower deck. He walked across the deck, pulled a chair out from the table, and sat with his back to the sun in the shade of his Cowboy hat. Big Bob Wilson rarely showed up at the lake house unless he was invited to dinner or a cookout or something else involving food.

"Nice shiner."

"Matches the bruises on my ribs."

He didn't smile. "You look tired."

"I am tired."

"Both brothers have been released from the hospital," he said. "They're in my jail."

"They're brothers?"

"Clint and Brodie Stern. They're ex-marines with honorable discharges. The one who came after you first is on crutches with a partially torn ACL and a fractured cheekbone. The other one has a concussion, a badly bruised back, and a fractured eye socket."

"I hope they hurt as much as I do," I said.

"What started the fight?"

"Probably my mouth. I told them to get their butts back in their SUV, and the blonder of the two took exception."

"That would do it," Big Bob said. "Why did you get in their faces?"

"It's personal."

"Well, if they were at the high school, this has something to do with Lacy," he said.

"Did you ask Mary about it?"

"I did."

"What did she say?"

"That you all would handle it."

"There's your answer," I said.

Big Bob exhaled in frustration and was quiet. But as he looked out on the lake, he seemed to relax a bit.

"Wish I could sit here all day and stare at the lake and enjoy this beautiful weather," he said. "But I've got to get back to it."

"Thanks for dropping by."

"I was in the neighborhood."

The lake house was nowhere near his jurisdiction. I knew he was worried about me and wanted to have a look for himself.

"Anything I can do for you?" he said.

"I'm good, but thanks for asking."

"You want to press charges on those two?"

"No, but I'd like you to hold them for a couple of days, if you can. Did they make a phone call?"

"No."

"That's interesting."

"It is," he said. "In fact, they haven't uttered one single word."

◆   ◆   ◆   ◆

I spent the next few hours in a semi-doze until Mary and Lacy came out with lunch. Turkey and Swiss on rye, chips, and a beer certainly improved my attitude. We talked about nothing in particular, and then they were off to town to run errands, confident I could make it on my own for a couple of hours. I listened to a Tennessee football game on the radio. Somehow, the Volunteers managed to win. The meds dulled my excitement.

After the game, I shuffled into the den to watch more football in high-def on my wide-screen TV. The women brought back fried chicken, Gorgonzola potato salad, and barbecued baked beans. We had a picnic on the coffee table in front of the TV watching football. How much better could it get?

I had a beer and meds for dessert and fell asleep. I woke up in the middle of the night in my own bed with no memory of how I got there. Mary slept peacefully beside me. My side didn't hurt much. I rolled over and went back to sleep.

47

Monday morning, I went to the office. I hurt less, but I still hurt.

Gretchen came in, took one look at me, and said, "Oh, my God, you look terrible."

"Don't spare my feelings," I said. "Tell me exactly what you think."

"That's some shiner."

"So I've been told."

"I could put some makeup on that for you. I'm real experienced with black eyes."

"Stay away from me," I said. "Back to your desk."

She laughed and went away. I had gone through pain and suffering for my badge of honor, and I certainly wasn't going to cover it with makeup.

A few minutes later, Gretchen was back in my office with the door shut.

"Elizabeth Durbinfield is here," she said. "Do you want me to get rid of her?"

"No, indeed. Let's see what she has to say for her boys."

When Gretchen showed Elizabeth in, her response to my face was immediate surprise. If she was acting, she was damn good at it.

"My goodness, what happened to you?"

"Your Elite Security boys decided to substitute me for a punching bag. Fortunately, it didn't work out too well for them. After they went to the hospital, they went to jail."

"Please tell me what happened," she said, all business.

As I told her all of it, her face reddened.

"I am extremely sorry this happened. They certainly were not following my instructions, and they will be terminated immediately. It sounds like you got the better of the altercation. I'm happy for that."

"As you can see," I said, "not without a price."

"Yes," she said. "You don't look so good. How do you feel?"

"About like I look."

She stood. With much effort, I did the same. *Manners are us.*

"We can discuss your employ at a later date," she said. "For now, get well. I'll be in touch."

She left without another comment, and I liked her a little better for it.

◆   ◆   ◆   ◆

Gretchen came into my office around lunchtime.

"You're aware the whole town is talking about your fight and what a tough guy you are," she said.

"I don't feel so tough."

"Nevertheless, Doris called and is sending you lunch on the house. It will be here around twelve-thirty."

"Fine," I said. "You have to stay and help me eat it. She'll send enough for two."

"I can do that," Gretchen said.

And that's what we did, sharing country fried steak with gravy, mashed potatoes, and green beans.

"Wish I was there for the fight," she said as we ate.

"You like fights?"

"Not especially. But it would have been nice to see the boss in action."

"Not a lot of action," I said. "It was over pretty quick."

"Still," she said, letting the word hang in the air.

We ate in silence.

"How did you get so experienced in covering up black eyes?"

She looked up at me. I waited.

"I've had a few."

"Husband?"

"I've never been married."

"Boyfriend?"

"For lack of a better word," Gretchen said. "More like boy enemy."

"Where is he now?"

"I have no idea. Dead, I hope."

"Ouch," I said.

"Hell hath no fury like a woman beaten. At least this woman."

"Good for you," I said.

◆   ◆   ◆   ◆

I thought about my conversation with Elizabeth Durbinfield and while doing so took an unexpected siesta. Big lunches will do that. I snapped awake a half-hour later, picked up the phone, and called Big Bob.

"How are you feeling?" he asked.

"Marginally better. I want to come over and have a chat with your prisoners."

"Come ahead," he said, not bothering to ask why.

"Have they made a phone call yet?"

"Not yet."

"See you in a few," I said.

❖   ❖   ❖   ❖

The act of leaving the office, going down the back stairs to the parking lot, and getting into my Pathfinder was an ordeal. In fact, the act of breathing was an ordeal. I was moving better but still very sore.

It took less than ten minutes to get to the Mountain Center Police Station. I started to park in a handicapped spot, figuring that I qualified, but then thought better of it. Big Bob would give me a ticket just for the hell of it. What were friends for?

The jail was downstairs. Thankfully, the building had an elevator. Sean Wilson took me down. The brothers were in a cell by themselves. Sean left me in front of it.

"I assume you can find your way back," he said.

"If you'll leave me a trail of breadcrumbs."

"I'm all out of bread," he said. "But it's nice to see you didn't lose that infamous sense of humor."

I stared at the brothers, and they stared back. The blonder of the two was sitting on his bunk and leaning against the back wall. The other one was sitting on the rubberized floor and also leaning against the back wall. We stared at each other a few minutes. I was in no hurry. I could wait.

Finally, the one on the bunk spoke: "Nice eye."

"Yours, too," I said. They both had black eyes.

"Shut up, Clint," the one on the floor said.

"Brodie," I said, looking at him. "The younger brother, I assume."

"Naturally," Brodie said.

"Screw you, Brodie," Clint said.

"Glad I never had a brother," I said.

"You didn't miss much," Brodie said.

"Thanks, Brodie."

"Shut up, Clint."

Clint pulled his bad leg up on his cot, again leaned against the wall, and sulked. Brodie got up slowly and came to the bars of the cell. He wasn't moving so well. He wrapped his hands around the bars and leaned toward me.

"He's not so bad," Brodie said. "Just a little impulsive."

"How's the back?"

"Hurts like hell, but no permanent damage. How about your ribs?"

"The same as your back."

"I couldn't believe you took that kick and came back firing on all cylinders. Showed some toughness."

"I had damage to my ribs a few years ago," I said. "Clint's kick made me mad as hell. I was running on anger and adrenaline."

"Pretty good fuel, if you can control it."

"I got lucky."

"Maybe," Brodie said. "Why'd you come?"

"Got a question."

"Ask it."

"Did Elizabeth Durbinfield know what you two planned?"

He paused. "No. We knew she wanted a DNA sample from your daughter, so we thought we could score some brownie points if we got one. Maybe get a bonus."

"What were you going to do, hold Lacy down and force her mouth open?"

"Nothing like that. We were going to tell her we were from an agency that specialized in finding biological parents of adopted kids. That the service was free and she had nothing to lose by giving us a swab."

I laughed. "And you thought the adopted daughter of a police officer and a private investigator would fall for that story from a couple of thugs wearing Elite Security shirts?"

Brodie shrugged. "In hindsight, it wasn't such a good plan."

"I was told you didn't exercise your right to make a phone call."

He shrugged again. "We're not in much shape for traveling, so I decided to wait and see how this plays out. I can always make a phone call."

"Here's how it's playing out," I said. "Elizabeth Durbinfield says you're fired, I'm not pressing charges for assault, and I'm telling the chief of police to cut you loose."

"Guess we'll lose our jobs," Brodie said.

I really didn't want to jam up two ex-marines who had honorably served their country, even if they did tune me up a bit.

"Not necessarily," I said. "When you get back to New York, tell your boss to call me, and I'll see if I can square it."

"Why would you do that?"

"In the big picture, we're all on the same side."

"Us against the world," Brodie said.

"Something like that."

He nodded, took a deep breath, and let it out. "Clint should have shown some restraint. Then you wouldn't have gone off like that."

"Yeah, blame it all on me," Clint said from his cot.

"Shut up, Clint," Brodie said.

48

In a perfect world, I would have had a week or two to heal before continuing my pursuit of CJK. I needed to get rid of the nagging soreness in my ribs. I needed for the black eye to fade and my upper lip to return to normal, not to look like I was made up for Halloween. But the world was far from perfect, and time did not stand still for Donald Youngblood.

Early the next morning, Nurse Nancy called.

"He's back," she said. "I don't know how long he'll be here, so you better hurry."

I had packed an overnight bag in case the call came. I left Gretchen a note and called Mary on my way out of town.

"Are you okay to drive that kind of distance?" Mary asked, concern in her voice.

"I'll soon find out. Anyway, I don't have a choice. I need to talk with Bret Sherman while he's lucid."

It was 285 miles from my office to the Maple Oaks Retirement Community. I made it in four hours with one stop for a bathroom break, a bacon, egg, and cheese biscuit, and a cup of coffee.

I arrived after one o'clock, but Bret Sherman was still in the dining hall. He was expecting me. He stood and extended his hand when I came into the room. We shook. He looked rested and alert.

"Don, it's so good to see you. What happened to your face?"

"It's good to see you, too, Mr. Sherman. I got hit with a racquet playing racquetball. It looks worse than it is."

"Well, that's good. And please call me Bret."

"Okay, Bret. It's nice to see you looking so well."

"Yes, it is," he said. "Nancy said I was gone for a while. It's funny, it's like waking from a dream you cannot remember. But for now, my memory is fine. And I do remember that the first time I met you, you brought me a picture of Sammy."

"That's right."

"And then I have a vague recollection that you visited me again later."

"Right again," I said.

Bret Sherman seemed as clear headed as I could hope for, so I got to the point of my visit.

"I don't think I told you before, but I'm a reporter for the National News Network." I was going to say I was a private investigator but changed my mind at the last second. I didn't want to do too much explaining, and the truth would hurt Bret Sherman more than my little white lie would.

"No, I don't think you told me that."

"Anyway, I'm doing a story, and I want to interview Matthew."

"Matthew," he said. "I haven't seen Matthew in years. I have no idea where he is. What's the story about?"

I started to say Cracker Jack and again changed my mind. I was really winging it.

"It's about older siblings who lost younger siblings before the age of ten, and the effects of the loss."

Bret Sherman was quiet. "I don't know if Matthew would talk about it even if you could find him," he finally said. "But I would certainly like the chance to see Matthew again."

"Did you sell your home in Lexington?"

"Yes, when I came here," he said. "I hadn't heard from Matthew in a long time and didn't even know if he was alive. I had a condo in Florida, and I sold that, too. I have all the money I'll ever need."

"Do you own any other property?"

"No."

Well, there goes my bright idea, I thought.

"There's a cabin in the eastern mountains that's in Matthew's name," he said. "I almost forgot about that. It was the only place he seemed to be happy, so when he turned eighteen, I gave it to him as a present. He was absolutely thrilled."

He paused as if he had gone somewhere else. For a brief moment, I thought I had lost him. Then he was back. He looked directly at me.

"I wonder if he's still there."

"Why don't we go find out?" I said.

"Indeed, why don't we?" he said excitedly. "I'm allowed to go out, although I never do. You'd never find the cabin without me."

"How far is it?"

"Oh, I don't know. I've never driven from here. I'd say about two hundred miles."

It was too late to make the trip, have some snooping-around time, and get Bret Sherman back at a reasonable hour. I had to gamble that he would have another lucid day tomorrow.

"I'll be back in a minute," I said, standing.

"I'm not going anywhere," Bret Sherman said.

I went looking for Nancy. I found her in the lobby.

"Is it okay if I take Mr. Sherman out tomorrow?" I asked.

"For how long?"

"Pretty much all day."

"His doctor would never approve," she said. "Mr. Sherman has conditions that need to be monitored and meds that have to be taken at specific times."

"What if you go with us?"

"I'm working the day shift tomorrow," she said.

"I'll pay you five hundred dollars and buy you breakfast and dinner."

She lit up. "Five hundred dollars?"

"Cash."

I carried an emergency fund of ten hundred-dollar bills in the center console of my Pathfinder.

"You got a deal," Nurse Nancy said. "I'll find someone to switch with me."

"I'll go tell Mr. Sherman," I said, turning back toward the dining hall.

"By the way," she said, "what happened to lunch? You said breakfast and dinner."

"We'll pig out at breakfast."

She laughed. "I can do that."

49

I spent the night at a nearby Residence Inn. The next morning, I picked up Nurse Nancy and Bret Sherman at seven. The sun was just coming up. Bret seemed as clear headed as the day before. They both were excited to be getting out. Mother Nature cooperated. The day had the promise of brilliance—cloudless, low humidity, temperatures near seventy degrees.

We drove across Kentucky, headed east on Interstate 64. We stopped at a Cracker Barrel and ate like lumberjacks.

After breakfast, Bret Sherman started a monologue about his older son. I learned everything I ever wanted to know about Matthew Sherman. Some of it I had heard a few years before, the first time I visited Maple Oaks.

"I got married late," Bret started. "We probably should not have had kids, but my Helen wanted to. She was younger than I was. I was almost old enough to be their grandfather. Matthew was seven when Sammy died. He worshipped Sammy like Sammy was the older brother. Sammy's death killed something in Matthew, brought out the dark side of him. He was never the same after that. None of us was. Then my wife died of cancer, and Matthew went to an even darker place, one with no hope and no joy and lots of anger. He didn't like being around people, only my Helen and me, and then Helen was gone. Matthew constantly got in fights at school. I finally had to take him out and have him homeschooled by a private tutor. That seemed to please him, not having to go to school. He was much better. He liked his tutor. She was like a second mother. Matthew was smart. He did well with his studies. When he finished high school, he wanted to get a degree by correspondence in computer science. Then his tutor died in a car accident, and he lost all direction. I didn't know him anymore. He started drinking, and that led to more fights and then some jail time. I tried to visit him in jail, but he wouldn't see me. The last time he got out of jail, he was twenty-one, and I haven't heard from him since. To be honest, until recently, I didn't want to hear from him."

I drove in silence. Bret Sherman then switched to "I remember when" stories about Matthew and Sammy before Sammy died. He was lost in the past, and we didn't try to bring him back.

We got off I-64 and headed south as Bret directed me down a series of narrow paved roads. The last turn was on to a gravel road that climbed through thick woods, finally reaching a clearing that revealed the Sherman "cabin," which proved to be a large log home that looked in good repair. No one seemed to be around. We got out of the Pathfinder and stretched our legs.

"Do you have a key?" *Fine time to be asking that, Youngblood,* I thought.

"I brought all my keys, but we may not need to go through them," he said.

He walked over to a large live oak, moved a rock, brushed at the dirt, and pulled out a small leather pouch. He fished inside with two fingers, produced a key on a ring with a leather fob, and held it up for me to see, smiling like a kid who had just discovered buried treasure. He walked back and handed the key to me.

"Hard to believe it was still there," he said.

"You want to go in?" I asked.

"Now that I'm here, I don't think I do. Too many memories." Bret had tears in his eyes. He was starting to get that distant look.

"Why don't we walk around a bit?" Nurse Nancy said.

"Yes," Bret said, "I'd like that. There's quite a view about a hundred yards in that direction." He pointed to a path leading up and away from the cabin.

I left them and climbed a flight of stairs to the front porch. I put the key in the deadbolt lock, turned it, heard a click, pressed down on the thumb handle, and felt the latch release. I pushed the door open and stepped inside. The cabin had the damp, stale, musty smell of a place not recently lived in.

I had noticed when we arrived that there were no power or phone lines anywhere. I tried to turn on a lamp, without success. The cabin obviously had a generator somewhere, but I had no need for it. The outside light was more than enough for me to see as well as I needed.

I started snooping. The place was on three levels. I went upstairs, where I found three bedrooms and two baths. One bedroom had been converted into an office. The master bedroom had a private bathroom. I started there, searching the medicine cabinet in the hope that I'd find a prescription bottle with a last name on it. No luck. I opened drawers on the vanity—nothing. Everything was clean and neat.

I searched the master bedroom top to bottom, then the guest bedroom and the hall bath. Zip. I went into the office and immediately found what I was looking for. On the desk in plain sight was a five-by-seven picture of Matthew Sherman with another man. His companion was wiry— maybe six feet tall, maybe less. His close-cropped hair was light brown or perhaps gray; it was hard to tell. His eyes were dark, his skin pale. He had a tattoo on one arm, but I couldn't make out what it was. The man was probably ten years older than Matthew, though it was difficult to guess his age; some people age well, and others don't. I removed the picture from the frame and turned it over. It was dated five years ago and inscribed, *"Matthew and James."* They were smiling. I slipped the photo into my right front pants pocket.

The office had a desktop computer and a shredder. I took the top off the shredder. It was empty. Some paper strips were showing in the blades—not enough to do any good.

I came to an obvious conclusion. Two men had lived here, maybe for years. But the dust buildup on the furniture told me no one had resided here for at least a couple of months, maybe more.

I finished upstairs, went down to the main level, and continued downstairs to the game room, complete with dartboard and pool table. While I scanned the room, a chill went through me, as if someone had opened a meat locker door. Lying on a coffee table in front of a large couch was a book, *Cracker Jack Collectibles*. At that moment, I was sure I had found the lair of CJK.

◆   ◆   ◆   ◆

When I returned to the Pathfinder, Nurse Nancy and Bret Sherman were already inside. I had left the driver's-side window down.

I leaned in. "Ready to go?"

"Has anyone been living here?" Bret Sherman asked.

"It looks as if someone was living here, but not in the last couple of months," I said.

"Does it look as if they might be back?" he asked.

"Probably. It doesn't appear that things have been packed up for moving out."

Bret pulled a sealed envelope from his shirt pocket. A name was written on the outside: *Matthew*. He handed the envelope to me.

"Would you put this on the kitchen table, please? That's where I used to leave notes at home for Matthew when he was young and I left for work before the tutor came."

I turned, went back up the stairs, unlocked the door, and reentered the cabin. I placed the note that would never be read by Matthew Sherman on the table in the dining area. I felt lousy knowing Bret's expectations for the note would never materialize.

I locked up, returned the key to the pouch, and placed it back in the hidey-hole under the rock.

The return trip seemed to take twice as long, and much of it was spent in silence. My ribs let me know I was having a long day. A peek in my visor mirror revealed that my black eye was fading from black to a light shade of army green. Not a pretty sight.

It was near dinnertime when we arrived at Maple Oaks. Both Nancy and Bret decided they wanted to eat there. I said goodbye to Bret, thinking I'd never see him again. But I'd been wrong about that before.

Nurse Nancy walked me to the front door. I handed her an envelope containing five hundred-dollar bills.

"Somehow, I don't feel right taking this," she said.

"You deserve it. And I can afford it. Do something special."

"Thank you." She smiled. "I will."

•   •   •   •

On my way back to Mountain Center, I called David Steele.

"I found where CJK has been living."

There was a pause, as if he couldn't quite process what I said.

"How on earth did you do that?"

"Fortune teller."

"See if you can hire her," David Steele said. "We could use some help."

I told him about my visit to Maple Oaks, my talk with Bret Sherman, and our trip to the mountains of eastern Kentucky. I told him about searching the cabin and finding the book.

"You're making the bureau look bad," he said.

"It can be our little secret," I said. "Your office can take the credit. You need to get a remote camera up there in case CJK comes back. I think it's a long shot, but it's worth a try. It doesn't look like anyone has been there for a few months. And you need to dust the place for fingerprints. Maybe we'll get lucky. There's a shredder, but not much left in it. And a desktop computer. You might get lucky with that."

"How did you know about our remote cameras?" David Steele asked. "They're classified."

"Lucky guess."

"Yeah, I'll bet," he said. "What's the address?"

I laughed. "There is no address. Or electricity or phone service. This place is in the boonies. I made some notes on how to get there. I'll put them together and email you the directions. One more thing. I have a picture of a man with Matthew Sherman. His first name is James. He has to be our guy, and I'd bet a thousand bucks he left it on purpose."

"Why?"

"He wants me to find him. He just doesn't want to make it too easy."

David Steele paused. I heard a deep sigh.

"You sure you don't want to become a full-time agent? You can have my job."

"That would take all the fun out of it. Listen, I'll scan the picture, and maybe you can get a hit with a facial recognition program."

"Don't bother," David Steele said. "I'll send Buckley by first thing in the morning. Give the picture to him. I don't trust scans, and there could be a fingerprint on the picture. You can also give him the directions. I'll send him and a couple of techs up there right after he sees you. Good work, Youngblood. I'm starting to wonder who's working for whom."

◆   ◆   ◆   ◆

It was eight-thirty by the time I got back to Mountain Center. I went straight to the office, scanned the picture, and emailed it to David Steele.

Thought you might want to see what CJK looks like.
I'll give the original to Buckley tomorrow.
Tell him to meet me at the office at eight o'clock.

I didn't look at messages or sports news or the stock market but instead drove to the Mountain Center Country Club and had a late dinner with Mary.

We ate and drank unhurriedly and talked about local news and gossip. As a cop, Mary heard lots of rumors and was privileged to some insider information. As a private investigator, I led a sheltered life in my second-floor office. On certain things she shared, I had to promise secrecy.

"Lacy is spending the night with Hannah," Mary said on our way out of the club.

"Is that a euphemism for saying I'm going to get lucky tonight?"

"We're both going to get lucky tonight," Mary said.

50

When I got to the office at 7:45 the following morning, Buckley was waiting in the hall.

"Chompin' at the bit, I see."

"My first major case," he said. "Pretty damn exciting, and I feel we're closing in."

I unlocked the door, and Buckley followed me in. He was there just long enough to get the picture of Matthew and James and the directions to the Sherman cabin.

"Older than I thought," he said, looking at the picture. "Gotta run. I have two techs waiting in the car."

"Good luck. A fingerprint would be really sweet," I said. "But be careful going in. He could be back, and I'm sure he wouldn't mind shooting a rookie FBI agent."

"I'll keep that in mind," Buckley said.

◆　　◆　　◆　　◆

Later than morning, I returned a phone call from Elite Security in New York City. Before I did, I went online to find out as much as I could about the company. Elite Security offered services from bodyguards to house watching to wedding security. The company installed security systems and provided 24/7 security guards for various businesses. The owner, Jason Grace, was a decorated marine. I would bet many of his employees were ex-military.

When I decided I had enough information, I made the call. I was surprised by who answered.

"Jason," the voice said. *Answering "Grace" was probably out of the question.*

"Donald Youngblood," I said, "returning your call."

"Thanks for calling back, Mr. Youngblood. How are your injuries?"

Straight to the point and all business; I liked that.

"Healing nicely," I said. "Thanks for asking."

"I'm calling to apologize for the actions of my men. In the end, I'm responsible."

"Elizabeth Durbinfield read you the riot act, I assume."

"She did," Jason Grace said.

"I hope you'll let it slide. I was partly to blame."

"She was pretty emphatic that I fire the both of them."

"Tell her I made a special request for you not to do that, and that if she agrees, I'll take that into account when I make my decision on the matter we discussed," I said.

"She'll agree to that?"

"Most likely. I really don't think she cares one way or the other if you fire them. She's trying to get on my good side."

"I'll relay your request," he said.

"Anything else?"

"No, except you must be pretty damn good to inflict that kind of damage on Brodie and Clint."

"Beginner's luck," I said. "First time I fought two marines."

He laughed. "Luck counts."

"It does indeed," I said.

◆　　◆　　◆　　◆

That afternoon, Elizabeth Durbinfield called. I had expected her to wait a few days after she talked to Jason Grace. But Elizabeth apparently was a woman in a hurry. Gretchen buzzed me on the intercom to let me know Elizabeth was on line one. I let her wait a minute. I needed to make a decision.

"Mrs. Durbinfield," I said pleasantly. "I take it you've talked to Jason Grace."

"Yes, I have talked with Jason," she said. "And I have agreed to stay out of his decision whether or not to keep Brodie and Clint. It's kind of you not to hold a grudge."

"I extracted my revenge at the time," I said. "No need to do a victory dance."

"Very well put, Mr. Youngblood. I called to see if you've made a decision about my retaining your services."

"Before that happens, I need to share some information with you face to face. I can come to Long Island if you wish."

"Information about John," she said flatly.

"Yes."

"I see. When can you come?"

"Probably next week or the week after. I'm still working on that case with the FBI, and I think it's coming to a head. I have to resolve it before I talk to you."

"Is your case connected to John?"

"No, it's just very urgent."

"Very well then," she said. "Let me know when you're ready, and I'll send my jet."

I almost laughed. "Not necessary. I have a private jet at my disposal. I'll be in touch."

"I'll wait for your call," Elizabeth Durbinfield said, apparently unimpressed.

51

Friday morning, rain fell, steady and unrelenting. The clouds looked like a dark gray ceiling that could cave in at any minute. I sat at my desk and looked at Doppler radar. A massive front promised rain well into Saturday. I watched the rain form puddles on the street below my office window. My ribs still hurt, but my face was almost back to its old self.

Gretchen was still an hour and a half from arriving, and I thought I could relax and enjoy the rain. I wanted time to think about how to catch CJK and just how much I was going to tell Elizabeth Durbinfield. A rainy day was just the ticket.

But it didn't happen. My phone rang.

"Youngblood."

"You're in the office," Buckley said.

"I am."

"Let me in. I'm right outside."

I let Buckley in and locked the door behind him. He was carrying a Dunkin' Donuts bag. The kid learned fast. Buckley followed me into my office and made himself comfortable. He opened the bag and handed me a medium-sized coffee.

"Cream and sugar," he said.

"Is that in my file?"

Buckley laughed. "The lady across the street told me you come in there often. She knew how you take your coffee."

I took a drink and savored that first swallow for a few seconds.

"You just redeemed yourself for disturbing a rather peaceful day," I said. "I take it you have good news."

Buckley looked at me and smiled. He removed the lid from his cup and took a drink. He was playing the moment.

"I wanted to report on our trip."

"I'm all ears," I said, taking another drink.

"CJK wasn't there, so I didn't get shot at. We went over the place top to bottom, inside and out—not a clue, not a print. The place was wiped clean, especially the guest bedroom. We found some hair in the master bathroom, but I'll bet it belonged to Matthew Sherman. The computer appears to be wiped clean, but we took it just in case. There wasn't enough left in the shredder to make it worth our while. We were ready to leave when I spotted the picture frame you removed the photo from. We had already dusted it for prints, and there were none. Then it hit me."

He leaned forward and looked at me and waited to see if I got it. It took a few seconds.

"You didn't dust *the inside of the glass.*"

He pointed an index finger at me. "We got a nice print off the inside of the glass. It was old, but there was enough to work with. I stayed up half the night running it through various databases."

"Tell me you got a hit," I said, feeling a rush.

"I did. His name is James Walton Hyde. He was in the army for twelve years and then in prison for drug trafficking for five. There's a fourteen-year gap in between. Also a few arrests for assault in New Jersey, but nothing major."

"In prison where?"

"Upstate New York. Indian River Correctional. It's a maximum-security state facility for prisoners with a history of violent behavior."

"Sounds like Matthew Sherman might also have qualified."

"If he was there, it wasn't under the name of Matthew Sherman or Trevor Smith," Buckley said.

"We need to get up there and see if we can find anyone who remembers James Hyde."

"Way ahead of you," Buckley said. "I talked to the warden early this morning. He's been there for twenty-five years. He was assistant warden at the time. We're booked out of Tri-Cities Airport at 11:20. We should be back late tonight."

"What airline?"

"US Airways."

"Through Charlotte?"

"Right."

Not commercial, I whined to myself. I picked up the phone and called Roy's office number.

"Is the jet available?" I asked. "It's important."

Well, it was to me. I hated flying commercial, especially if it wasn't direct. *You're a spoiled little baby, Youngblood,* I thought.

I smiled widely when Roy said the jet was ready to go.

"Tell Jim to file a flight plan to Syracuse. I'll see him in an hour," I said. "I'll explain it to you later."

I hung up and looked at Buckley.

"Cancel that US Airways flight. You're about to be ruined for life."

◆　　◆　　◆　　◆

We were at twenty-three thousand feet. Buckley hadn't uttered a word. He was moving around the cabin, examining every aspect of the jet. He had spent some time on the phone at Gretchen's desk while I called Mary to explain why I'd be home late or possibly not at all.

"Try not to get locked up, Cowboy," Mary had said. "I'd hate to have to come get you."

"Not to worry. I'm with the FBI."

"Yeah, that's comforting," Mary had replied.

Buckley finished his tour and sat.

"Please tell me this is not yours," he said.

"It's not."

"Thank God. For a minute there, I wanted to be a private investigator."

"Not a bad thought."

Buckley ignored me. "What's this little joyride going to cost the FBI?"

"I'm not sure of jet fuel prices right now," I said. "I'd guess around twenty-five hundred."

"Not too bad."

"One-way."

"Oh," Buckley said.

"Don't worry, I'll take care of it with Agent Steele."

Jim Doak's voice came over the intercom: "We should be landing in about an hour and a half. Looks like a smooth ride."

"How do you have access to this jet?" Buckley asked.

"Long story."

"We've got time."

"The Fairchild case," I said. "That was my first major case. Sarah Ann Fairchild went missing with her husband and a lot of money. Joseph Fleet, her father, asked me to find her."

"Did you?"

"Sort of," I said. "When I found her, she was dead. Then I went after her killer."

I proceeded to tell the history of the Fairchild case, which ended in closure for Joseph Fleet. But the ending was not a happy one.

Buckley listened intently. "Might have benefited the greater good if you gave the killer to the FBI."

"Sometimes, you have to screw the greater good and do what's right," I said, a little steel in my voice. "I didn't regret it then, and I don't regret it now."

"Can't say I blame you," Buckley said.

52

One thing I learned at the Indian River Correctional Facility was that I didn't want to spend any significant time there. The place was bleak. It sat on the knob of a hill overlooking nothing. Barren land lay all around it. If a convict managed to get outside the razor wire, he would be a sitting duck for the tower guards. I had no doubt that existence inside those walls was a living hell. Or at least it would be for me. I didn't want to think about it.

We had landed in Syracuse on schedule and picked up a rental from Hertz—a Taurus, no less. The FBI was so predictable. The drive was forty-five minutes through thinly populated, scattered-tree back country on a two-lane road that seemed to be an afterthought in the New York State highway system. Buckley drove.

We showed our creds at the main entrance and were directed to parking, after which we were met and escorted to the warden's office. It wasn't every day the FBI came calling.

We sat in front of the warden's desk. The office was large but sparsely furnished. Behind us was a conference table with eight chairs. The warden peered at us over his reading glasses. He looked like a character from a 1940s prison movie: grim, skeptical, and all business. His hair was white, his face craggy, his eyes tired. I guessed he was close to retirement. Buckley introduced me as a prominent FBI consultant. I felt important. The warden was unimpressed.

"I pulled the file on Hyde," he said, looking directly at Buckley and ignoring me. "I remember him. We called him Dr. Jekyll because he could be an angel one minute and a devil the next." He put the file on his desk and picked up another. "Also, when you asked me if we ever had a Matthew Sherman here, the last name rang a bell."

"Why?" I asked.

"James Hyde's cellmate was *Sammy* Sherman," the warden said, still looking at Buckley.

Buckley gave me a quizzical look.

"The younger brother who died of leukemia," I said to him. "I guess Matthew had a second alias."

The warden handed Buckley the files. Seconds later, the phone rang. The warden picked it up.

"I said I wasn't to be disturbed," he growled. "Oh, yeah, right, I forgot. I'll be right out." He stood, took off his reading glasses, and laid them on his desk. "I'll give you boys some time to look at the files. I have a little something I need to take care of, but it won't take long."

He left, closing his office door behind him. Buckley handed me the file on James Walton Hyde. It was thick. We took the files to the conference table and proceeded to read them.

James had been arrested and convicted of drug trafficking in New York. He had spent other stretches in jail on assault charges in New Jersey, which could have influenced his being sent to a maximum-security prison. In his first two years at Indian River, James had spent the majority of his time in solitary confinement for fighting. Each fight was documented. Each trip to solitary was documented. There was a lot of documentation. Also documented were visitors. James had the same visitor about every three months his final few years at Indian River, a woman by the name of Josie Daniels. She always signed in to see Jimmy Hyde. In the third year of James Hyde's incarceration, the trips to solitary stopped. Either they quit doing the paperwork or James quit fighting, a question worth asking.

Buckley and I switched files.

Sammy Sherman had arrived at Indian River a little over a year after James Hyde. He was convicted of armed robbery and assault. He, too, spent many of his early days in solitary for fighting. Then Sammy was transferred to James Hyde's cell, and the fighting stopped for both men. Sammy had no visitors during his entire five-year stay.

"Did you see what I saw?" Buckley asked.

"They were bad guys until they became cellmates. Then they were good guys."

"Exactly."

The warden returned and sat with us at the conference table. He had been gone nearly half an hour.

"Sorry," he said. "That took longer than I expected."

"Not a problem," Buckley said. "It gave us a chance to look thoroughly at the files. Tell us what you remember about these two."

"Both were angry at the world," he said. "Who knows why? They were both mean, but James was meaner by far. I think James liked solitary so much that he got into fights just to get there. Sammy spent some time in solitary right after he arrived, and somehow they made a connection. I dealt with James on more than one occasion, and we got along fine. He never gave me any trouble. So one day, I got word that he'd requested Sammy as his cellmate. When I asked him about it, he told me if I could make it happen, he would never get into another fight. He gave me his word and told me he never went back on his word. Allen Dunn, the warden at the time, was against the arrangement, but I convinced him that if we put them together and they stayed out of trouble, it would be worth it. He finally agreed. Neither one got into a fight from that time forward."

"What if someone picked a fight with one of them?" I asked.

The warden laughed. "James was the meanest con at Indian River. The other cons avoided him like the plague. He put the word out that he would kill anyone who started a fight with Sammy Sherman. No one knew about our little deal, and I kept it that way."

"Josie Daniels visited James Hyde on a regular basis," I said. "Any idea who she is?"

"Sister, or so she said. She came about once every three months from someplace in North Carolina."

I had noticed in his file that James Hyde's place of birth was listed as Boone, North Carolina. I looked at Buckley.

"We need to talk to the sister."

"We do," Buckley said.

He had been making notes in a spiral notebook the whole time we were there. He wrote something else down.

"Sammy never had any visitors?" Buckley asked.

"None that I know of," the warden said. "If he did, they'd be in the file."

We had run out of questions. Buckley looked at me. I shook my head. Buckley then stood. I did likewise. We shook hands with the warden and thanked him for his time and started for the door. Then one final question popped into my head. I turned back.

"Did James Hyde collect Cracker Jack charms?"

The warden looked stunned, as if I had guessed the answer to a riddle he thought no one could figure out.

"Why, yes, he did. His sister used to send him boxes of Cracker Jack, and James started collecting the charms. How the hell did you know that?"

53

Most Saturday mornings, I was at the lake house sitting on the lower deck, drinking coffee, and listening to the day wake up. This particular Saturday morning, I was in the office with two FBI agents planning our next move in the pursuit of CJK.

I wanted to interview Josie Daniels. According to Buckley's late-night research, Josie lived in Boone, North Carolina, and was a manager at a local supermarket. She was a widow with no children. The full name listed on her employment application was Josephine Hyde Daniels.

"Be one hell of a coincidence if she's not the one," David Steele said.

"It would," I said.

"She's the one," Buckley said.

"I'd like to talk to her alone," I said.

"Too dangerous," David Steele said. "He might be there and shoot you dead."

I ignored him. "If she gets a hint of FBI, she might shut down completely. We need to move fast. I can feel this thing coming to a head."

"I agree with Don," Buckley said.

David Steele gave him a withering stare. "You're supposed to agree with me. You've been hanging around Youngblood too long."

"He's not much good if he agrees with you all the time," I said.

David Steele shook his head, took a deep breath, and let it out. "What have you got in mind?"

"I'm a reporter doing a story on reform for prisoners with violent behavior," I said. "I want to interview relatives. Maybe we could get the warden to call and set up my cover story and tell her it would be a paid interview."

"What if she says no?"

"Then I show up anyway. Since when does the press take no for an answer?"

"You'd need some ID for that," David Steele said.

I smiled.

He shook his head again. "I don't want to know."

"He can wear a wire," Buckley said.

"You need to be carrying something," David Steele said. "Just in case."

"How about the .32 with the ankle holster?"

"Worked once," he said. "Could work again. I'll call the warden." He looked at Buckley. "Set it up. We go tomorrow."

◆   ◆   ◆   ◆

"Your face looks better," Mary said. "How are your ribs?"

"Healing faster than last time," I said.

We sat at the kitchen bar finishing our drinks. Lacy and Biker were in the den. Mary had cooked a crockpot beef roast with potatoes, carrots, and onions. She made brown gravy and homemade biscuits. It was comfort food of the highest order.

"Knocking on doors you don't know what's behind can get you killed," Mary said, none too happy about my upcoming venture to North Carolina.

"I'll wear a vest and carry the .32 in my ankle holster," I said. "I'm ninety-nine percent sure James is nowhere near his sister's house."

The second it came out of my mouth, I knew I shouldn't have said the ninety-nine percent thing. I waited for the obvious response, and got it.

"It's the one percent I'm worried about," Mary said.

"He won't be there," I said firmly.

"Maybe the sister will shoot you," Mary said, her protest losing steam.

"A local supermarket manager."

"Okay, probably not."

"I'll be fine."

"You better be," Mary said. "Lacy and I are going to the lake house, and I want you showing up tomorrow afternoon in one piece."

"Yes, ma'am," I said.

54

Sunday afternoon, a white van with an electrical company logo was parked down the street on the opposite side from Josie Daniels's house when I pulled into her driveway behind a late-model Chevy Malibu. The van's windows were heavily tinted, so as to conceal the three FBI agents inside. David Steele, Buckley Clarke, and a techie from Knoxville were waiting to listen to my conversation with Josie. I was wired for sound.

I got out of the Pathfinder and walked to her front door, feeling the weight of my .32 Ruger snug in its holster above my right ankle. Underneath my shirt, I wore a custom-made white bulletproof vest, a thank-you gift from Jared Gray, assistant director of the CIA.

I pushed the doorbell and heard it ring somewhere inside the house. Seconds later, a pleasant-looking woman of medium height, dark hair, and a few extra pounds opened the door.

"Mr. Youngblood?" she asked through the screen door that separated us.

"Yes," I said. "Alexander Youngblood with the National News Network. Thanks for seeing me."

My forged press credentials were clipped to my sports coat. My jeans had the appropriate fade, and my boots were clean but unshined.

I'm using this persona so much, I actually may have to write something, I thought.

She studied me for a moment. "Josie Hyde Daniels. Pleased to meet you." She unlatched the door and stepped out onto her porch. "Let's sit out here. It's such a nice afternoon, and my house is a mess."

We took chairs on opposite sides of a small table with a glass top. The table and chairs appeared recently cleaned. I flipped open my notebook. *Youngblood, ace reporter.*

"I don't mean to be rude," she said, "but could you give me the money before we begin?"

"Sure," I said, fishing in the back left pocket of my jeans and taking five twenty-dollar bills from my wallet. I folded them and handed them to Josie Daniels.

"What can you tell me about your brother?"

She hesitated. "Well, Jimmy was ten years older than me, and he was out of the house by the time I turned nine, so I don't remember much. He was a really nice, sweet older brother, always looking out for me."

"I know he was in the army. Did he join right out of high school?"

"I suppose so," she said. "I'm not really sure."

I scribbled some notes. "How did he end up in prison?"

"Drugs," she said. "I don't know the details, but Jimmy told me he got involved in selling drugs after he got out of the army. He never did drugs, so I was shocked."

I kept at it, scribbling unrecognizable notes. All through the interview, she continued to refer to her brother as Jimmy. I learned that James and his sister had reconnected when he came to her high-school graduation. After that, he sent her money from time to time and helped her with college. They talked at least once a month on the phone and saw one another about once a year until James was arrested. He lived in New Jersey and later somewhere in Upstate New York before he went to prison. He was always vague about what he did for a living and exactly where he lived. He told his sister he moved around a lot.

She knew he got into trouble in prison, since his visitor privileges were revoked on a regular basis. She'd call the prison to find out if he could have visitors and was always told no. Then that changed, and she was able to visit him on a regular basis.

When Jimmy got out, she said, he lived in Kentucky with his best friend from prison, a man named Sammy Sherman. After that, they didn't talk much.

"When is the last time you talked with Jimmy?"

"I'm not really sure," she said. "Two, maybe three years ago. He called to tell me Sammy had been killed. He was very upset and very angry. He was like a different person. He didn't sound well, like maybe he was sick."

"Do you know where he is?"

"I'm sorry," Josie Daniels said. "I don't."

I finished the interview, said goodbye, and drove to a McDonald's on Blowing Rock Road. I parked in a far corner of the lot and met David Steele and his junior G-men. They were kind enough to let me into their inner sanctum.

"Nice interview," David Steele said.

"Thanks. The warden's cover story must have been convincing. She never asked why I chose her brother as a subject."

"I'd say it had less to do with the cover story than with the hundred dollars," David Steele said.

"You're right about that," Buckley said.

"I'm not sure we learned anything," I said. "I'll have to think about it."

"Curious that she didn't invite you in," David Steele said. "I think we'll keep an eye on the house a few days, just to make sure James isn't there."

"I'm pretty sure he isn't," I said.

I was right. As it turned out, James Hyde was nowhere near Boone, North Carolina.

◆   ◆   ◆   ◆

There was no easy way to get from Boone to my lake house—no interstate, no four-lane. I took a series of curvy, two-lane state highways with speed limits ranging from forty-five to fifty-five miles per hour, and convinced myself I was in no hurry. On the way, I listened to my interview with Josie Daniels. David Steele had given me a copy of a CD they had recorded. When I finished listening a second time, I had a couple of ideas.

◆   ◆   ◆   ◆

Mary and I sat at the table on the lower deck finishing our drinks and discussing my trip. For dinner, I had grilled chicken and basted it with Cardini's Caesar salad dressing, a happy accident I had discovered one night during bachelorhood upon running out of barbecue sauce. Hannah, Alfred (who now was being called Al), Biker, and Lacy had taken the barge out after the meal.

"Alfred is turning into a nice-looking boy," Mary said.

"Al."

"Oh, right. I forgot."

Al had grown taller than Biker. Under the influence of the other three, he had discarded his glasses in favor of contacts and was dressing "cooler." He and Biker worked out at Moto's three times a week, and it showed.

"Think he and Hannah are long-term?"

"Without a doubt." Mary's instincts concerning affairs of the heart were miles ahead of mine, and I always deferred to her opinions in such matters.

"Still think Biker and Lacy are long-term?"

"No question."

"That's good."

Mary arched an eyebrow. "I thought you just tolerated Biker."

"He's growing on me." In truth, I liked Biker. He was tough, smart enough, and respected by his peers. I thought Biker and Lacy made a good pair.

"You're just an old softie."

55

When Buckley told me James Hyde was in the military, I had disregarded it because he had immediately followed that up with the news about Hyde's prison term. But the more I thought about it, the more I wanted to know why an apparent career military man left the service after twelve years. I was in early that Monday morning, and I knew the man I was about to call would also be in early. I dialed his private cell-phone number.

"Culpepper," he answered.

Lieutenant Colonel Bradley Culpepper worked at the Pentagon. I had met him during the Crane case. He had proven to be a valuable source of information regarding things military.

"Lieutenant Colonel," I said, "it's Don Youngblood."

"Youngblood!" he exclaimed as if greeting a long-lost friend. "How the hell are you?"

"I'm fine, sir. And yourself?"

"Likewise," he said. "Same old routine. The most excitement I had in years was when I helped you out on the Walter Crane affair."

"I appreciated that, sir."

"Glad to do it," he said. "What can I do for you today? I hope it's something interesting."

"It is, and it's confidential. That's why I dialed your private number. I'm working with the FBI on a serial killer case. Our suspect's name is James Walton Hyde."

"Hang on," Bradley Culpepper said. There was a pause. "James Walton Hyde. Got it."

I gave him a brief synopsis of the case and the dates Hyde was in the military. I could tell he was making notes.

"I need to find out what branch he was in, what his job was, and the name of his last commanding officer," I said. "I'd like to talk with that officer if possible."

"I'll see what I can do," Bradley Culpepper said. "I assume you're in a hurry."

"That would be an affirmative."

"I'll be in touch," he said.

•   •   •   •

It was still a couple of hours before Gretchen would arrive, so I locked up, went down the back stairs, and turned north up the alley toward the Mountain Center Diner. I slipped in the back door and went to my table. Nothing got by Doris Black in her diner. Within thirty second of my backside's touching the chair, I had a mug of steaming coffee and two preowned newspapers.

"I haven't seen you around lately," Doris said.

"I've been traveling," I said. "I have two cases going, and they're keeping me busy."

"Well, it's good to see you. Want the usual?"

"That would be great."

The usual arrived in five minutes. I ate my feta cheese omelet with home fries and rye toast, my only company a *USA Today* and the *Mountain Center Press*.

"How Far Can the Dow Go?" That was the headline on the financial page of *USA Today*. *Pretty damn far*, I thought. The Dow had roared past thirteen thousand, paused to catch its breath, and then kept going. Fourteen thousand was doable, and maybe even fifteen thousand, but climbing too far too fast always concerned me. At some point, a correction was inevitable.

"Local Team Stays Undefeated," the sports-page headline in the local paper proclaimed. The Mountain Center High football team had won its first seven games, and none was close. The team was on a collision course for a season-ending game against an undefeated team from Greeneville.

I read and ate slowly. None of my inner circle showed up to harass me or pick my brain about my involvement with the FBI. I enjoyed the peace and quiet.

I'd soon learn that peace and quiet were going on a vacation without me.

◆　　◆　　◆　　◆

Back in the office a few minutes after nine, I checked my financial to-do list. With two cases going, I had ignored Wall Street and let Gretchen take up the slack. She had a natural talent for it. I was checking the latest projected dividends for blue-chip stocks when I heard the click of leather heels on the marble floor outside my office, a sound that usually announced the arrival of Big Bob Wilson. The door opened and closed. I heard the sound of coffee being made. A minute later, the big man sat across from me, his Cowboy hat tossed in my other chair.

"Haven't seen much of you lately," he said, taking a sip of coffee.

"I've been on the go."

"So I hear."

"What's new with you?"

"Same shit, different day," Big Bob said.

"Maybe you should retire. Take some of your old man's money and buy a house on the lake near me. We'll drink beer and fish all day."

He laughed. "I could do that for maybe a month. Then I'd want to do this again."

He drank more coffee.

"Quit stalling," I said. "I know you. This isn't a social call."

"What's the FBI doing in town?" Big Bob asked.

"How did you know?"

"One of my guys saw a gray Taurus with government license plates parking on Main Street near here. Two suits got out and headed toward this building. It didn't take a brain surgeon to figure out the rest."

"I'm still working that serial killer case with them," I said. "I think we're closing in."

"Anything else you can share?"

"Not while it's ongoing. I'll tell you all of it when it's finished."

"Fair enough. But if anyone in Mountain Center is in danger, I want to know about it."

"Only me," I said, the words making me feel uncomfortable as I uttered them.

◆　　◆　　◆　　◆

Gretchen arrived promptly at ten and left promptly at four. In between, nothing much happened. She fielded a few phone calls, and I did some financial research. It was a boring day. It got a little less so after Gretchen left. That's when I received my return call from Lieutenant Colonel Bradley Culpepper. He got right to it.

"Hyde was a marine," he said. "He did his basic at Parris Island, scored high on the intelligence test. He attended the U.S. Army Military Police School and went on to be an MP. Expert marksman with rifle and pistol. He was an MP for six years and rose to the rank of master sergeant. Faced a few complaints for excessive force, but no charges. He did tours at Camp Pendleton and Camp Lejeune and in Germany. Then he completed the required course and became a drill instructor at Parris Island. A few notations about being too aggressive, but no apparent disciplinary action. He was honorably discharged after twelve years. His commanding officer at Parris Island was Captain Jaden Reese. He's retired and lives in Jupiter, Florida." He gave me Reese's phone number. "I've already called him. Paved the way, so to speak. He's expecting to hear from you."

"I appreciate that, Lieutenant Colonel."

"Not a problem. Call me when this is over and fill me in. I'd be interested."

"I'll do that," I said.

◆　　◆　　◆　　◆

I brewed a cup of green tea and added an ample amount of local honey. Okay, I admit I'm not a tough, hard-drinking private eye. Most of us aren't. Those guys can be found in books and movies, but not so much in the real world. I didn't need the money, and sometimes the job still felt like a hobby, though not recently. Over the last two months, it had felt deadly serious.

I'd half-finished my tea by the time I made the call.

"I was expecting to hear from you, private detective," Jaden Reese said. He made *private detective* sound like a military rank—undoubtedly a few notches below captain.

"Thank you for agreeing to talk with me, Captain."

"You're welcome. I've been making some notes on Master Sergeant Hyde since I talked with the lieutenant colonel. He emailed me the file, and I went through it."

"Any remembrances or observations will be much appreciated," I said.

"James reported directly to me for six years," Captain Reese said. "During that time, it was like commanding two different people. There was the by-the-book nice guy, who liked to be called Jimmy when he was off duty, and the mean, tough-as-nails drill instructor, James. I had to speak to him more than once about what I considered abusive behavior toward his men."

"How did he respond to that?"

"Like a typical marine. 'Yes, sir,' he'd say. 'I'll try to dial it back, sir.' Like that."

"But did it happen again?"

"Eventually, but with a long time of acceptable behavior in between. Something would set him off, and he just couldn't help himself. Then, in the last year, the incidents became more frequent. I finally had to tell him that if he re-upped, I would transfer him. So he took an honorable discharge and left. I'll tell you one thing, though: he turned out some damn fine marines." I could hear the admiration in his voice.

"Did he ever have a psych evaluation during his time as a drill instructor?"

"Yes, a couple, and he passed them with no problem. That surprised me. Either he really didn't have a problem or he was smart enough to get around the psych eval."

"And you think it was the latter."

"Let me put it this way," Captain Reese said, seemingly irritated. "I was damn sure he had a problem or I wouldn't have sent him on his way after a twelve-year stint."

I let that hang for a few seconds.

"Anything else come to mind?"

He paused. "The only other thing that stands out is this: when James gave you his word on something, you could count on it."

Guess he never gave his word about not mistreating the grunts, I thought.

56

"You usually don't come on Tuesdays," T. Elbert said. "What's up?"

"I need to go over this CJK case with someone who understands the fine points," I said.

"I'm honored you chose me."

We were on T. Elbert's front porch on a cool fall morning having our usual coffee and bagels.

"Don't get giddy about it. You're the logical choice."

"That's true," T. Elbert said. "So tell me all, and don't spare the details."

I didn't time myself, but I probably talked for half an hour. T. Elbert grunted a few times and a few other times said, "That's interesting," but other than that, he kept quiet. When I finished, we sat awhile in silence.

"So what do you think?"

"Let me talk this through," T. Elbert said. "CJK goes into the army out of high school and is making a career of it. Most of the time, he's a model soldier, but he occasionally has anger management issues that eventually force him out."

"Technically, he left voluntarily," I said.

"Right. So there's this fourteen-year gap when he's probably in the drug-trafficking business. Then he gets arrested and shipped off to a maximum-security prison, probably influenced by his anger management issues. Once there, he spends lots of time in solitary for fighting until Matthew Sherman—a.k.a. Lucifer, a.k.a. Trevor Smith, a.k.a. Sammy Sherman—shows up. Then James Hyde becomes Mr. Nice Guy again, and all's well. James and Matthew get out of prison and live in the woods. Think something homosexual was going on there?"

"Maybe, or maybe they were just two bad-asses that liked to hang together," I said. "We'll probably never know for sure."

"So anyway, they're living happily ever after when something sets off Matthew Sherman, and he starts the killing game. What do you think set him off?"

"No idea."

"Then you track him down and kill him. Less than two years later, CJK kills three nurses. Obviously, the number three is significant. Probably related to the Three Devils case. And you're at the center of all this. He blames you for Matthew's death, and I'm guessing he's seeking some kind of payback."

I waited. I knew T. Elbert wasn't finished. He had that faraway look.

"Here's what I'd like to know," T. Elbert said. "First, why does CJK seem to vacillate between Mr. Nice Guy and Mr. motherfucking badass?"

"Such language."

T. Elbert ignored me. "Second, what actually happened in that fourteen-year gap? Third, why did Matt Sherman start playing the deadly Three Devils game with high-school kids? Finally, what did CJK mean when he emailed you that he was going to be away for a while?" He paused, staring into space as if to consider that he might have missed something. Then he looked at me. "Got any answers?"

"Guesses."

"Let's hear 'em."

"Okay. First, I think maybe CJK could be bipolar or have some other mental disorder that makes him seem like two different people. I'm going to talk with Sister Sarah Agnes about that. Second, I have no idea what happened in the fourteen-year gap. Think that's important?"

T. Elbert stared at me.

"Better to know than not to know," I said.

"Most of the time," T. Elbert said. "This being one of those times, I think."

"As for the Three Devils, maybe James left Matthew for some reason, and the Three Devils game was Matthew's response. Maybe something about his little brother's death set him off. I don't know. It could have been anything."

I stopped to eat some bagel with cream cheese and drink some coffee. The coffee, despite being covered by a lid, was lukewarm.

"The last note is interesting," I said. "Maybe he got in another fight and received some jail time, maybe under an alias."

"Not a bad thought," T. Elbert said. "That might be an angle worth pursuing."

"This case is giving me a headache," I said.

◆　　◆　　◆　　◆

"I haven't heard from you since Vegas," Sister Sarah Agnes said. "Did you get out in one piece?"

"Yes, believe it or not."

I had called her as soon as I was settled in my office with a second cup of coffee.

"I take it this is not a social call."

"Not entirely," I said. "But before I forget to ask, did Regina Capelli ever leave?"

"No, she's still here," Sarah Agnes said. "I did all I could for her addiction, and then she surprised me by asking for a job, so I gave her one. She practically runs the place. That girl can really get things done."

"She's got a few connections."

"She does indeed," she said. "You have a problem?"

"I do. I need to put those high-powered degrees of yours to work."

"Tell me about it."

"I'm tracking a serial killer who I think might have multiple personality disorder."

"Mercy," she said. "How on earth do you get involved in such bizarre cases?"

"This one seems to be a spawn of the Walker case. You remember the Three Devils?"

"Indeed, I do."

"You have to treat what I'm about to tell you as if I were a patient."

She chuckled. "So what else is new? I will regard this as if I'm a priest and you're in the confessional."

"Forgive me, Sister, for I have sinned."

"Tell me, my son."

I told her all of it.

"Well, first of all," she said when I finished, "he could also just have extreme anger management issues. Multiple personality disorder is an old term. We now call it dissociative identity disorder. It's still controversial, and hard to diagnose definitively. From what you've told me, your serial killer could be a candidate. But DID, as we call it, occurs more in women than men."

"How much does one personality know about the other or others?"

"It varies," Sarah Agnes said. "Sometimes nothing at all, other times a lot. You have to remember that the data collected is from patients, and sometimes patients lie."

"Could this guy go from one personality to the other on demand?"

"Doubtful. Usually, there's an outside trigger."

We talked a few more minutes about DID. When Sarah Agnes started getting so technical that I grew confused, I stopped her.

"I think I get the picture. My brain is overloaded. Thanks for sharing."

"Anytime."

"I'm sorry, but I have to run," I said. "I'll call soon, and we can talk about more pleasant things."

"Don," she asked sadly, "why did he have to kill three nurses?"

"I have no idea why he chose nurses. But the number three was a personal message. I think he's playing a game with me in honor of his dead friend."

◆   ◆   ◆   ◆

The pieces of the puzzle were floating around in my head like Salvador Dali images, distorted and undefined. I needed to see them more clearly, to fit some of those pieces together. Was the note a clue? I pulled CJK's note from the center drawer of my desk and looked at it: "I'll have to be away for a while, but I'll be back." Be away where? I thought about it. He sure as hell wasn't taking a vacation. And then something Josie Daniels said broadsided me: "He didn't sound well, like he was sick."

"That's it," I said out loud. I picked up my portable office phone and dialed David Steele's direct line.

"Steele," he answered.

"It's Don."

"I see you finally learned how to block caller ID."

"Gretchen, not me. Listen, Dave, I think James Hyde is sick. It fits. His note to me said he was going to be away for a while, and then Josie Daniels mentioned that the last time she talked with him, he sounded sick. Since all his notes came from the D.C. area, I think you should check the hospitals there."

"Not a bad idea," he said. "I'll put Buckley right on it. It might take a day or two."

"Start with Johns Hopkins."

"Why?"

"The only reason I can see why he'd go to the D.C. area is that he wanted the best," I said. "Johns Hopkins meets that qualification."

"Sounds expensive."

"Maybe he has insurance from his army days. Maybe he put away money from his drug days. Maybe this is a wild goose chase."

"I trust your hunches," David Steele said. "We'll be in touch."

◆　　◆　　◆　　◆

The call came after lunch.

"How do you do it?"

"Meaning?"

"Meaning you're making us look bad again," David Steele said.

"You found him," I said.

"Yes! You were right about Johns Hopkins. He's there now being treated. At least there's a James Hyde being treated. It sure as hell better be CJK. We have a team on the way to apprehend him. I'll call you as soon as I hear something."

I hung up and called Mary's cell. In my excitement, I had to tell somebody. After all, it was still partly her case.

"You never call me at work," she said. "Is everything okay?"

"Everything is fine. Can you talk?"

"Sure. I'm just investigating a break-in. The crackheads are long gone. You must have good news."

"Your husband, the ace private eye, may have just cracked the CJK case."

"Tell me."

I did.

"The D.C. hospital thing is a really good insight on your part, Don. But is sounds a little too easy."

"It does, doesn't it?" I said, having second thoughts and hoping I hadn't jinxed anything by jumping the gun and calling Mary.

"When will you know?"

"Soon," I said. "Maybe we can celebrate with a drink or two."

"Or three," Mary said.

◆   ◆   ◆   ◆

Gretchen was two hours gone, and I still hadn't heard from David Steele. I knew the news wasn't good. I was going to be late for cocktail hour. When I could no longer stand the waiting, I called him.

"Talk to me."

"I was about to call."

"You don't sound pleased."

"I'm not," David Steele said. "It was CJK. As best we can figure, he left about thirty minutes before our team got there. They locked down the building and did a thorough search but didn't find him. We were so damn close." I could hear the tiredness and frustration in his voice. "He must have been tipped off. His doctor said he was scheduled to have a chemo treatment later in the day and then to stay overnight. He has cancer, an aggressive type. He was scheduled for six chemo treatments over six weeks. He's completed five. They're hard on him physically, so he's been staying somewhere locally, but neither the doctor nor the staff knows where. We're canvassing area hotels and motels. I'll know more in the morning when I get the written reports. Go have a drink someplace. We can't do any more today."

"Good advice," I said. "I know just the place."

57

I tossed and turned for most of the night, then got up early and went to the office. Neither the dogs nor the females took any notice. I had a half-finished first cup of coffee in front of me when the phone rang.

"Youngblood."

"It's Steele," he said. "He's in the wind. If James Hyde was registered at a nearby hotel or motel, it was under an alias."

"Did you try Matthew Sherman or Sammy Sherman?"

"Damn it, Youngblood, you're worse than my wife."

"How's that?"

"Always coming up with good ideas a day late."

"Sorry," I said. "It just occurred to me."

"Well, it's a good thought," he said. "Another one I should have had. I'm losing my touch. Hang on a minute." Thirty seconds later, he was back. "Buckley is going to call our guys in Baltimore to have them follow up on that."

"What else have you learned?"

"He has insurance. Good coverage. A discount policy he got through the army. What his insurance doesn't pay for, he pays in cash."

"That's why he didn't use an alias at the hospital," I said.

"Get this," David Steele said. "He hates the female nurses, and they hate him. He wants only male nurses, and that isn't always possible. Maybe that's where the dead nurse thing fits in."

"Is he terminal?"

"Yes."

"How long?"

"Dead man walking," David Steele said. "The doc said he'll be dead in three months, maybe sooner."

"He's got nothing to lose."

"Precisely what I was thinking," David Steele said.

◆   ◆   ◆   ◆

CJK was coming to Mountain Center unless I could find him first. I was sure of it. I needed to pull out all the stops. *Better to know than not to know.* I needed to call in a favor.

I dialed his private number.

"Vincente," the voice said.

"It's Don Youngblood."

"Mr. Youngblood," Carlo Vincente said. "Always a pleasure."

Carlo Vincente was a New York mob boss I had met while working my first big case. We had exchanged information that proved mutually beneficial. I wouldn't say we were friends, but we weren't enemies either. Carlo wasn't much involved anymore in the day-to-day but still had his finger on the pulse of his operation. Recently, I had helped his granddaughter out of a jam and recommended therapy for her gambling addiction. Regina Capelli now worked at Silverthorn with Sister Sarah Agnes. Carlo felt he owed me. I was about to collect, and I didn't waste time asking.

"I need a favor."

"I'm glad to hear that," he said. "I owe you more than one. What can I do for you?"

"Write down the name James Walton Hyde."

There was a pause.

"Done," he said.

"James Walton Hyde supposedly worked for the Jersey mob back in the nineties and early two thousands until he went to prison. I need to find out all I can about him."

"Why are you interested?" Carlo Vincente asked.

"I killed someone he was close to. He's coming to settle the score. I'd like to find him before he finds me."

"Can you come to New York if you have to?"

"Yes."

"I'll call you back," he said.

◆   ◆   ◆   ◆

The call came late in the day. Gretchen had left five minutes earlier.

"Cherokee Investigations."

"Can you come tomorrow if I send my jet for you?" Carlo Vincente asked.

"What time?"

"Eight o'clock at Tri-Cities Airport."

"I'll be there," I said.

58

We sat alone at a back table at Le Alpi, one of Carlo Vincente's New York restaurants. His World Wide Imports jet had arrived on time at Tri-Cities and whisked me away to Teterboro, New Jersey, where Frankie, Carlo's jack-of-all-trades, waited with the limo. Frankie now sat out of earshot at another table with his longtime sidekick, Gino. The first time I met Gino, I broke his nose. I wondered if he still held a grudge.

Carlo and I shared a calamari appetizer and engaged in small talk. We were drinking Peroni beer, a premium lager brewed in Rome. Carlo hadn't mentioned James Hyde, but I knew he'd get around to it.

"I guess you've heard Regina is doing well," he said.

"What I heard is that she's practically running the place."

Carlo Vincente's chuckle sounded almost like a growl. "Yes, that would be her."

"Takes after her grandfather."

Carlo smiled but didn't comment.

We finished the calamari. Another round of beer showed up as soon as we set our empty bottles on the white tablecloth.

"You are a patient man, Mr. Youngblood," Carlo Vincente said. "I like that. It shows discipline."

"When someone does you a favor, you're on their time and not yours."

"Well spoken." He leaned forward and lowered his voice. "Now, we are here to meet Anthony Brunello. Close friends call him Lucky. He wins a lot at the track, although I think it has nothing to do with luck. He's the head of the northern New Jersey branch of our organization. We'll have lunch, and then I'll ask him some questions about James Hyde. You keep quiet unless you get a cue from me. Understood?"

"Understood," I said.

A few minutes later, Anthony Brunello arrived with two bodyguards. He sat with us at the back table, and the bodyguards joined Frankie and Gino. Brunello was maybe six-two and wide, like an NFL offensive lineman. He had dark hair combed straight back, but it was thinning. Introductions were made. I was introduced as a good friend of the family.

Carlo ordered veal parmigiana with a side Caesar salad, and Anthony and I followed suit. Lunch was excellent. I was mostly ignored as Carlo and Anthony caught up on news of what was going on in their respective territories. Anthony was loud and extroverted, and I thought at times he was trying too hard to impress Carlo. Every now and then, they looked at me as if to bring me into the conversation. I smiled and ate. After our meal, the table was cleared and a bottle of Disaronno Originale Amaretto and three apéritif glasses were brought to us. Carlo poured.

"Good health," he said.

"Good health," Anthony and I responded.

We drank.

Carlo set his glass down and looked at Anthony. "Remember a guy who used to work for you named James Hyde?"

I thought I saw concern register on Anthony's face, but it was instantly gone. A man didn't do what he did without being able to mask his feelings.

"Yeah, what about him?" Anthony asked, more subdued now.

"What can you tell us about him?" Carlo asked.

"Mind telling me what this is about?"

Carlo looked at me and nodded.

"I'm looking for him," I said. "He killed three nurses, and I'm trying to find him before he kills anyone else."

"Three nurses," Anthony said. "That cocksucker. I should have whacked him before he got sent to prison."

"Too bad you didn't," Carlo said.

Anthony shrugged. "Most of the time, he was a mean son of a bitch, I'll tell you that. He was a real Southern redneck. There was something about him that made people afraid. I liked that, so I brought him in as a collector. He worked for me maybe five, six years and then moved on. I think he started a little drug operation of his own. Not in my territory, of course. Someplace in Upstate New York, I think."

"You said he was mean most of the time," I said. "Was he nice some of the time?"

"Yeah, like a different person. But I think it was an act. It made him look crazy and made people even more uncomfortable being around him. You felt as if he was going to explode any minute." He paused as if trying to remember anything else. "But he was one hell of a collector."

"I'm surprised you let him leave," Carlo said.

Anthony shrugged again. "Well, he wasn't a made man. To tell you the truth, I wasn't that unhappy to see him go. He was kind of like having a cobra for a pet. Your never knew when he'd turn on you and bite."

"This him?" I asked, sliding a picture of James Hyde I had photo-shopped from the one I found in the Sherman cabin.

"He looks older, but yeah, that's him," Brunello said.

"Do you have any idea where he might be?"

"No. If he was anywhere in northern Jersey, I would have heard about it." Anthony settled his gaze on me. "You a cop?"

"Private," I said.

Anthony looked at Carlo. "He's a friend of the family?"

"A very good friend," Carlo said sternly. "He found Joey Avanti and turned him over to me and not the feds. That information does not leave this table."

"Okay, no problem. It's between us." Anthony turned his gaze on me. "You watch yourself. James Hyde is one mean motherfucker."

◆   ◆   ◆   ◆

"Did you learn anything?" Mary asked.

"Not much," I said. "James Hyde is a badass, but I already knew that. On the other hand, lunch was great, and it was enlightening to see Carlo and Anthony Brunello interact."

"Did they know you're working with the FBI?"

"Brunello didn't. If Carlo suspected, he didn't say anything."

We were at the kitchen bar in our Mountain Center condo. Mary and Lacy had already finished dinner by the time I arrived back from New York. Still feeling the effects of lunch, I had opted for a snack of cheese, breadsticks, peanuts, and tarragon chicken salad with almonds. I ate slowly and washed it down with a Michelob Amber Bock.

"You look tired," Mary said.

"I am tired. I need to get this thing resolved."

Mary stood, pulled me off my barstool, and kissed me. "It's a shame you're so tired."

"Probably not that tired."

"After Lacy is asleep, maybe we'll find out."

Unfortunately, by the time Lacy was asleep, so was I.

59

That Friday, the Youngbloods of Mountain View condo 5300 all seemed to awaken at the same time. I slipped on shorts, a T-shirt, and running shoes and took the dogs for a walk. It was a quiet morning until I had an epiphany of sorts. I pulled my cell from my back pocket and brought up Buckley Clarke's personal cell number.

"Hello," he said, none too enthusiastic.

"You awake?"

"I am now."

"Alone?"

"Not exactly," he said. "Hang on."

I had fond memories of those "not exactly" days, but I was glad that phase of my life was over. I heard mumbling.

A few seconds passed.

"Okay," Buckley said. "What's up?"

"Get the Tattoo Killers file, look up the address for the farmhouse where I killed Matthew Sherman, and find out who the owner of record is."

"You think CJK may be there?"

"Or on his way there. Or it could be another wild goose chase. We need to cover every possibility."

"You have a pretty good record with wild goose chases," Buckley said. "And I like this one. I'm on it. I'll call you back."

◆　　◆　　◆　　◆

Once I showered, dressed, and escaped the sound of hair dryers and the smell of soap, shampoo, deodorant and hair spray, I went straight to the Mountain Center Diner. I called Big Bob on the way and asked him to meet me there. He arrived ten minutes after I did. We ordered, and I filled him in on what was going on.

"I need your people to be on the lookout for this guy," I said, handing him a folder containing a couple dozen copies of the James Hyde picture I had photoshopped from the original at the Sherman cabin.

He took out one of the pictures and looked at it. "He doesn't look like a serial killer. Is this the guy killing the nurses?"

"That's him," I said. "We think he has a split personality. What you're seeing there is probably the good guy."

Our food arrived.

"I'll tell you one thing," Big Bob said. "If he gets caught in Mountain Center, he leaves in a pine box."

I smiled. "I like your attitude. Breakfast is on me."

◆　　◆　　◆　　◆

I was expecting Buckley to call me back. He didn't, but his boss did.

"You're on target again, Youngblood," David Steele said. "Guess who owns the farmhouse in question."

It hit me like a bolt of lightning. It couldn't be James Hyde. That would be way too easy.

"Josie Daniels," I said.

"Bull's-eye. I'm putting together a SWAT team now. Want to come?"

"Wouldn't miss it," I said. "We'll need a helicopter."

"How do you figure?"

"You remember the place. You can see incoming ground vehicles from a mile away. There are woods not more than fifty yards in back of the farmhouse. They're big enough to get lost in. If James Hyde is there, he'll have an escape route."

"Sounds reasonable. We have a Eurocopter AS350 at McGhee Tyson Airport. Where can I pick you up in Mountain Center?"

"We have an emergency helicopter landing area beside the North Mountain Center Fire Station. I'll be sure they know you're coming."

"Shouldn't be more than two hours," David Steele said.

"See you there."

◆   ◆   ◆   ◆

I called Big Bob.

"The feds will be landing a helicopter at the North fire station in about two hours. You might want to give them a heads-up."

"What's going on?"

I told him.

"I'll take care of it," he said. "Watch your ass."

I left Gretchen a note, went back to the condo, changed into jeans and a T-shirt, and strapped on my Glock nine.

I called Mary and told her about the farmhouse.

"Don't forget your vest," she said.

"Yes, Mother," I said as I grabbed a black Kevlar vest from the front-hall closet and headed out the door. We were still on the phone when I got in the Pathfinder.

"Think he'll be there?" Mary asked.

"I hope he is. I'd like to end this."

"Be careful," Mary said.

◆   ◆   ◆   ◆

I arrived at the firehouse ahead of the helicopter and went just inside the open doors to say hello to the chief and the few paid firemen on duty. The chief was a local boy a few years older than me.

"Youngblood, how the hell are you?" he said.

"It's been awhile," I said.

"Big Bob said an FBI helicopter is on the way to pick you up. What's this all about?"

"Training exercise," I said, smiling.

"Yeah, I got it," he said. "Need to know only."

We played catch-up until we heard the distant thumping of the helicopter. The sound continued to grow until the copter, black with *FBI* emblazoned on the side door, hovered over the landing field and gently set down on the newly mowed grass. The pilot throttled back until the rotors were lazily turning. The side door opened, and David Steele got out and walked toward me. The chief and the firemen watched with rapt curiosity.

"Got a permit to carry that thing?" he said loudly, looking at my Glock. I knew he was kidding, but he acted deadly serious. He was getting his game face on.

"A couple."

"You ready?"

"You bet," I said.

Behind me, I heard a car pull in. I turned to see a black Crown Vic owned by the town of Mountain Center. The driver parked on the grass beside the firehouse and got out. All eyes were on the six-foot blonde in the black jeans and white sleeveless top. Her hair was in a ponytail. Her badge was on her belt near her Glock. She walked toward us carrying a Kevlar vest. She ignored me and looked directly at David Steele.

"Got room for one more?" Mary asked.

"Sure do," he said. "As long as it's you."

Mary put the vest on and looked at me with a wry smile. "Didn't want to miss the fun." She walked away from us toward the helicopter.

"Mama comes to protect her man," David Steele said in a bad Southern hillbilly accent.

"Shut up," I said, but I couldn't help laughing.

◆   ◆   ◆   ◆

By the time I boarded the helicopter, Mary was wearing a black FBI baseball cap and headphones. She had the attention of every male on board. One of the SWAT team members handed me a cap and headphones and pointed to an empty seat. I sat and buckled in. The SWAT team guy extended his hand. We shook. There were six of us, plus the pilot and David Steele. Dave was up front with the pilot.

"They call me Wolf," the SWAT team guy said through my head-phones. "I'm the team leader. I hear you know the layout. Would you brief us, please?"

"I assume you've seen pictures of the man we're looking for."

"Yes, sir, we have. James Hyde."

"We're headed to a farmhouse that sits in the middle of quite a few acres of land. Woods are in the back maybe fifty yards from the house. If there's a barn, I don't remember it. We'll want to drop in quickly so we have a good view of the back. That would be our target's only escape route."

"Unless he has an underground route," Wolf said.

"Anything's possible. But I don't think so. I've been in the basement. Unless a tunnel was added in the last couple of years, it's not there. Mary and I can cover the woods, if you want."

Little did I know that decision might later save my life.

"That would be good," Wolf said. "You two are here for backup only. Only my team and I will approach the house. I'll be the first out, followed by my team, then you two. Agent Steele will come out last."

"Sounds good," I said.

Mary nodded and looked at me. "I'll follow you."

"I'm taking us to ten thousand feet," the pilot said. "It'll be harder to hear us coming, and we'll have a better view of the area. We'll come in fast from the rear and set down on the closest acceptable ground."

I noticed the team was carrying assault rifles, M4 carbines. If CJK put up a fight, he wouldn't survive.

◆　　◆　　◆　　◆

Twenty minutes later, we spotted the farmhouse. It was a speck in the distance, but we were closing fast.

"Drop to five thousand and do a wide sweep," Wolf said.

The pilot did as ordered. As the chopper turned its 360, Wolf surveyed the area with his field glasses.

"Looks deserted," he said. "No vehicles in sight, and no barn. Let's go in."

We dropped fast. It was like riding a roller coaster to the top of the tracks, then having the bottom fall out. I looked at Mary. She gave me a sly smile. I could tell she was pumped. I was feeling a little excited myself.

"Get ready," Wolf said as we hit the ground with a jolt.

The team unbuckled. Mary and I did the same. Wolf slid the door sideways, and they were out, like a basketball team bursting through the locker-room door and onto the court. They went for the house. Mary and I were right behind them. We headed to the woods, went in about twenty yards, and spread out, keeping each other in sight. We waited, watched, and listened.

"This is the FBI," David Steele said over a megaphone. "Anyone in the house, come out with your hands up, and you will not be harmed."

We waited. No one came out, as far as I could see. I scanned the woods. No movement anywhere.

"Let's go in," Wolf said over the headphones. I heard footsteps and a door opening and more footsteps. Then came sporadic calls of "Clear!" and finally Wolf's voice: "All clear, nobody home. Youngblood, anything in the woods?"

"Nothing," I said. "See any other exits?"

"None."

We took one more look around.

"We're coming in," I said.

◆　　◆　　◆　　◆

It was like preparing for the big game and then having it called off. We had to come down from our adrenaline and testosterone high. The disappointment was noticeable. We searched the house but didn't find anything connected to James Hyde. There was a refrigerator that was unplugged. The hot water heater was also unplugged. But the lights worked. I found that curious.

"It's been awhile since anyone was here," David Steele said.

"At some point, he was here," I said. "I'd bet on it. You need to check with the power company and see how long the power's been on."

Buckley arrived with a tech to take fingerprints. I looked around but didn't see anything interesting or incriminating. I glanced at the basement door and decided going down those stairs once in my lifetime was enough. I turned around and walked outside. Mary followed me. We sat on the front steps and waited for the team to wrap up.

"Having some bad memories?"

"Déjà vu," I said. "I think I did some good work here, but it's still unsettling."

"You did do some good work here," Mary said, putting a comforting hand on my leg. "You saved a young girl's life."

David Steele came out and sat beside me. "Doesn't seem that long ago we were here."

"No, it doesn't," Mary said.

"Don't feel bad, Don," he said. "It was a good thought. We're going to get this guy."

"Damn straight, we are," I said.

"Can you two ride back with Buckley?" David Steele asked. "We're getting low on fuel, and the pilot wants to go straight back to Knoxville."

"Sure," I said.

David Steele stood to leave. "It's going to end soon. I can feel it."

◆　　　◆　　　◆　　　◆

Buckley dropped us at the firehouse to pick up our cars, after which Mary and I went our separate ways. It was after lunch when I went through the outer office door.

Gretchen looked up from her desk. "Jeans and a T-shirt. Nice look. I especially like the Glock on your belt."

"We were going to have a party this morning," I said. "But the guest of honor failed to show up."

"Who is *we*?"

"Mary and I, David Steele, and an FBI SWAT team whose leader is called Wolf. It was a total waste of government resources."

"Too bad. Would you like a cup of coffee?"

"That sounds really good."

"Go get settled in and I'll bring you one," she said.

60

The end game started with a phone call an hour later. My intercom buzzed.

"The man on line one won't give his name but says you'll want to talk to him," Gretchen said. "Don, this guy's voice creeps me out."

I felt a rush, knowing it had to be James Hyde.

"Youngblood," I answered.

"Well, at last I get to talk to the famous Donald Youngblood, the stone-cold-killer private detective."

His speech was slow and measured, his voice like a sandy whisper mixed with honey—Southern redneck with a whole lot of sinister. Gretchen was right, it was creepy.

"You got the stone-cold-killer part confused with yourself," I said.

He started to say something, then began coughing.

"You don't sound so good, James. You better get back to the hospital."

"Pain in the ass, the feds showing up like that. I missed my last treatment. I'll bet that was your idea."

"A real shame," I said. "Who tipped you?"

He ignored the question and coughed again. It was the cough of a dying man.

"I'm coming for you, Youngblood," he said. "But first, I'm going to visit with your ladies."

I fought to control my anger. "We'll be anxious to see you. Please come soon."

"On my way," he said just before disconnecting.

I called Mary.

"Time to get out of Dodge," I said. "He's coming. Get Lacy, go to the lake house, and pack a few things for Florida. Take some MCPD backup. Meet me at the private hangar at Tri-Cities Airport as soon as you can. Be extremely careful. He may already be in town."

Mary didn't ask questions. We had talked about the possibility of leaving town.

"See you there," she said.

I called Roy Husky.

"I'll need the jet in an hour or so."

He already knew why. "It'll be ready. I'll call Jim."

I called Big Bob.

"James Hyde called me and said he's on his way. I'm taking Mary and Lacy out of town for a few days. Mary is on her way to get Lacy. Give her some backup."

"We'll be on the lookout," Big Bob said. "I'll have Sean and John follow her."

"If you catch him, try not to kill him. I'd like to have a little chat."

I called Scott Glass.

When he answered, I got straight to the point: "Is anyone in your Florida condo?"

"No," he said. "What's up?"

I hit the highlights.

"You have a key," Scott said. "It's all yours. Go take care of your family."

I started shutting down as I buzzed Gretchen on the intercom and asked her to come in.

"Close up the office and don't come back until I tell you to," I said.

"Why?"

"The guy on the phone was the guy we've been looking for. I don't want him trying to get to me through you. Pack your bags and take a vacation. Take what money you need from the business account."

"I can take care of myself," she said. "I carry a gun, and I know how to use it. I don't need to close up the office, and I certainly don't need to leave town."

I felt myself getting angry. I didn't have time for this. I gave her the hard stare. "You do what I tell you or you're fired. Take your kid and go."

"Okay, okay," Gretchen said. "Now you're scaring me."

On my way to the airport, I called David Steele.

When he picked up, I hit him with the news that James Hyde had called to chat. "I'm taking Mary and Lacy and lying low for a day or two. If he really is coming but can't find me, he'll call me again. When he does, I'm going to set him up to take him down."

"He might be all talk," David Steele said.

"I don't think so. This is all about getting revenge for Matthew Sherman. He wants a confrontation, and I'm going to give him one."

"Let me know when he gets in touch."

"I will, sooner or later."

"Youngblood," David Steele said sharply.

Whatever he may have said after that was lost when I snapped my antiquated cell phone shut.

◆   ◆   ◆   ◆

Jim Doak's voice came over the intercom. "Welcome, ladies and gentleman. This is your captain speaking. We have now reached our cruising altitude, and it is safe to move about the cabin."

"Does he do that all the time?" Mary asked.

"No," I said. "He's just showing off for you and Lacy."

"You said you'd tell me when we were in the air what's going on," Lacy said. "So what's going on?"

"A nice weekend vacation to Florida," I said. "We're going to stay in Scott's three-bedroom condo—lots of room. We'll have a great time."

Lacy looked at Mary and then to me. "Bullshit," she said. "Tell me."

Well, we did encourage her to speak her mind.

I looked at Mary. "I'm tired of telling this story," I said.

So Mary told Lacy as much as she could.

"Thank you," Lacy said, looking at me when Mary finished. "Was that so hard?"

"Don't get smart," Mary said.

"Sorry." Lacy looked down at her lap, then up again. "Thanks for watching out for us."

I swallowed the lump in my throat.

"Always," I said.

◆   ◆   ◆   ◆

After we landed at Palm Beach International Airport, I rented a Navigator from Hertz. On the way to Scott's condo, we stopped and bought groceries. We were ready to hunker down.

I didn't think there was one chance in a million James Hyde could find us, but I played it safe anyway. The single-tower condo complex was called The Seagull. I had made the purchase for Scott years ago from his growing portfolio before the complex was finished. He had gotten in on the ground floor, so to speak, except that his unit was an ocean-view penthouse on the top floor. Security was tight. A gate with an electronic eye was activated by remote control. Visitors had to stop by the guardhouse or call the unit they were visiting to get buzzed in.

I introduced myself to the guard and was surprised he knew who I was. He looked ex-military.

"Agent Glass called ahead," he said. "I know the situation. He said to get a picture from you."

I gave him one. "I doubt you'll ever see this guy, but if you do, call me. And remember, he's dangerous."

"I'll do that," he said. "I've got a .45 in the guardhouse." He handed me a visitor hang tag for the Navigator. "Agent Glass's spot is in the parking garage, number 201."

We parked, unloaded, and settled in for the night.

◆   ◆   ◆   ◆

We walked on the beach, came back, and prepared a dinner of grouper Francese with saffron rice and baked green beans seasoned with lemon and garlic. The madness that CJK had created seemed like a bad dream.

Later, we sat on the balcony talking under a brilliant full moon and listening to the surf below. Lacy finally tired of the old folks and headed to her room to call Biker.

"You cannot tell him where we are," I said.

"I know," she said, subdued by having to keep that secret.

An hour later, Mary and I went to the master bedroom. I watched her undress and get ready for bed, a sight I would never tire of. She always wore panties and one of her many XXL T-shirts to sleep in. We slipped into the king-sized bed and turned out the light. A nightlight cast a dim glow from the bathroom.

"Do you remember the first time you made love to me?" Mary asked.

"Of course. It was in the bedroom where our daughter is now sleeping."

"Correct."

"As I remember, you seduced me."

"Correct again."

"Is this leading somewhere?" I asked.

"It is if you can be real quiet."

"As a church mouse," I said.

Well, almost.

61

For two days, we mostly hung out by the pool or at the beach on lounge chairs under two umbrellas. We played some tennis, watched a few movies, ate great seafood, and waited. The weather was perfect, the surf aggressive. A tropical storm was brewing far out in the Atlantic. Singer Island was safe, as the storm was tracking toward Bermuda.

The call came Monday, late morning.

"It's not nice to invite someone over and then not be there, Mr. Youngblood. Word is, you're out of town—wife and daughter, too. Your office is locked up tight, and your assistant is in parts unknown. I suspect you're in Florida or Utah—New York, maybe. I thought we had a date."

If snakes could talk, I thought, *they'd sound just like James Hyde.*

"Something came up," I said. "How are you feeling, James?"

"Poorly," he said. "Thanks for askin'."

"You certainly seem to know a lot."

"Money talks," he said.

"Listen, James, I'm sorry, but I'm going to be away for a while. By the time I get back, you might be dead. It's been nice knowing you."

"You need to come home now, Mr. Youngblood. Otherwise, I start killing innocent people, and that would be on you. I have plenty of Cracker Jack charms left, got 'em on Amazon. Be a shame to let 'em go to waste. So we're going to have a showdown while there's still time, or people start dying. Don't lie to me, now. I know a showdown is what you want."

I had no intention of letting James Hyde kill anyone else. And he was right, I did want a showdown.

"Where?"

"The cabin," he said. "I know you know where it is."

"No way." The cabin I'd visited with Bret Sherman was too remote and too far away. "Too many places I could get ambushed," I said. "It has to be somewhere more open."

He paused. "The farmhouse. That's open. I'll be in the house watching. You drive down the road, and I'll come out and walk toward you. It'll be like a Western movie, handguns only. Better man wins. I hear you can shoot. I can shoot a little myself."

"When?"

"Tomorrow at dawn," he said. "Duel at dawn, you gotta love it."

"I'll be there."

"And you have to give me your word you'll be alone."

"I'll be alone," I said. "I wouldn't have it any other way."

◆　　◆　　◆　　◆

We headed home that night, except we flew into Knoxville's McGhee Tyson Airport and not Tri-Cities. As Adam had learned in the Garden of Eden, one should never trust a snake. I most certainly didn't trust James Hyde. He obviously had eyes in Mountain Center, and the less he knew about our whereabouts, the better.

Oscar picked us up and drove the hour and a half to the Fleet mansion, where we would spend the night. Joseph Fleet had an excellent security system, and I doubted James Hyde could breach it or would even be interested in trying. Oscar and Roy had moved my Pathfinder, so I'd have wheels the following morning.

That night, after an excellent dinner, Mary and Lacy went up to the third floor to settle in for the night. Joseph Fleet and I adjourned to his study for an after-dinner drink, as was our custom when I had dinner at the mansion. The nights were getting cooler, and there was a fire in the fireplace. The room gave me a safe feeling. I relaxed a little.

"It's nice to have you, Mary, and Lacy with us," he said. "Roy was a little vague on the details."

"I'm working an FBI thing that might be dangerous for Mary and Lacy. I hope to resolve it tomorrow morning."

"Stay as long as you need to," he said. "You're always welcome."

We drank in silence and watched the fire. For the first time in days,

I felt tired. After running on adrenaline, I knew that sooner or later I was going to crash.

"Do you know how old I am, Don?" Joseph Fleet asked.

The question caught me off guard. I wondered where it was leading.

"I've never given it much thought."

"Pushing eighty. I'm probably too old to be running this empire." He sounded as tired as I felt.

"What else would you do?"

"What I'd like to do is take a year off and travel. See some things I've always wanted to see, go places I've always wanted to go."

"Alone?"

He smiled. "No, not alone. I may be old, but I'm still . . ." He paused.

"Active," I said.

"Exactly."

"So go," I said.

"That would put it all on Roy's plate."

"What does Roy say?"

"He says go. That I've earned it."

"So?"

"So we'd both feel more comfortable if Roy had someone he could consult with every now and then. Someone he could trust, who has no agenda."

"Me."

"You," he said. "We're losing a board member."

"I'd be honored to fill that position."

"Welcome aboard," Joseph Fleet said.

I was about to retire for the night when Roy poked his head into the study. "You have a visitor," he said.

He stood to one side as Billy came in. He was in uniform. Joseph Fleet stood, and they shook hands.

"Good to see you again, Billy."

"You too, sir."

"I take it this is not a social call," Joseph Fleet said.

"No, it's not," Billy said. "I need to speak with Blood."

Joseph Fleet stood. "Gentlemen, I'm turning in. Billy, you're welcome to stay."

He left us alone.

I looked at Billy and waited.

"Agent Steele called me this afternoon looking for you," Billy said. "He said you're not answering your cell phone, that your office is closed up tight, and that you, Mary, Lacy, and Gretchen are in the wind and out of touch."

"Sounds about right."

"Mind telling me what's going on?" Billy asked, not hiding the fact that he was upset with being kept out of the loop.

"Sorry, Chief," I said. "I didn't want to involve you. Now I want to. I could use your help tomorrow, although you'll probably want to lose the uniform."

Billy smiled. "I did bring a change of clothes. Let's hear it."

◆   ◆   ◆   ◆

Billy and I left the study and went to my third-floor room to plan our strategy for tomorrow. I thought I knew exactly where James Hyde would set up for me. Mary didn't seem surprised to see Billy. I started to share my plan with Billy when Mary interrupted.

"About tomorrow," she said, her voice determined, "I'm going with you, and it's not negotiable."

"I promised him I'd come alone," I said with little conviction.

"He doesn't deserve your promise," Mary said. "And besides, I didn't promise him a damn thing."

"Me either," Billy growled.

It was pointless to argue, and something about having Mary with me felt right. I showed her our route in and how we'd play it. I told Billy his part. We all agreed.

"You think he's going to try and ambush you?" Mary asked.

"I do."

Billy nodded. "In the end, they're all cowards."

"I thought he wanted a face-to-face," Mary said.

"He wants me dead," I said. "He doesn't want to gamble with me out in the open. This is his version of a face-to-face."

We went over it a second time, then Billy left for his room and Mary and I took some time getting ready for bed.

Well, Mary took some time. I was ready in five minutes.

◆   ◆   ◆   ◆

"Mr. Fleet asked me to be on the Fleet Industries Board of Directors," I said to Mary.

We were in bed. Our bedside lamps were on.

"What did you say?"

"What could I say? I said yes."

I told her about my conversation with Joseph Fleet in his study.

"I think that's great," Mary said. "You can be a big help to Roy."

"I'm not sure Roy needs my help. But I'll be there if he does."

I cut my light off. Then Mary cut hers.

"I love the fact that you'll be with me tomorrow," I said. "Together, we're unstoppable."

She moved close. "It took me a long time to find you. I'm not taking any chances on losing you, Cowboy."

62

We left before dawn. Billy dropped us off at the side of a back-country road where we could come at the farmhouse from the rear. We were dressed all in black and wore Kevlar vests with upper-arm guards. Mary and I both wore holstered Glocks on our belts. Mary also carried a sniper rifle with a scope, and I had a twelve-gauge short-barreled shotgun. We were armed and dangerous.

I hoped James Hyde hadn't considered posting a lookout at the back of the woods. I was counting on his believing that I was so naïve that I would do exactly what I said.

We moved quickly off the road and found cover. I carefully scanned the area with night-vision binoculars for any sign of life. A low-lying mist made visibility poor, but that worked both ways. I saw no movement.

We moved carefully through a field of high grass toward the woods. Once there, I headed silently toward the place where I felt certain James Hyde would be hiding. Mary stayed a few yards behind me, trying to mimic my footsteps. I grew up in the woods around my house and had learned how to move quietly. Periodically, I stopped and surveyed the area with the binoculars. Still no movement. Finally, in the distance, I could see the farmhouse. We moved slowly at a right angle to it. And then I saw what I was looking for: a camouflaged deer blind. I had spotted it the day we landed in the FBI helicopter. It was about a hundred feet in front and to the right of us and offered a clear view of the road. The barrel of a rifle protruded from the front opening in the blind.

"We wait," I whispered to Mary.

We settled in and watched the deer blind for signs of James Hyde. All we saw was the rifle barrel. *I hope to hell that's him in there*, I thought. It was easier to see by the minute. Dawn was fast approaching. Five minutes later, the rifle barrel extended farther from the opening.

In the distance, I saw my white Pathfinder stop at the dirt-road entrance to the farm, its headlights cutting through the morning mist. As the Pathfinder slowly turned and crept toward the farmhouse, the rifle barrel extended a little farther from the opening of the deer blind. A shot rang out. Through the binoculars, I saw a mushroom the size of a silver dollar appear on the Pathfinder's windshield in front of the driver. The Pathfinder veered off into a field, as if the driver no longer had control, and coasted to a stop. There was no sign of life from the Pathfinder. We waited.

After a few minutes, I heard movement in the deer blind, and then James Hyde emerged. He carried a rifle with a scope. He moved carefully out of the woods toward the Pathfinder. We followed silently, gaining ground on him as we went. I was thirty feet behind him when I yelled, "Drop the rifle, James!"

He turned slowly to see a shotgun and a rifle leveled at him. I noticed that, like us, he carried a holstered handgun. He lowered the rifle but didn't put it down.

"You said you'd come alone," he hissed. The snake was cornered.

"You said you'd be in the farmhouse."

"Change of plans. And I didn't give you my word on it."

"My plans also changed," I said. "But we can still do this. Put the rifle down or I'll cut you in half right now."

"What about her?" he asked, looking at Mary.

"She's here only as an observer."

"She puts her rifle down first," he said.

I nodded at Mary, and she laid her rifle in the grass. James Hyde placed his on the ground. I laid my twelve-gauge down.

"Go for it," I said. "You know you want to."

"If I kill you, she'll kill me," he said.

"I doubt it. She's a terrible shot."

In the distance behind James Hyde, I saw Billy get out of the Pathfinder and start toward us.

"Don't chicken out now, James. You're supposed to be a tough guy. You kill innocent women, remember."

Suddenly, I saw fear in his eyes, the bravado gone.

"Pull your weapon, soldier!" I yelled. "Come on Jimmy, do it!"

His mouth went slack, his eyes wide. The color drained from his face. The transformation was unbelievable. If this was an act, he had missed his calling.

"No, no, no," he said. "I don't like guns."

It was not the voice of the snake. When he went for the gun in his belt, I drew my Glock but didn't fire. He fumbled the gun away like a kid with a hot potato. It fell harmlessly to the ground.

"James likes guns," he said frantically. "James is gone now. I don't like guns. I am afraid of guns."

I raised the Glock and took dead aim.

"Please don't shoot me!"

"Don," Mary said. "Don't do it." She stepped past me and walked toward him. "He won't hurt you," she said. "Put your hands behind your back."

Jimmy Hyde did as he was told, and Mary cuffed him and led him toward the farmhouse. Billy walked past them to where I was standing.

"You were right," he said. "He was where you thought he'd be. Your plan worked."

"More or less. At least it's over."

"You okay, Blood? For a few seconds there, you had me worried."

"I wasn't going to kill him, Chief. I just wanted him to stare death in the face like his victims did. I wanted to scare the hell out of him."

"Looks like you accomplished that."

"How's my Pathfinder?"

"Going to need the front windshield replaced again." Billy smiled. "That bulletproof glass is a lifesaver."

◆   ◆   ◆   ◆

Billy retrieved the Pathfinder and drove it to the front of the farmhouse. He and Mary took Jimmy Hyde and sat him down against the trunk of an oak tree. Billy pulled out a large knife and waved it in front of Jimmy's face.

"You try to run and I'll cut your throat."

"I won't move," Jimmy said in a panic.

Billy opened the passenger-side door of the Pathfinder and sat. He left the door open. Mary stood talking with him as I removed my cell phone and made the call.

"Damn it, Youngblood, where are you?"

"I miss you too, Dave."

"Talk to me."

"I have our guy."

There was a pause, as if he was having a hard time processing what I said.

"That's great news. Dead or alive?"

"Alive," I said. "Come and get him."

"Where are you?"

"The farmhouse. And don't come in here like storm troopers. Just you, Buckley, and the FBI's version of a paddy wagon to transport the prisoner."

"Do we need a doctor?"

"No, you'll need a psychiatrist," I said.

◆   ◆   ◆   ◆

"Terrible shot!" Mary said, sitting down next to me on the front steps. "What was that all about?"

"I was trying to make him feel less intimidated," I said.

"So he'd draw and you could kill him."

"I would have only wounded him. I want him dying from his cancer. That's a whole lot worse than a bullet."

We sat in silence. I'm not sure she believed what I said. I'm not sure I believed it myself. I knew part of me had wanted to kill James Hyde then and there.

"What are the odds you would end the careers of two serial killers in the same place?" Mary asked.

"Like hitting the lottery."

"I'm proud of you."

"Me, too, you," I said, and kissed her to prove it.

◆　　◆　　◆　　◆

The cavalry arrived in less than an hour. A black Taurus followed by a black van. Neither had *FBI* emblazoned on the doors, or anywhere else, for that matter. David Steele got out and came walking toward us. Buckley and a couple of other agents went to fetch Jimmy Hyde.

"I'm about to get a lecture," I said softly to Mary.

"If he gets too far out of line, I'll shoot him," she said.

She was kidding, of course. *I think.*

"You hung up on me, Youngblood," David Steele said.

"Nice to see you, too, Dave."

"Don't change the subject."

"We were at thirty thousand feet," Mary said. "We lost your signal."

"For three days?" he shouted.

Mary shrugged. "Sit down, David, and relax."

Agent Steele recognized a hopeless argument when he saw it. He acquiesced and sat beside Mary.

"Fill me in," he said resignedly.

I kept quiet and let Mary talk. She told it well. When she was finished, Dave sat silently.

"If anyone asks," he finally said, "I knew all about this."

"Works for us," Mary said.

"I'll talk to you later, Youngblood," he said. "I have to go take a few bows, thanks to you."

David Steele headed back toward the Taurus. Buckley, who had been hanging in the background, came over quickly.

"Good work, Youngblood," he said.

"Thanks."

"Ma'am," he said, nodding at Mary. He turned and walked away.

"Who's that?" Mary asked.

"Agent Buckley Clarke," I said. "Junior G-man."

"He's cute."

"Way too young for you."

"Watch it, Cowboy," Mary said, jabbing me in the ribs.

Thankfully, it wasn't my sore side.

63

We spent Monday afternoon and all day Tuesday at the lake house. Lacy stayed with Hannah. I called Gretchen on Monday afternoon and gave her the all-clear.

Wednesday, Mary and I went back to the real world. I spent an hour on T. Elbert's front porch telling a much-embellished story of the capture. He loved every minute of it.

"Did you see Agent Steele made CNN?" T. Elbert said.

"Nope, guess I missed it."

"Got credit for heading the investigation that led to the capture of the serial murderer the FBI now refers to as the Cracker Jack Killer," T. Elbert said. "You were not mentioned anywhere in the story."

"Good for me. National press is the last thing I want."

"Well, at least I know the true story. But you should have gotten some credit."

"You, too."

"Didn't want any."

"Me neither," I said. "We toil in silence, and justice is our reward."

"That's us," T. Elbert said.

•   •   •   •

I was in the office by nine and had a visitor by nine-thirty. We drank coffee and talked.

"You sure you don't want to be a full-time FBI consultant?" David Steele asked.

"I'm sure. Sounds like an FBI agent with a different title. I do not want to work for Uncle."

"Don't blame you, but I had to ask."

"Heard you made the news," I said.

"None of my doing. But the bureau never misses a chance at positive press. Sorry you weren't mentioned."

"Don't be. Once is enough in my lifetime. If it hadn't been for all that press in the Tattoo Killers case, James Hyde would have probably been gunning for you and not me."

"Well, James—or Jimmy or whoever the hell he is—is history. He'll die in prison, and that will be the end of CJK."

"Where are they sending him?"

"Wallens Ridge," David Steele said. "It's in Big Stone Gap, Virginia. Used to be a supermax prison, but they've downgraded it. He'll be in solitary twenty-three hours a day when he's not in the infirmary."

"Have you notified the families of the victims that we got the killer?"

"Buckley is in the process of doing that now," David Steele said.

"That's good."

My intercom buzzed. "I'm in," Gretchen said.

"Agent Steele is here," I replied. "I'll talk to you after he leaves."

"I'm out," he said, standing. "No offense, Youngblood, but I hope we don't have to work together again for a very long time."

"I understand completely. How about never?"

"That'll work. But stay in touch." We shook hands. "Take care of your-self, Don."

He turned and walked out of my office. That was the last time I worked a case with FBI Special Agent in Charge David Steele.

◆   ◆   ◆   ◆

After lunch, Buckley Clarke came by. When he entered my office, he handed me a folder and then sat.

"That's the complete file on the CJK case," he said. "I thought you should have it. You're mentioned quite often."

"Does Agent Steele know about this?"

"He does. In fact, his final report is in the file. He gave you most of the credit. Naturally, the higher-ups preferred not to mention a part-time consultant when handing out the story to the media."

"You're too young to be so cynical," I said. "It was nothing personal, just politics. Better get used to it."

"I guess," he said, standing to leave. "Anyway, it was nice working with you, Mr. Youngblood."

"I don't want to ruin your sense of protocol, Buckley," I said, "but you can call me Don."

"Right," Buckley said. "Don it is." He walked toward the closed door, stopped, and then turned around to face me. "Your assistant, Gretchen, is she married?"

"Divorced," I said.

He nodded before disappearing into the outer office and closing the door behind him.

A few minutes later, Gretchen came in.

"Buckley asked me out," she said.

"What did you say?"

"Well, he *is* really good looking."

"Yeah, so I've heard. What happened to Chase?"

"Ancient history."

"So what did you say?"

"What do you think I said?"

"You said yes."

She just smiled and went back to her desk.

◆   ◆   ◆   ◆

After Gretchen left for the day, I made the phone call I had been putting off. Believe it or not, the butler answered.

"Durbinfield residence," the British-accented voice announced.

"Elizabeth Durbinfield, please."

"Whom may I say is calling, sir?"

"Donald Youngblood. Of the Mountain Center Youngbloods."

"Will she know what this is in reference to, sir?"

"She will."

"Very well, sir. Please hold."

It took a minute or so before Elizabeth Durbinfield came on the line.

"Mr. Youngblood. Sorry to keep you holding. I take it from news reports that you've concluded your FBI case."

Elizabeth Durbinfield didn't miss much, I thought.

"Yes," I said. "I would like to pay you a visit and tell you what I know about your son's death."

"I would be most grateful. When can you come?"

"Is Friday convenient?"

"Friday would be fine. Will you need transportation? I would be glad to send our jet."

I quickly decided there was no need to involve the Fleet Industries jet when I had the offer of comparable transportation.

"I think I'll take you up on that offer," I said.

"Splendid. Will it be acceptable if I give my pilot your number and he calls to work out the details?"

"That will be fine. Tell him to call tomorrow after ten o'clock and speak with my assistant, Gretchen. She'll work with him on the arrangements."

"Very well," she said. "Until Friday, then. I look forward to speaking with you, Mr. Youngblood."

◆   ◆   ◆   ◆

That night, I sat with Mary at the kitchen bar finishing my second Amber Bock and relishing the memory of the pizza and Caesar salad I had just consumed. Lacy was having dinner at the McBrides', as she was now doing about once a week.

"I'm going to see Elizabeth Durbinfield on Friday," I said. "I'm being picked up in her corporate jet."

"My, my, aren't you important?" Mary said.

"For a minute or two."

"How much are you going to tell her?"

"Most of it. I'll clean it up a little. I won't mention the possibility it was rape. I really don't think it was."

"We need to tell Lacy she might have a living grandmother," Mary said.

"Elizabeth Durbinfield wouldn't be your run-of-the-mill grandmother. If Lacy is her granddaughter, it could get complicated."

"Doesn't matter," Mary said. "Lacy needs to know and make the decision on whether or not she wants to pursue it."

"You're changing your tune from the last time we talked about this," I said.

"I've been giving it a lot of thought," Mary said. "It's the right thing to do."

"When do we tell her?"

"This weekend," Mary said. "Let Elizabeth Durbinfield know you'll come on Monday instead."

64

Saturday morning was crystal clear. The sky was as blue as it gets, the air cool, the breeze light, and the lake as quiet as a Tibetan monastery. Late that morning, we sat on the lower deck with Lacy.

"There's a possibility we might know who your father is," Mary said.

"Don's my father and you're my mother," Lacy said. "End of story."

"Of course we are," I said. "That's not going to change. Even if this person was your biological father, he's been dead a long time and never knew you existed."

"So why are we even having this conversation?" Lacy said. "All that's in the past, and I don't want to think about it."

"We're having this conversation because you may have a living grandmother," Mary said. "And if she is your grandmother, she's very much interested in her granddaughter. We didn't think we should withhold that information from you."

Lacy was silent. "You said *if* she's my grandmother," she finally said. "You're not sure?"

"We'd have to do a DNA test," Mary said.

It didn't take Lacy long to put the pieces together. "Those two men at school," she said, leveling her gaze at me. "That was all about getting my DNA."

"Yes," I said.

"And you didn't want them to have it," she said.

"No, I didn't. I had already told them no."

"Why?"

"I didn't want to complicate your life," I said. "Mary saw it differently, and after discussing it with her, I had second thoughts. I agreed we should let the decision be yours."

"So this potential grandmother sent the two guys you got in a fight with," Lacy said.

"Sort of," I said.

"Guess she really wants to know," Lacy said.

"She does," I said. "But whether or not you decide to give her a DNA sample is up to you."

"I'll think about it," Lacy said.

◆   ◆   ◆   ◆

If the weather could possibly have gotten any better, it did—mid-seventies, fresh-smelling, gentle breeze coming off the lake, bright sunshine. Biker came over around lunchtime, and he and Lacy took the houseboat out for the afternoon. Later, we cooked out—boneless chicken breasts, hamburgers, grilled pineapple, and baked beans. We sat on the lower deck and ate and watched the sun go down.

Much later that night, I was in my office surfing the web and checking football scores. Tennessee had won, so I was happy. I had recorded the game and hoped I'd find time to watch it.

Lacy came in and sat in a chair beside my desk. I looked up at her.

"I had a talk with Biker, and he helped me make a decision," she said.

65

I started the week by going to the Mountain Center Diner. A familiar face was at my table.

"Glad you could make it," I said.

"Wanted to hear about your adventure," he said.

Doris arrived and took our orders.

I told Roy how the takedown had unfolded and how James Hyde morphed into Jimmy Hyde right in front of our eyes. I told it slowly and with as much detail as I could remember. While I was telling it, our food arrived.

"Think it's an act?"

"If it is, it's a damn good one," I said. "But I think it's real. He's severely screwed up. Sarah Agnes called it dissociative identity disorder—two or more distinct personalities."

"Well, it's good you got him off the street," Roy said.

"It is. But for a second or two, I wanted to blow him away. Then I heard Mary's voice and came to my senses."

We ate in silence.

"I hear you're going to be our newest board member," Roy said.

"An honor."

"I'm glad. Since I'm going to be running the company, having you around to bounce things off will give me peace of mind."

"You'll do fine," I said.

"I think I will," Roy said.

"You've come a long way, my friend."

"I have, haven't I?" Roy said.

◆　　◆　　◆　　◆

After breakfast, I went to the office and called the Durbinfield mansion. I went through the same routine with the butler. A minute later, Elizabeth Durbinfield was on the line.

"Yes, Mr. Youngblood. I assume your schedule has changed again."

I had left a message with her answering service that I would be coming Monday, not Friday. Then Mary had texted the number we had for Elizabeth Durbinfield's pilot, and we received an immediate response that he would wait to hear from us before he made further plans.

"It has," I said.

"And someone notified my pilot?"

"Yes, someone did."

"Very well, but I don't like all these delays."

"I think you'll like this one," I said.

"Explain, please."

"I'd like you to come here."

"Why?"

"I have someone who wants to meet you."

I thought I heard a gasp.

"Lacy?" she asked, hesitantly.

"Yes."

"When?"

"This weekend. Can you fly into Tri-Cities Airport Saturday morning?"

"Most certainly," she said.

"Let me know your schedule, and I'll pick you up. Pack for a couple of nights, Mrs. Durbinfield. We dress casual down here."

"Thank you," she said. "I very much look forward to meeting your wife and daughter, Mr. Youngblood. And please call me Elizabeth."

"Only if you'll call me Don or Donald."

"Donald will work just fine," she said.

Why was I not surprised?

"I'll let you know our estimated time of arrival," She said, excitement now in her voice.

"Until then, Elizabeth," I said.

"Until then, Donald."

66

We arrived early in a light rain. The guard at the gate to the area for private aircraft waved us through without a second thought, no doubt recognizing Oscar and the Fleet Industries limousine. We waited, the motor of the big car idling to maintain the air conditioning, which we hardly needed.

Oscar had picked me up at the lake house that Saturday morning.

"Brought you a local paper, boss," he said. "I thought you might want to kill some time on our way to the airport."

"Thanks, O-man," I said.

I read the sports first, naturally, and saw where the high-school football team had won another game to remain undefeated. Then I read the local news, which was both sad and disturbing. The police blotter was full of drug arrests, DUIs, assaults, drunk-and-disorderlies, and robberies. According to Mary, many arrests were of good people doing stupid stuff. The rest were habitual dopers and career criminals who didn't know any other way of life. When I'd read enough, I closed the paper and enjoyed the ride. The glass partition between the front and back seats was closed. When we arrived at the airport, I tapped on it, and Oscar slid it open.

"*How have you been, Oscar?*" I asked in Spanish. Oscar and I often conversed in Spanish, since I rarely got to practice. Mary was learning but was not yet ready to carry on a conversation.

"*Good, boss,*" Oscar said. "*Real good. Love the job.*"

"*Family okay?*"

"*Family is fine,*" Oscar said. "*Are you all right, boss? I heard you brought down another bad guy.*"

"*I'm okay now. I'm sure glad it's over.*"

We made small talk until I saw a sleek little private jet set gently down on the tarmac and taxi toward private hangar number two. Once the jet was positioned as instructed, the pilot cut the engines and Oscar drove out to within a few feet of the jet's folding stairway, which was on its way down. When the stairs were in place, the door opened and Elizabeth Durbinfield descended. Oscar opened the rear passenger-side door, and she got in.

"Well, that's what I call service, Donald," she said. "How are you?"

"I'm fine. How was your flight?"

"Uneventful."

"The best kind," I said.

◆   ◆   ◆   ◆

On the way to the lake house, I told her what I knew about the death of her son, leaving out a few details she didn't need to know.

"What I'm going to tell you I heard secondhand," I said. "I know none of it as absolute fact."

"But you believe it to be true," she said.

"I do."

"Please continue."

"Johnny was killed in a fit of passion while having sex with an under-age girl."

"Lacy's mother."

I nodded. "The body was buried to conceal the crime, and Lacy's mother, Tracy, left town with her mother. No one missed your son. He was a drifter, and it was assumed he had just moved on. I uncovered all this when I was searching for Tracy, who abandoned Lacy."

Elizabeth Durbinfield showed no emotion. I could have been giving a stock report. But I knew a woman in her position would be good at covering up her feelings.

"The killer was a jealous lover," she said.

"Yes."

"Another woman?"

"Yes."

"Where and how?" Elizabeth asked.

"With a pitchfork in a barn," I said.

"So it wasn't premeditated."

"Probably not. A fit of rage, I would guess. Caught them in the act."

"Is this person who killed my son still alive?"

"No. Everyone connected to the death is dead."

She was silent a long time. "So Lacy is probably my granddaughter," she finally said. "But that is not an absolute certainty."

"Correct," I said.

"Thank you for telling me, Donald. We shall not speak of this again."

I inwardly breathed a sigh of relief. She had not asked the name of the killer.

"There's one other thing," I said. "In my closet at the office, I have a leather jacket that belonged to John, and a friend is storing John's motorcycle."

She thought about that. I waited. I was in no hurry.

"Hold on to the jacket and motorcycle," Elizabeth said. "There will be plenty of time to decide about those things later."

◆   ◆   ◆   ◆

We sat at the table with the umbrella on the lower deck and had coffee and Danish. The rain had stopped, and the day was clearing and held the promise of being glorious, full of sunshine and fall color. Elizabeth Durbinfield and Lacy did most of the talking; Mary and I listened. Elizabeth was a good listener who was adept at finding things out.

"Would you like to go out on the lake?" Lacy asked. "Just you and me. We have a houseboat."

"Certainly," Elizabeth said. "That sounds like fun, but I'll need to change my clothes."

Lacy showed Elizabeth to her room. Fifteen minutes later, they were back on the lower deck. Elizabeth now wore jeans and a white shirt with the sleeves rolled up.

"Have you ever been fishing?" I heard Lacy ask as they headed to the dock.

"Why, of course. But it's been a long time."

We watched in silence as they untied the barge and boarded. Lacy started one of the engines, and they moved slowly away from the dock.

"I think I like her," Mary said.

"Me, too."

"Might be nice for Lacy to have a grandmother."

"Might be," I said. "And it never hurts to have a rich one."

67

Monday morning, Lacy and Elizabeth hugged fiercely before Lacy left for school. They had obviously bonded during the weekend.

Oscar picked us up and drove Elizabeth and me to Tri-Cities Airport. Elizabeth was silent for most of the ride. It was probably a half-hour before she spoke.

"You're comfortable with silence," Elizabeth said.

"I am."

"And you are very observant."

"Sometimes."

"Most of the time, I suspect."

"Part of the job," I said.

"The last two days have been the happiest I've had in a long time," she said, her eyes moistening. "Lacy is a wonderful girl, and she's lucky to have you and Mary as parents."

"We feel lucky to have her."

"I hope all of you will visit me sometime."

"We'd love to," I said.

"I was never a very good mother. I always pushed my sons in the direction I wanted them to go. My older son, Andrew, seemed to want to go in the direction I chose. John certainly did not. Long after he left, I realized it was my fault. John and my mother got along famously, and I hope Lacy and I can do the same."

"I have a feeling you'll do just fine," I said.

Oscar pulled through the gate and drove out on the tarmac, where Elizabeth Durbinfield's private jet was waiting.

I tapped on the partition. "Give us a few minutes, Oscar."

Oscar got out and stood by the limo.

"Still want to do that DNA test?" I asked.

"Of course not," Elizabeth said. "I certainly know my own granddaughter when I see her. Besides, Lacy and I have unofficially adopted each other. But I have no doubt she is John's child."

I nodded, got out, opened the door for Elizabeth, and helped her out. We walked to the jet's stairway.

"If there's ever anything you or your family need that I can provide, it's yours," Elizabeth Durbinfield said.

"I'll keep that in mind," I said.

"I hope to see all of you soon."

"I suspect you will. Safe travels, Elizabeth."

"Thank you, Donald."

She turned and walked up the stairs and into the jet without looking back.

Epilogue

My life returned to dull normalcy, as it often did after a big case. I dove back into my investment accounts headfirst and reacquainted myself with runaway Wall Street. New record highs were being set daily, and I wondered where it would end. I continued to make more money than I could spend.

I called Bradley Culpepper and gave him the highlights of the CJK case. I never knew when I might need a favor from a lieutenant colonel at the Pentagon. He seemed pleased to hear from me.

"Your life is certainly a hell of a lot more interesting than mine, Youngblood," he said. "Anytime you need a favor, call."

"I will, sir," I said. "Thanks again."

The following week, Sheriff Phillips called to say that Johnny Cross's Saddle Boot landlord had informed him that she had some of Johnny's belongings stored in her basement. With Elizabeth Durbinfield's permission, I had them sent to Mountain Center. Among the belongings were two finished paintings, along with one that was unfinished. I had them repacked and sent to Elizabeth.

◆　　◆　　◆　　◆

A few weeks later, David Steele called.

"James Hyde died yesterday," he said. "He saved the taxpayers some money. I hope the murdering son of a bitch suffered."

"I'm sure he did," I said. James/Jimmy Hyde was a troubled soul, and I took no pleasure in the news of his passing. Then again, he hadn't killed anyone I was close to.

"I tried again to retire," David Steele said. "All it got me was a promotion, to associate deputy director. We're moving to D.C."

"Sounds like a major leap. Congratulations."

"Thanks," he said. "It's a big pay bump."

"Who's taking your spot?"

"Don't know yet. But I'll be sure to let him know you're available as a consultant."

I didn't laugh. I was already starting to get bored.

◆   ◆   ◆   ◆

Lacy and Elizabeth Durbinfield talked a few times a week. As it turned out, Elizabeth Durbinfield was interested in basketball and insisted Lacy call her after every game. There was a lot to report. Lacy and the Lady Bears were tearing up the competition, winning every game, none of them close. Elizabeth made plans to come down for a holiday tournament in Johnson City. The Mountain Center Lady Bears were one of six undefeated teams invited. The field included sixteen teams, some from other states. The competition would be fierce.

Elizabeth again made it quite clear that a DNA comparison of Lacy to John Cross Durbinfield was unnecessary. Not actually knowing whether or not they were related seemed to be a unique part of Lacy and Elizabeth's relationship, and I had no intention of sabotaging that.

I had a DNA analysis done anyway. *Better to know than not to know.* Wanda sent me the report unopened. I sat at my desk and read the results. I promptly went downstairs to the bank and put the report in my safe-deposit box.

The test results would remain my little secret.

Author's Note

Most of the places in this story are real. Mountain Center, however, is not one of them. I chose a wide-open space on a map of East Tennessee and decided that's where Mountain Center should be. You might recognize places from Gatlinburg, where I reside, and Johnson City, my hometown. I have transplanted them to Donald Youngblood's Mountain Center. Sometimes I get confused and think it's a real place.

Don's lake house is very much like my mountain home in Gatlinburg, except that below my bottom deck is not a lake but a tennis court. Beyond the court lies hundreds of acres of undeveloped land that is home to deer, black bear, coyotes, wild turkeys and a host of other wildlife too numerous to mention.

Just over the ridge is Ober Gatlinburg, Tennessee's only ski resort. At night, when it's cold enough to make snow, I can hear the snow guns from my back deck, music to a skier's ears.

The Tail of the Dragon, sometimes referred to as *The Dragon*, is an infamous piece of U.S. highway 129. This snake-like roadway is said to consist of 318 curves within 11 consecutive miles that runs from Rock Overlook in Tennessee to Deals Gap in North Carolina. Serious bikers know it well. Safely negotiating this sadistic stretch of highway is sometimes referred to as "Slaying the Dragon." Quite by accident, I drove it once. Once was enough. I did not count the curves.

I spend several months of the year on Singer Island enjoying the beautiful beach, playing tennis, eating great seafood and working on the next Donald Youngblood mystery. As I write this author's note, book six is well under way. As always, I have no idea where it is going.

Stay tuned.

Acknowledgments

My thanks to:

Todd Lape, Lape Designs for continuing to turn out brilliantly designed jackets.

Ron Lawhead, web master, for attending to my website: www.donaldyoungbloodmysteries.com.

Buie Hancock, master potter and owner of Buie Pottery, who has given Donald Youngblood and friends a spotlight in the Gatlinburg community. Come see us when you're in town.

My wife, Tessa, proofreader *extraordinaire*, who catches mistakes others cannot.

Mary Sanchez, my publicist, who continues to work tirelessly to introduce Donald Youngblood to the masses.

The Folletts, Nancy and Rob, of Park City, Utah, for allowing me on the premises to put the finishing touches on this book. Your home is wonderful, the view breathtaking, the skiing superb.

Steve Kirk, my editor at John F. Blair, Publisher, for his help on four books and counting. Great job, as always.

And finally to:

All those Donald Youngblood fans who support the work. Without you, this series could not continue.

On the Internet

Visit the Donald Youngblood Mysteries website at:
www.donaldyoungbloodmysteries.com

You may write the author at: DYBloodMysteries@aol.com

Like us on Facebook:
Donald Youngblood Mysteries by Keith Donnelly

E-book readers:
The first four books in this series are available for Kindle and
Nook e-book readers. *Three Dragons Doomed* will be
available by the end of 2014.

Praise for Keith Donnelly's
Donald Youngblood Mystery Series

"Boston has Spenser, East Tennessee has Donald Youngblood. [Don] represents the private investigator profession well—he is believable, tough, honest, professional, intelligent, and determined to do what is right."

—**Ron Head,** private investigator, Kingsport, TN

"*Three Devils Dancing* is a fast-paced and riveting read that should prove hard to put down."

—*Midwest Book Review*

"... a good crime/drama series that keeps you invested in the characters themselves, not just the final 'whodunwhat.'"

—**Kinah Lindsay (aka "Idgie"),** "Dew on the Kudzu" online magazine

"Keith Donnelly has hit the trifecta with *Three Devils Dancing*, the third installment in the Donald Youngblood Mystery Series."

—**Bill Noel,** author of the Folly Beach Mystery Series

"Keith Donnelly cruises through another funny, engrossing tale of Donald 'Don' Youngblood's mysteries with *Three Devils Dancing.* . . . Before you know it, the pages are flying. . . . It's a whirlwind of words worth riding."

—**Joe Tennis,** *Bristol* (VA) *Herald Courier*